RUN

OUTMATCH, OUTSMART, OUTLIVE

A THRILLER BY
CHRISTY COOPER-BURNETT

Black Rose Writing | Texas

This is a work of fiction. Names, characters, businesses, places, events, and incidents are either the products of the author's imagination or used in a fictitious manner. Any resemblance to actual persons, living or dead, or actual events is purely coincidental.

ISBN: 978-1-68513-440-2
PUBLISHED BY BLACK ROSE WRITING
www.blackrosewriting.com

Printed in the United States of America
Suggested Retail Price (SRP) $21.95

Run is printed in Minion Pro

OTHER TITLES BY
CHRISTY COOPER-BURNETT

The Christine Stewart Time Travel Series

No Way Home

Finding Home

Escaping Home

The Passport Time Travel Series

Passport to Terror

RUN

PROLOGUE

Kendra Thompson woke up suddenly, fully alert. Bolting upright, then remaining motionless, she held her breath as her heart pounded like a wild animal trying to break free. She struggled to hold on to whatever it was she heard, but it had already vanished from her memory.

Did she just imagine it?

She closed her eyes and let her head fall back against the headboard, easing further out of her sleep induced fog.

She had to get a grip. If she didn't stay calm, she wouldn't be able to think rationally, and she already felt like she was losing it. Although she would bet money that anyone in her situation would struggle to remain composed.

That's when she heard it again. The doorknob rattled as the chair wedged beneath it shifted a little. Kendra reacted immediately. She rolled out of the motel bed and fumbled in the dark for her go bag filled with cash. Grabbing it, she crawled across the cold floor while her son Kyle stirred in the bed next to hers. Reaching for her son's bed, she gripped the mattress and pushed herself up to place her hand over his mouth. The moment he woke up, he started flailing his arms wildly, trying to fight her. Her free hand shoved him down when he attempted to sit up.

"It's me, Kyle! We need to leave. Grab the bags. Now!" she whispered.

Her son detected the desperation in her voice, and she knew it. Her vision had adapted to the darkness, enough to see the expression on his face, which devastated her. His fear was palpable, and although she felt the same, she couldn't let him see that.

"It's all right, we'll be fine. Let's just go as fast as we can," she whispered, trying to project some confidence.

Kyle blinked once, then with one swift motion, grabbed the duffel bags next to his bed and rolled to the floor beside his mother. Kendra crawled to the bathroom while the door handle jiggled behind them. She glanced back after a few feet to ensure Kyle was following closely. A stronger push on the door made her heart rate escalate and caused a scream to lodge in her throat.

Kyle flinched at the sound, so Kendra quickened her pace, shoving her bag over the threshold and rapidly covering the last few feet to the bathroom. Moonlight streamed through the tiny window, casting an eerie glow. She closed the door quietly and wedged a rubber doorstop firmly underneath it. That wouldn't stop someone from breaching the room, but it would slow them down. And she intended for her and Kyle to be long gone before that happened. Tracing the edge of the tub, she stood and opened the window as quietly as possible, hoping no one had come to the back of the motel. They would be trapped if there was someone waiting for them there. She signaled to Kyle to stand up and follow her before dropping their packs to the ground below, one by one. Although she couldn't see anyone, Kendra was aware the situation could change at any time. She stepped aside so Kyle could go first then pulled herself up and over the windowsill. Squeezing through the small opening, she fell to the ground with a thud as the cold air seeped through her t-shirt.

Leaving the bathroom behind, they jogged across the dirt divide behind the motel and entered a thick strand of trees. Quickly and silently, mother and son made their way forward. All Kendra could think about was making it to the truck undetected. Then, a sudden loud

CRACK broke the silence, making her jump. She knew their pursuers were inside the motel room.

Kendra quickened her pace and looked over her shoulder to make sure Kyle was keeping up with her. Bushes scraped their arms as they ran past, and tears stung her eyes when a low-hanging branch raked across her face. But to be fair, the tears were there before she caught the branch. The sight of light up ahead gave her a glimmer of hope that they could still escape.

When they reached the tree line's edge, they stopped to catch their breath while Kendra surveyed the parking lot for dangers. She'd become quite skilled at that in the past week. The neon sign above the diner was the sole source of light in the nearly deserted lot. With half of the sign burned out, it was just enough to guide them to their vehicle. Running from under the trees, they sprinted across the empty space, completely vulnerable and exposed. Every passing minute outside the motel increased the likelihood of being caught by their pursuers.

It felt like much longer, but they reached the truck in under one minute. Kendra opened the door and tossed the bags inside as Kyle climbed into the truck and reached for the baseball cap and the gun in the glove box. Kendra adjusted the rearview mirror, started the truck, and sped out of the parking lot.

"They're going to be looking for two people, so you need to get down, out of sight," she said.

Kyle didn't reply, but still did what his mother asked. They turned onto the two-lane highway and drove away, putting as much distance as possible between them and the motel. Kendra had to control her urge to push the accelerator to the floor, as driving too fast would attract unwanted attention. She forced herself to drive at a moderate speed, even though she didn't want to.

"You can sit up now," said Kendra, breaking the silence.

Hoping for a response, Kendra glanced over at Kyle. He straightened upright in the seat but remained silent. Sixteen was too young to deal with this, and a now familiar stab of guilt shuddered through her.

"Do you want to pick something to listen to? You can have complete control of the radio, and I promise I won't complain," she asked, hoping to lighten the mood.

Kendra got no reaction from Kyle. Not even a glance in her direction. A week ago, her typical response would have been to launch into a lecture on manners. But right now, nothing was normal about their lives, and she decided neither of them was ready to delve into that. So she stayed silent.

The minutes ticked by as they drove, rushing toward an uncertain future and an unknown destination. Kyle's silence was deafening, and fresh tears filled Kendra's eyes. Not for the first time that week, she found herself questioning her actions.

Was she doing the right thing? Should she turn around, drive back home, and take a chance with the police protecting them? Could she trust anyone at the LAPD or the FBI?

It turned out that the answers weren't that simple, although Kendra desperately wanted to trust someone.

Anyone.

She needed help, but had no idea where to turn now that they had left Sam behind. Nothing felt safe. The entire situation was steeped in countless unknowns, and in a world seemingly full of options for everyone else, she had none. She was completely lost and without direction.

Which was a first for a self-professed micromanager like her.

Driven by nothing more than a primal urge to protect her son, Kendra did what she had learned to do so well over the past week. She did what she *needed* to do. She had no other choice.

She ran.

ONE

Kyle Thompson sat on the concrete bench outside the movie theater, his knee bouncing up and down in a nervous dance.

"What if they don't show?" he asked Brendan.

"I dunno. I mean, they said they'd be here. That would be pretty messed up if they ghosted us," Brendan replied. "But seriously, I wouldn't blame Brittany if she stood up your ugly ass," he said, tossing a twig at Kyle.

"Yeah, I'm sure the only reason Casey is coming is because Brittany made her. No girl is gonna wanna hang out with you if they don't have to," Kyle replied, launching an old candy wrapper at Brendan.

Brittany Carpenter and her friend, Casey, were supposed to meet Kyle and his best friend Brendan five minutes ago. She was one of the cutest girls in school, and Kyle couldn't wait to hang out with her. Especially since they had never been on a legitimate date. They always hung out with a group of friends, so Kyle hoped tonight was a real date.

"Girls are like, always late. Right?" Kyle asked, turning to Brendan.

Brendan shrugged and didn't answer. Kyle wasn't sure why he was asking. Brendan was more clueless about girls than he was. But Brendan *did* have an older sister, so maybe that gave him a slight advantage.

"Kyle, look. Is that them? Over there by the pizza place."

Kyle squinted against the setting sun and searched the parking lot.

Yes!

They showed up. His heart raced as soon as he saw her. The girls walked toward them, and Brittany raised her hand in a wave. Kyle smiled and lifted his chin slightly.

"Hey, Kyle," said Brittany, flipping her hair over her shoulder.

"Hey. It's going."

Brittany frowned at him, and Kyle felt his face flush red.

Hey. It's going?

He immediately regretted what he considered to be a completely lame greeting, and wondered, not for the first time, why he struggled to act normal around Brittany. That didn't even make sense, and he cursed himself for saying something that made him sound like a complete moron.

"So, are we gonna get tickets, or what?" said Casey, looking less than pleased as she eyed Brendan.

"Let's do it," said Brendan, rising.

An awkward silence enveloped them as they walked the few feet to the ticket booth to stand in line, and Kyle shifted nervously from foot to foot. He knew he should say something but had a hard time coming up with anything to say and ended up with nothing.

At least the girls started talking about a friend of theirs Kyle didn't know. He listened halfheartedly. Something about her being grounded for sneaking out. Maybe a movie was the best kind of first date, he thought. He wouldn't have to stress about filling any more stretches of silence. Afterward, they could talk about the movie or school or whatever. Kyle hoped he'd be less nervous by that time. Brendan didn't seem nervous at all, which only made Kyle continue to question why he couldn't seem to act at all chill around Brittany.

They reached the front of the line and Kyle took his debit card and school ID out of his wallet and slid them under the glass partition to the cashier. He felt stupid using his student ID, but it gave him a ten percent discount, which he needed. He knew he only had about forty bucks available on his card, and if Brittany wanted something from the snack bar, that would be cutting it close. The idea of his card being declined in front of her was so humiliating.

As they waited for their tickets, Kyle glanced over at Brittany. He could have sworn she rolled her eyes at Casey. He wasn't sure if it was the choice of movie or that he used his student ID card. Either way, he was beginning to feel like this wasn't going to go as well as he'd envisioned.

He needn't have worried though, because things picked up when they got inside. They all enjoyed the movie, and Brittany leaned her head on Kyle's shoulder and let him kiss her. That kiss was the best thing that happened to him lately.

After the movie, Casey's mom picked the girls up while Brendan and Kyle started their walk home. The boys lived in opposite directions to each other and were ready to part ways after a few blocks.

"Dude, you wanna come over and play some video games or something?" asked Brendan.

"Nah. My mom will freak if I'm not home pretty soon," said Kyle, rolling his eyes.

"Okay, see you tomorrow at school," said Brendan, slapping Kyle's hand in a loose high five.

"Yeah. Later, bro," Kyle replied, taking off toward home.

Kyle was still riding the high from his date with Brittany as he walked along the busy street. He thought about how he would act toward her in school now. Did she think they were going out after this? Like a couple? He wasn't sure and decided to just go with the flow and see how things went tomorrow.

He turned onto Walnut Street and decided to cut through the abandoned warehouses that had shut down a few years ago. It would be a lot less walking if he took this route. His mom didn't like him to go that way, but she wasn't there, so it didn't matter. His phone rang, and he pulled it out of his pocket quickly, hoping to see a call from Brittany.

Mom - Incoming call.

It was like she knew he was doing something he wasn't supposed to. Irritated, he pushed the phone back into his pocket.

"Nope, not picking that one up," Kyle muttered to himself.

He wasn't down to give her a blow-by-blow account of his day, even though it was her second call in twenty minutes. He'd be home soon enough, and it wouldn't be the end of the world if he hadn't picked up before then. His mom might not agree, but he really didn't care. He was practically an adult. He'd be seventeen in a few months, so it totally got under his skin that she felt the need to check up on him constantly. It just made him dig his heels in deeper and refuse to answer his phone. He heard the voicemail chime, but ignored it and continued walking. He only hoped his mom didn't give him crap for being late and spoil an otherwise sick night. She was on his back about everything lately. It seemed like he couldn't get anything right in her opinion.

Kyle made his way through the maze of buildings, checking out the graffiti-covered walls. Empty beer cans and fast-food wrappers were scattered around the pavement everywhere.

He was lost in thought when the sound of voices stopped him in his tracks as he rounded a corner. He hadn't expected to find anyone else there on a Thursday night. The area had a reputation as a party spot on weekends, but during the week, it was usually deserted. And he walked this route home from Brendan's often. He strained to hear what they were saying, but all he could make out was the rise and fall of voices. It sounded like a group of guys. Heading to the edge of the building, he took a quick look around the corner. Three guys were kicking something on the ground. Two men were clapping and cheering their friend on, while another stood away, watching. They repeatedly kicked at a dark, motionless shape as they continued to yell and laugh. Using a garbage bin as cover, Kyle crept closer. It was only after one of the guys moved that he realized it was a person on the ground. Trying to defend himself, the man on the ground covered his head with his arms, but it wasn't doing much good, as he was bleeding from more than one wound.

It took Kyle a moment to fully understand what he was seeing. They were beating the crap out of some dude, three guys to one. Kyle took out his phone and started recording a video, thinking that Brendan would never believe he saw this without proof. He hardly believed it himself. He continued recording for roughly two minutes and got a clear shot of each of the guys. He tried but couldn't get a good line on the guy's face on the ground because the man's arms covered his head, still trying to fend off the blows.

Just as Kyle's low battery symbol started to flash on his phone, the guy who had so far only been watching the others stepped forward. The rest of the group stopped kicking and beating the man on the ground and turned to face him. He lifted his chin at one of them and Kyle very clearly heard what he said.

"Finish it, Baby G."

The guy who had been cheered on by the others reached into the back of his waistband, pulling something out that stopped Kyle from cutting off the video. Crouching beside the garbage bin, he was frozen in place, muscles tense. He couldn't make sense of what was happening. When he saw the gun, a sense of dread started at the base of his spine and traveled through him as goosebumps formed on his arms. The guy drew the gun upward and pulled back the slide. Kyle was too stunned to make a sound, even though he knew he should yell at them to stop. Before he could react further, the guy aimed the gun at the man on the ground in front of him and pulled the trigger.

CRACK!

The sound bounced off the nearby buildings, making Kyle's ears ring. The man on the ground was suddenly still. Kyle let out a gasp as a pool of blood slowly formed around the man's head.

Panic swelled inside of him. The fear stunned him into a state of shock. There was only one thought playing on a continuous reel in his head as he watched them.

Did they just kill him? What the *actual fuck!*

He knew he had to get out of there and call the police. Or his mom. Someone! But fear still had him rooted to the spot.

The guy who gave the order to finish it, who seemed to be the leader, stepped forward.

"Take care of him," he said, as he spit on the man at his feet. "Joker, call our guy at LAPD and let him know it's done."

The others took their turn to spit on him as well. Then the leader put his arm around the shooter and patted the guy's chest with his free hand. "You did good, Baby G. You're one of us now. For life."

With arms raised and fists pumping, they each slapped the shooter's back and then started chanting. It was then that Kyle realized he was still recording.

South Side Sinners! Pecadores del lado sur!

The gang's name echoed through the air as they sang it out over and over. No one messed with the South Side Sinners. Least of all, a kid like Kyle. It was beginning to register with him just how deep a pile of shit he had stepped in.

And that was the exact moment his phone rang.

The ringtone echoed as loudly as the gunshot had just a few minutes earlier. Kyle hit the ignore button as fast as he could, but it was already too late. The group turned toward him in unison, and within seconds, they saw him. He was paralyzed with fear. He gripped the phone in his hand, suspended in midair, the screen glowing and the video still playing. He knew he was close enough for them to see he was shooting a video of them.

"He's fucking recording us!" yelled one of them.

That was enough to jolt Kyle back to life, and he didn't hesitate. Shoving his phone into the front pocket of his jeans, he sprang to his feet and ran faster than he ever had, managing to bolt away a few seconds before the group of gangbangers. He heard the sound of their shoes slapping the pavement behind him as they gave chase.

"Get him! Get that little motherfucker!" one of them yelled.

Kyle zigzagged through the buildings of the deserted lot as fast as he could, with no idea where he was going. Panic and sheer terror propelled him forward in a blind run, while the adrenaline surging through him gave him a burst of speed. He had a close call when he skidded around a corner too fast, rolled his right ankle and fell, but managed to scramble to his feet quickly.

"Son of a bitch!" he cried out under his breath.

Kyle's student ID popped out of his t-shirt pocket when he fell, but he couldn't see it in the dark. He took a few steps in each direction, but it was no use, and he knew he was wasting precious time looking for it. He didn't care about the card, but it had his name and picture on it, so he didn't want one of the bangers to find it, either. The sound of nearby voices forced him to give up his search and take off again.

Pain engulfed Kyle with each step, his twisted ankle sending sharp, shooting pain up to his knee. But he couldn't stop, so he did his best to ignore it. It didn't help that this area of the lot was much darker. He hadn't entered this way and wasn't sure how to get back to the street from where he was.

Kyle's mind raced with regret for not walking home with Brendan and calling his mom to pick him up. He needed to find his way out of there. He had lost his pursuers for the time being, but he knew if he didn't make his way out soon, they'd track him down eventually. They were close enough for him to hear one of them tell the others to split up and find him. He knew that was very bad. They had much better odds of finding him if they were all searching in different directions. Stopping to call the police wasn't an option. Help would never get there in time. Plus, he had no idea exactly where he was in the maze of buildings. He had to keep moving every second. He turned a corner and swerved to avoid running face-first into a five-foot block wall.

Kyle cursed under his breath as he looked for another way out. Someone was near enough that he heard their ragged breathing. He ducked behind a stack of wood pallets. It was far from perfect, but he was out of time. Someone could see him between the slats of wood if they looked closely enough, but it was the only cover available. He slowly reached into his pants pocket and pressed the button on the side of his phone to turn it off as he watched his pursuer start down the alley toward him. His heart was beating so hard he was sure the other man could hear it. With his arm hanging loosely at his side, the gun twitched in the shooter's hand. He looked around with wide eyes, trying to find

Kyle. Kyle knew the gunman would find him any second. There was nothing in the alley but stacks of worn pallets, and there was no way his pursuer would leave them unsearched. As the gunman approached his hiding spot, Kyle mentally cursed himself again for not walking home with Brendan. None of this would be happening if he had just done that, like he had a thousand times before. His second thought was that no one would ever know who murdered him.

The shooter kicked one of the pallets, and the pile of wood toppled over. Kyle's time was up. There was no doubt his pursuer could see him. Kyle remained crouched on the pavement, looking up at the gunman. He was just a kid, not much older than Kyle. His eyes narrowed as he raised the gun, but his trembling hand was the only sign Kyle needed to see. Maybe he could use the other guy's hesitation to his advantage, catch him off guard and get the jump on him. He hadn't called out to the other bangers yet, so Kyle still had a chance. His self-preservation instinct kicked in and he pushed against the stack of wood as hard as he could, knocking the gunman backward onto the pavement. The gun slipped from his hand and skittered onto the ground a couple of feet away. With that, Kyle had all the incentive he needed to leap over the block wall. He landed on the other side in a heap, a white-hot pain shooting up his leg from his injured ankle. He scrambled to his feet and took off like a bullet, pushing through the burn.

Kyle didn't stop running until he saw light from the street. A chain-link fence topped with barbed wire blocked his way out, but he shimmied through an opening in the fence and was back on Walnut Street within seconds. He sprinted toward the strip mall where he knew there would be crowds, giving him the chance to disappear. Old Navy was the first store he came to, so he quickly ducked inside. Grabbing a couple of random t-shirts from the clearance table, he headed straight to the dressing rooms. There was no attendant, so he took the room that was farthest away at the end of the row, locked the door, and fell onto the bench. It was only then he relaxed enough to fully catch his breath. Resting against the wall, he lifted his foot to look at his ankle when he caught his reflection in the mirror. Unsurprisingly, he looked like crap. His face was red from exertion, his sweaty hair plastered to his forehead. And he looked scared.

Kyle grabbed his phone from his pocket and turned it on. The cell pinged with another voicemail message while the red, low battery symbol still blinked in the corner of the screen. Just as he pulled up his mom's number, the phone went black.

He cursed out loud and pushed his hair off his forehead. He couldn't stay in Old Navy all night; they were going to close soon. He had to call his mom. He also had to change clothes to avoid standing out. Wearing a red t-shirt with a picture of Lil Nas X on it wasn't exactly low key, and the bangers would be looking for someone in a red shirt. One of the t-shirts he grabbed on his way in was a basic gray one on clearance for $4.99. It was perfect for blending in. He pulled off his sweaty shirt, rolled it into a ball, and launched it at the corner of the dressing room. Putting the new shirt on, he tore the tag off and left the room.

He stood at the changing room entrance, where he quickly scanned the store. Only a few people were still shopping, and he didn't notice anything unusual. No gangbangers searching the clothing rounders for him, so he took that as a good sign. Kyle walked up to the cash register and placed the tag on the counter, silently praying his card had at least six bucks or so left on it. He couldn't remember how much he spent at the movies, but he knew there was a chance it could be declined.

"I, um, I'm gonna wear it out," he said to the young cashier.

"Sure," she said, without looking up.

"Hey, my phone died, and I need to call my mom for a ride home. Do you think I could use your cell for a second?"

She looked up at Kyle and shook her head. "Sorry, we can't bring cells up here with us. Mine is in the back and I can't leave the register."

"Sure, I get it. What about the store phone?" he said, pointing to the phone on the ledge behind the counter.

"You can't make outgoing calls on that. Guess they're paranoid that we'll spend our time talking and not working."

"Yeah. Okay, well, no worries. My bad," he said, handing her his debit card and trying his best to sound casual. Although he was sure he sounded anything but normal, and he imagined he looked like a tweaker, he was so jittery.

The cashier rang Kyle up and he sighed with relief when the transaction went through. He stuffed the receipt into his jeans pocket and headed for the entrance, where he stood outside for a couple of minutes to make sure no one was coming for him. He found a *Rams* logo baseball cap someone had forgotten on the bench in front of the store, so he put in on and took off for home.

He ran for a bit, then had to switch to walking when his ankle began to throb too much. He didn't stop again until he reached his neighborhood, then rested for just a minute at the nearest corner to his house. He lifted his ankle to ease the pressure as he looked up and down the deserted street.

Kyle was so relieved when he saw nothing out of the ordinary that he laughed out loud. Then he limped the remaining half block home. He couldn't believe he just saw the South Side Sinners carry out a hit. Or *something.* He didn't know exactly what had gone down. All he knew was that some guy was dead. He could identify the killers, and even worse, they knew he had video of the murder on his phone. And someone at the police department was involved. He heard the leader tell one of his guys to let their guy at the LAPD know the job was done.

The Sinners would leave no stone unturned to find out who he was and then hunt him down. Of that, he was certain. He silently prayed that wherever his student ID card was, it remained out of sight, because he knew there was no way the gang would let him walk if they found out who he was. They were the infamous South Side Sinners. Everyone in Los Angeles heard the rumors about how they took revenge and took care of their business. None of the stories were good, and now he was their target. He knew he didn't have much time to waste before he had to come up with a solid plan to get himself out of this mess.

The bad news was, Kyle had no idea where to start. What he knew with certainty was that the video was his only leverage. He wasn't going to tell anyone that he had that for the time being until he could figure some things out. Not even his mom. And especially not the police.

He just hoped his mom would know what to do in the meantime.

TWO

Kendra glanced at her watch, the dial glowing 6:30 p.m. Only another thirty minutes left on her shift at the hospital. Kendra loved being a nurse. She really did. The job paid well, but it was never about the money for her. It was about helping people. But days like today, where she had been on her feet for twelve straight hours, were rough. It also didn't help that she hadn't eaten anything since wolfing down a protein bar between patients at 11:00 a.m.

"41B's wife is on the phone for you, Kendra. Again." Kendra turned to face Erika, a nurse who had been at the hospital for almost twenty years.

"Can you tell her we're in the middle of shift change and the incoming nurse will return her call later?"

"You sure that's all you want me to tell her? I have some ideas if you need them," said Erika.

"We're nurses. We have to be kind and empathetic. Even if the family are tactless oafs," said Kendra.

"You keep saying that. I think you're beginning to believe it."

"It's my motto. One day I'm going to have it embroidered on a throw pillow as a reminder."

"Well, I'd like to place my order for one of those when you do," Erika chuckled as she walked back to the nurse's station phone.

Witnessing patients who had spent years abusing their bodies with drugs and alcohol, expecting doctors to work miracles and cure them, was frustrating for Kendra. That perfectly described her patient in room 41B. He believed they could fix what took him four decades to destroy. It was even more frustrating that his family put the blame on the medical community when nothing but comfort care could be done for him.

Overworked nurses were a common issue at the hospital, which was understaffed like many in the greater Los Angeles area. Management had no clue what it was like to deal with an ever-increasing patient load, and yet they kept assigning the nurses more from their plush offices on the top floor. Although complaining would have been pointless. It was clear things weren't going to change anytime soon.

After Kendra finished updating her patients and completing the handoff to the incoming nurse, she grabbed her purse and sweater from her locker and headed outside. The cool night air was refreshing and a welcome relief after being inside all day. She walked across the vast parking lot while rummaging through her purse for her phone. She called her son once she was in the car, but it went to voicemail after only ringing twice. She knew what that meant; he had ignored the call. She would have kept calling until he turned off his phone or answered if she had the energy, but she was too exhausted. It wasn't as if she called him every hour throughout the day. She only wanted to touch base and make sure he was okay. Nor did she want to cramp his style, and she certainly was *not* a helicopter mom. A mother wanting to know what her sixteen-year-old son was up to on a school night didn't strike her as inappropriate or unreasonable.

She and Kyle had been sniping at each other for days now, and having just one conversation with him that didn't go up in flames would be nice. Apparently, asking that of him was too much, given his current state of teenage angst.

Twenty minutes later, Kendra pulled into her driveway, where she found the house shrouded in darkness. Kyle wouldn't have fallen asleep yet, so he must still be out with his friends. She tried his cell again, and the call went directly to voicemail this time. They were definitely going to talk about this when he got home.

It was hard to be a single parent, and a familiar pang of anger shot through her as she thought of Kyle's father. Where was Trent now? She sure didn't have a clue. She didn't even have a current phone number for him. He traveled around the country like a drifter in search of his next big opportunity. To be honest, he was a dreamer, with unrealistic expectations. And it made her angry that he wasn't more involved with their son. He rarely called Kyle, only once every few months at most. Remembering Kyle's birthday wasn't a priority for him either. There were several years when Kendra bought a gift for Kyle and said it had come from Trent. Many times, she wished she had chosen a better father for her son.

Despite Kendra's best efforts, she couldn't bring herself to hate Trent. He gave her their son, after all. And there was a time when she had loved him. But that felt like a lifetime ago now. Trent just wasn't cut out to be a husband or a father. There was a part of her, deep down, that knew that from the start. But she believed she could change him. Looking back, she realized now how foolish that had been. He embraced the nomad lifestyle and refused to be tied down. And as for Kendra, she just didn't. She longed for stability and routine. He used to tell her that her focus was so intense it frightened him. No one had ever described her single-minded drive as nicely as focused. Although she hoped his comment was a compliment, she knew it probably wasn't. She needed to be the best at everything she did and control everything in her orbit.

Before meeting Trent, Kendra had navigated her way through the delights of several unpleasant relationships. So when he declared his love for her, she fell fast and hard for him. She had everything planned out for their perfect life by the time she found out she was pregnant with Kyle. Unfortunately, Trent's perfect life involved going on tour with his band, and that didn't include a wife and child. When Kyle was seven years old, Trent walked away without ever looking back. Coming to terms with that was difficult for Kendra. No woman wants to think a man can get over her without so much as a second thought. Yet that's precisely what Trent did. Within a month, he had already moved on and found a new girlfriend.

Her name was Porsche. Every time Kendra thought of her name, it conjured up images of some bouncy cheerleader barely out of high school who fixated over Pilates, woke up with a full face of make-up and ordered fat free lattes.

Or a stripper.

Partying with his friends to cope with their separation, she could *almost* understand. But hooking up with someone new so soon? She hadn't even filed for divorce yet, and it blindsided her. It was a punch to the gut when she should have been happy to see the back of him. Instead, she built walls to protect herself and left them there. She did her best raising Kyle on her own, with no family to offer advice. Both her parents were gone, and she had no siblings. Despite everything, she managed to build a good life for herself and Kyle, with a great job and loyal friends. Her life was simple, sometimes boring, but still decent in her eyes.

Tonight was a different story, though. She felt like a failure as a mother. Kyle wouldn't even answer her calls, and lately, most of their conversations began and ended with him gracing her with his entire collection of eye rolls.

She pulled into the garage and shook her head to clear her thoughts. Walking into the kitchen, she called Kyle's name on a whim. No answer. She took a quick peek into his bedroom and turned on the light. It was no surprise that his bed was unmade. A cereal bowl, yogurt carton, and a banana peel balanced precariously on the edge of the dresser. She grabbed the trash and dishes and set off for the kitchen to make herself something to eat.

By 9:30 p.m., Kendra was furious because Kyle hadn't contacted her yet. She was exhausted, but obviously couldn't sleep while her teenager was still out running the streets doing God knew what.

He was so grounded.

She tried his phone and got his voicemail again, but decided to leave him a message anyway while she paced the living room.

"Kyle, I have been trying to call you. Where the hell are you? It's a weeknight and you have school tomorrow. Get your butt home, now! Oh, and by the way, you are *so* grounded. And I may take your phone away too, since you can't be bothered to answer my calls. So I hope staying home with me and weeding the backyard sounds like a little slice of heaven, because that's where you're going to be all weekend."

She knew her reaction to him being out later than usual was a little on the melodramatic side. But it was still not without merit. She needed her son to understand he wasn't free to go wherever and whenever he wanted, especially without checking in with her. He was still a minor, and she was still the mom. She pressed the end call button, tossed her phone on the couch, and settled in to find something to watch on TV as she waited for him to return home. She tried to avoid worrying before giving herself a massive migraine, but thirty minutes later when she still hadn't heard from Kyle, she was both worried and livid.

Kendra was pacing again when she heard a key in the front door. She let out a sigh as the worry disappeared and was immediately replaced by anger. Her lecture began before the door was completely open.

"Where have you been? And why haven't you returned any of my calls? I have been—"

Kyle stumbled into the house, out of breath and red-faced, causing her to cut her sentence short at the sight of him. He locked the door after himself, something he never did. He wiped his sweaty forehead across the sleeve of his t-shirt then took two steps toward the lamp, switched it off, and then peeked through the front window blinds. He turned and limped toward Kendra, wrapping his arms around her neck.

"Mom, something really bad happened tonight," he said.

"Hey, calm down. What's the matter?" she asked, pulling away to look at him.

His eyes brimmed with tears as he trembled.

"I saw someone murdered tonight."

THREE

Gilbert "Baby G" Ruiz got up quickly and checked that none of his fellow Sinner's combat soldiers were around to witness the kid take him by surprise. He grabbed his gun and scaled over the block wall after the little *joto*. He let out a loud curse after landing heavily. That *hijo de puta* was dead when he got him. He would make sure he knew he had fucked with the wrong people. The gang initiated Baby G tonight, and he didn't need some *chavalo* screwing it up for him. He had worked too hard promoting his name and their set to let that happen.

"You're dead, motherfucker!" he yelled into the empty alley.

All the men in Baby G's family had been members of the South Side Sinners. It was a family tradition passed down through the generations, and if he messed this up, there would be hell to pay. His father, brothers, and uncles would kill him if Big Boy didn't do the job himself. His chapter, or set as it was known to his fellow gang members, of the Sinners was led by Frank "Big Boy" Delgado, who had always been good to Baby G, but he knew that it wouldn't make a difference if he screwed up his first job. Baby G would meet the same end as the man he shot moments ago.

Running in the direction the kid had gone, he gave up when he came to a chain-link fence with a barbed-wire top. No way did that skinny white *puto* get over that fence. Turning around, he quickly darted down another alley. After half an hour, he had to come to terms with the fact that the kid had evaded him. That wouldn't go over well with Big Boy. But maybe he didn't have to reveal that *he* was responsible for letting him escape. He had to keep that information to himself. Admitting his mistake would be a suicide confession. It was also possible that one of the others caught him, so there was nothing to worry about, anyway.

Baby G traced his steps back to where his evening had begun. He used his phone light to navigate his way through the back area of the warehouse, which was devoid of any ambient light from the street. While he was rehearsing what he would say to Big Boy in his head, the light from his phone reflected on something partially covered by an old fast-food bag. Curious, he bent down and picked it up. He couldn't believe his luck when he held it under his cell flashlight. It was a high school student body card for the kid they were after. The picture confirmed it. He looked at the name on the card.

Kyle Thompson.

"We're coming for you, *cabrón*," he said to himself.

But his excitement was short-lived as it dawned on Baby G that he was the only one who got a clear look at the kid. He couldn't go back to the others and tell them he knew this was the kid. They would want to know how he could be so sure. Lots of teenagers partied here on the weekends and the card could belong to any one of them. But at least it was something he could give to Big Boy. Then Big Boy could call one of his contacts at the LAPD and have them run this kid down. The kid was sure to go to the police with what he saw.

Baby G returned to find that none of his fellow soldiers had found the kid. Their attention shifted to him as he approached.

"I didn't see him," lied Baby G, looking at the ground. "But I found this," he said, holding out the student body card to Big Boy.

Big Boy flipped the card over and glanced back at Baby G.

"What the fuck is this?" asked Big Boy.

Baby G licked his lips nervously. "I, I found it on my way back here. It was on the ground. It was in the same area where that kid took off. I dunno. I thought maybe one of your cops on the payroll could check it out. If it's the kid's, then the cops would know, right? 'Cause he would probably call them about what he saw. Right?"

Sweat started to bead on Baby G's forehead as Big Boy continued to stare at him. Baby G was more frightened by Big Boy's silence than if he had gotten angry. It was Big Boy's lack of emotion and coldness that made him a great captain. He made sure to handle his business, no matter the task. Despite feeling like he would piss himself any minute, Baby G maintained eye contact with Big Boy. To look away would show weakness.

A minute later, Big Boy stuffed the card into his pocket and tapped the body on the ground with his shoe.

"Take care of this *pendejo*. Dump him in one of those bins and bury it in trash," he said.

Baby G helped Joker and Spyder lift the dead man by his feet and shoulders, carrying him to the same garbage bin the kid had hid behind earlier. They tossed him over the side and Joker climbed into the bin, burying him under the trash. The buildings hadn't had any trash service for a while, and the smell from the bin was overwhelming. It would conceal the scent of a decaying body for a while. Not that it would matter. They left a trail of blood that led straight to the bin.

"*Chingado*," muttered Big Boy, glancing down at the blood splatter on his shoes.

He withdrew a rag, a bandana with the gang colors, from his back pocket and wiped the top of his shoes clean. "Let's go. I have business to take care of."

The Sinners followed Big Boy out of the parking lot, climbing into his restored Chevy Impala to make the trip across town to South Central LA.

The trip back to the trap house took less than thirty minutes, and when they arrived, the typical nightly party was in full swing. Outside, Sinners were drinking from beer bottles, while inside their girlfriends were either strung out or passed out. Baby G passed through the living room where a poker game was heating up. Two Sinners were accusing each other of cheating, and he didn't want to be around if things turned physical. He needed time to think, and joining a fight wasn't going to help that happen. When he got to the kitchen, he noticed his road dog, his closest friend, Joey "Lil' Loco" Martinez.

"*Ese*, what's the word, cuz?" said Lil' Loco, when he saw Baby G.

"All good, cuz," replied Baby G. He lifted his chin in the direction of the bedrooms to let Lil' Loco know he wanted to talk to him alone.

They grabbed a couple of beers and headed toward the back of the house. The first bedroom they tried was occupied, and Baby G felt the heat rush to his face when the woman asked him if he wanted to join them.

Entering an empty room at the end of the hall, Baby G collapsed on the worn couch and took a long swallow from his beer bottle.

"Joker told me how shit went down tonight, bro. Heard Big Boy was pissed."

"Yeah, man," said Baby G, peeling the label from his beer bottle.

"Sup, cuz?"

"Nuthin'. Just had a fucked-up night," said Baby G.

"Nah, I know you. Something's on your mind, cuz. Tell Loco your troubles. We're family, *ese*."

Baby G hesitated for a minute. Loco was his closest friend, and he was right. He *was* family. Sinners family. And the family was loyal to one another.

"I saw the *culero* up close, man. I had him cornered. But I choked, *ese*. I fucked up! He came at me, I dropped the gun and he bolted," said Baby G, downing most of his beer.

Lil' Loco's eyes widened. "*Ay dios mio. Joder.*"

"Don't look at me like that, Loco. I know I fucked up. You got any smoke, man?" said Baby G, draining the last drops of his beer.

"Yeah, sure. I can get weed in a minute. So, what did Big Boy say?"

"I didn't tell him, bro. I found the *puto*'s ID and gave it to him. He'll find out who he is with that. I couldn't tell Big Boy I fucked up so majorly the first time I put work in for the set. I'm gonna become a ghetto star, *ese*. I can't mess that up."

"G, you should have told him. If he finds out, it's gonna be worse for you."

Baby G shuddered, thinking about the violation that might come his way. The punishment for breaking gang rules.

"Yeah, I know that, *pendejo*. But no one knows. It's not like the fucking kid is gonna tell Big Boy when we get him."

Lil' Loco chugged his beer and got up. "I'm gonna go get my smoke, man. You want another beer while I'm up?"

"Yeah, sure."

Lil' Loco left his friend sitting alone on the stained sofa in the back of the house. He didn't go to his car to get his weed. Instead, he went to find Big Boy. He thought back to the day he courted-in Baby G. His friend just got his full membership tonight, and already he had screwed it up. Too bad he had to snitch him out now, he thought, but his loyalty to his set ran deep. Lil' Loco did whatever was necessary for his gang, earning his name through his actions. He knew the Sinners couldn't have Baby G out there promoting his name, and therefore their set, after what he had done tonight. He should have just put his work in and kept his mouth shut. But it was done now, and there was no way he would keep Baby G's secret. If he did, and Big Boy found out, he would retaliate against Lil' Loco in the same way he would Baby G. And there was no way Lil' Loco would allow that to happen. He had his sights set on advancing his street rank. Joker had just gone up the ranks and there was no reason Lil' Loco couldn't do the same.

He seethed with anger at Baby G for even confessing to him. Doing that brought Lil' Loco's devotion to the gang into question. It was a low-key insult. Baby G should know Lil' Loco's loyalty would always be to the South Side Sinners. And now Lil' Loco would be held in high esteem for his allegiance to his set and to Big Boy.

When Baby G heard the door open, he looked up, expecting Lil' Loco, but instead saw Big Boy's massive figure filling the frame. Baby G stood, bewildered as to why Big Boy was there. Joker, Spyder, and Lil' Loco followed the large man into the room. Baby G shifted his gaze from Big Boy to Lil' Loco, who refused to make eye contact with him.

In an instant, Baby G understood that Lil' Loco had betrayed him and handed him over to their captain. It made no difference to Baby G whether Lil' Loco did it to save himself or gain points with Big Boy. His family member, someone he considered his own flesh and blood, had betrayed him in the worst way.

"I want to hear it from you, *ese*," said Big Boy, staring directly at Baby G.

Baby G struggled to find words. It didn't matter that he couldn't speak. Big Boy was aware that he had lied to him. He couldn't talk his way out of it, no matter how hard he tried. When Baby G didn't answer, Big Boy reached into his waistband and pulled out a gun. Warm dampness ran down Baby G's leg, staining his pants, as he trembled uncontrollably.

Big Boy glanced down at Baby G's pants with disgust. He lifted the gun and fired it unceremoniously. Baby G slumped onto the filthy couch, a lone bullet wound marking his forehead.

"What a shame. I liked him. Adios, Baby G," said Big Boy. "Clean this up and get rid of him," he said before he walked out.

It surprised Lil' Loco that Big Boy took the shot himself. Joker was the designated shooter for this one, but Lil' Loco wasn't about to question Big Boy's actions. He showed no emotion as he gazed at his dead friend on the couch. Blood ties, friendships, none of that made any difference to Lil' Loco. The Sinners were the only family that mattered to him now. Betray the Sinners, and you betray Lil' Loco.

FOUR

Kendra was at a loss for words. It took her a minute to grasp what Kyle had just said.

"I'm sorry, I'm confused. Did you just say that you saw someone murdered? What are you talking about? And why are you limping?" asked Kendra, her uneasiness escalating with each word.

"Mom, I saw four guys, and they were beating the crap out of some other dude."

Relief flooded through her. It was a mistake. He thought he saw something he didn't.

"Okay, hang on. You saw someone being jumped. Maybe getting injured pretty badly, but you don't know that anyone was killed, Kyle. I'm still calling the police either way, but let's not jump to any conclusions just yet."

"Mom! Listen to me, please! I saw the South Side Sinners murder someone in cold blood."

"Calm down, Son. We don't know anything yet. Tell me exactly what you saw."

"Yes, I do! Oh my God! Will you please stop talking and listen to me for one second, Mom?" his eyes pleaded with her as the words rushed out of him.

"One of them shot the dude in the head. There was so much blood. And then he went completely still after they shot him. There's just no friggin' way he lived. They shot him *in the head*! Then they all started cheering and yelling their gang's name. Then my phone rang, and they saw me. They chased me, and I thought they were going to catch me, but I got away."

The panic crept in again as she tried to make sense of what Kyle was telling her.

"Oh, my God. They saw you? Are you all right?" said Kendra, pulling him close again.

"There's something else too. I lost my student body card there when I fell. That's when I messed up my ankle. If they find it, I'm dead."

"Okay, let's think for a minute. I'll call the police and we'll be safe. Where the hell is my phone?" said Kendra, as she felt between the couch cushions for it.

"There it is!" she said, grabbing it from under a pillow.

Kyle's anxiety skyrocketed when his mother picked up her phone. Part of him wanted to scream at her to stop, but he was also unsure if he should tell her what he heard the gang say about calling their contact at LAPD. He ultimately decided that the chances were very low that the officer dispatched to their house tonight would be involved. He would stick to his plan to play it by ear for the time being.

Kendra dialed 911 and gave the dispatcher a quick outline of their emergency. She ended the call and went to get a wrap, ice, and ibuprofen for Kyle's ankle.

"Here, elevate your ankle and put this ice pack on it until the police get here," she said, handing him a bottled water and two pills.

Kendra hastily changed into jeans and a t-shirt while Kyle leaned back on the couch with his ankle propped on two large pillows. She examined his ankle and found nothing broken.

"You sprained your ankle pretty good, but I don't think you completely tore a ligament. You don't have any bruising or tenderness in your arch, so that's a good sign. You probably have what we call a grade one sprain. It'll be swollen and tender for a few days. I'll wrap it for you later, and that will help. You can use your crutches we got when you broke your leg last year.”

They waited for thirty minutes for the police to arrive, which wasn't surprising for Los Angeles. The two responding officers called in an officer from the gang detail task force unit after hearing Kyle's story. Within twenty minutes, gang unit officer Gutierrez arrived, and the responding patrol officers left him with Kendra and Kyle to repeat their story.

Kendra needed to know what she was dealing with, so she got straight to the point.

"Will we be safe here or should I be worried about that?" asked Kendra.

"I think you'll be fine here, Ms. Thompson. We don't know what, if anything, has happened yet. As soon as I have any information, I'll be in touch. The responding officers took your contact information and your identification information, correct?"

"Yes. So when do you think I'll hear from you, then?"

"Hard to say. I'm going to meet another task force officer at the site, and we'll walk around the area to see what we can find. If we locate something, we'll call in the crime scene unit. If we don't find anything, I may need you to meet me there tomorrow, Kyle, so we can go over the area together. I can come and pick you up."

Kyle swallowed hard and looked at Kendra nervously.

"Is it really necessary for my son to go back there? I'm not sure I'm comfortable with that."

"I doubt it will come to that, Ms. Thompson. If Kyle's depiction of events is accurate, we shouldn't have any trouble locating the spot."

"What about the fact that he thinks he may have dropped his student body card there? That concerns me."

"I *did* drop it there. I *know* I did," said Kyle.

"Well, that area is a well-known hangout for minors, lots of parties, and such. The chances of one of the men you saw tonight finding it and linking it to you as a potential witness would be a long shot. With the number of kids through there on any given weekend, I'd say the odds of that are pretty slim. I don't think you have anything to worry about right now. Plus, we're just a phone call away if you need us."

The task force officer assured Kendra that he would provide them with an update the following day and left them alone again.

Kendra was too anxious to fall asleep. She wrapped Kyle's ankle and settled him in her bedroom, insisting that her king size bed would be more comfortable for him with his ankle elevated. The truth was, she was running worst-case scenarios through her mind, and she didn't like what she came up with. She was unwilling to let Kyle out of her sight, not even for a minute. She entered his room and grabbed his backpack from the bed. After emptying it, she packed a few days' worth of clothes for him. She felt suddenly uneasy in her own home and wanted to be prepared to leave.

She dropped Kyle's backpack at her bathroom door and grabbed an empty overnight bag from her closet.

"What are you doing?" asked Kyle.

"I just thought now might be a great time to go on a little road trip. You know, maybe head up to see Yosemite or something. Just until Officer Gutierrez has some news for us. I didn't think you'd argue about a few days off from school. It's almost summer break, anyway. You won't be missing much."

"Okay. I'm down for that."

"All right. Get some sleep. I'm going to stretch out on my chaise here and read for a while."

Kendra could hear Kyle's rhythmic breathing within minutes. Watching him sleep reassured her, just like when he was a baby, and she was reminded of how effortless it was to love your child more than your own life.

Packing without much thought, she made her way to the back of her walk-in closet. Reaching into the pocket of an old coat, she pulled out a roll of one-hundred-dollar bills. Her emergency cash stash. She wrapped it in a blouse and stuffed it in the bottom of her overnight bag and made a mental note to herself that their first stop in the morning would be the bank to get more cash. She didn't feel secure with her emergency cash fund being only a few thousand dollars. With a plan in place, she covered herself up with a throw and settled into the chaise in the corner of the room. She tried to concentrate on reading, but it was no use. Putting the book aside, she closed her eyes and was drifting to sleep when the sound of a car door woke her up. Without disturbing the curtain, she crept to the window and peeked through the open space in the corner. Alarm gripped her as she stared out of the slit in the curtain to see four men emerge from a car in her driveway. The restored older model was gleaming with fresh, new paint. As the driver exited the car, his t-shirt rose slightly to reveal a gun in his waistband. Fear and panic mixed in her stomach like a bad cocktail. Her head echoed with a loud *CRASH,* indicating that the front door had been kicked in. Kyle sat straight up in bed and called out for her. She hesitated for only a moment until her brain caught up, then sprang into action. Tossing her overnight bag and Kyle's backpack toward the bookshelf on the far wall, she grabbed Kyle's hand.

"Quick! Get in the hiding place, now!" she whisper-shouted to him, dragging him from the bed.

When Kendra rented the house, one of things she genuinely detested about it was the large niche in the master bedroom designed to house a dresser or desk. It screamed the 90s to her, but the landlord wouldn't allow her to drywall over it. Placing a tall bookcase against the wall was her solution. The bookcase concealed the empty space behind it flawlessly. She always told Kyle if they were ever the victims of a home invasion, that would be their hiding space.

Kendra and Kyle pushed the shelving aside, threw the bags inside, scrambled into the empty space, then dragged it back into place, concealing themselves. Crouched in the darkness, they huddled together. Kendra could make out the sound of men ransacking the house. Voices drifted into the room, but the words were indistinguishable. Kyle flinched at the sound of a loud crash coming from his room. With a reassuring squeeze of his hand, she whispered that everything would be okay and she would protect them. It was a promise she couldn't guarantee she could keep, but it was what he needed to hear at that moment. She was unsure who she was trying to convince at that point, Kyle or herself. Maybe both of them.

The voices got louder, and seconds later, the bedroom door crashed open. Kendra tightened her grip on Kyle as her heart pounded in her throat. She heard them opening the closet and searching the room. Her mind raced with all the possibilities. Was this a random home invasion or burglary? Were these the gangbangers? A random home invasion seemed too coincidental to Kendra, in light of the earlier events.

"Fuck!" one of them yelled as something banged against the wall. "This is a fucking shitshow. I want this little *pinche pendejo* found and dealt with. And his mother too. Do you hear me?" he shouted.

That statement confirmed Kendra's suspicions. The Sinners were searching for her son. She didn't realize those words were all it would take. A couple of sentences from the Sinners' captain, and their fate was sealed. A hit on their lives was green-lighted.

Although they were still searching the house, the voices receded after a minute. They were no doubt trying to find a clue about their location or find out if they had run. Kendra and Kyle stayed in the cramped, dark space for an extra ten minutes after they heard the car leave the driveway, just to be safe.

When Kendra pushed the bookcase off the wall, cool air rushed into the confined space, a welcome relief. Kyle limped to the bed, lifted the pillow, and grabbed his phone, while Kendra quickly retrieved their bags from the niche.

"Hurry up, put on something from the clothes I packed you. We need to get out of here," said Kendra.

"Where are we going?" asked Kyle.

When Kyle looked at Kendra, the look of hopelessness etched on his expression almost broke her. Walking up to him, she hugged him tightly. "I don't know yet. I don't have all the answers, but we'll figure it out as we go. I just know we can't stay here."

Kendra just hoped luck would stay on their side. Hope and luck. Neither of which she had much confidence in just then. She knew she couldn't lose Kyle. She couldn't go on if she did. She wouldn't want to laugh. Feel. Live. All Kendra was certain of in that moment was that somehow, someway, she was going to keep her son safe.

FIVE

Kendra grabbed her purse and overnight bag while Kyle got dressed. Before heading to the garage, she gave her room a final sweep to ensure nothing they needed was left behind, then grabbed her car keys and led Kyle to the garage. Peeking through the garage door window, she scanned for unfamiliar cars. Once she was convinced it was safe, she quickly started the car and pulled out. She floored the accelerator and watched the speedometer climb as they sped away, leaving their neighborhood behind. If only there had been some kind of sign to tell her that today would be the day that everything would fall apart. But life was never that easy.

Kendra drove until she found an unimpressive-looking motel situated on an obscure side street, which she was sure would accept her cash with no questions asked. It wasn't the Ritz Carlton by any stretch of the imagination, but right now, anywhere was better than staying at their house.

Once she checked them in, she pulled the car around the back of the motel, where it was out of sight from the street. After entering the room, she collapsed on the desk chair and pulled out her phone, feeling drained.

"Who are you calling?" asked Kyle.

"Officer Gutierrez." she said, pulling out the officer's business card and starting to dial.

"No, wait!"

She pulled the phone away from her ear and frowned at her son. "What?"

"Mom, think about it. How did they find us so fast? I mean, seriously, like we just told the police, and what, less than two hours later, the Sinners are at our house? Even if they found my student body card and figured out it was me, that's too fast. What if the gang has someone on the inside, you know?"

"Kyle, you've been watching too many police shows. I mean, I agree it was fast. But I just can't believe the police are part of it. Especially not an officer in the gang detail unit."

"Mom, please, you don't know what you're doing. This could make it worse for us."

"It'll be okay. Officer Gutierrez will help us."

Kyle sighed and sat on the bed. "Okay, so there are a couple of things I didn't tell you before," he said.

"What are you talking about?"

"Don't get mad at me, please. I just couldn't tell the police."

"Tell them what, Kyle? If you know something else, then you had better tell me right now! These people aren't playing."

"Yeah. No, duh, Mom. All right, so the guy with the gun caught up to me. I was hiding, but he found me. He pulled the gun on me, and I pushed my way out from behind a stack of pallets. He fell and dropped the gun, and that's when I got away."

Kendra was left speechless as she stared at her son, realizing how close this came to ending disastrously. She was shocked that he didn't tell her this before.

"So he saw you, then. And if the gang found your ID, then they know who you are. Your name. That's probably how they found us so fast."

"Yeah. Well, maybe."

"Oh, my God. I can't believe you waited until now to tell me this! What were you thinking?" Kendra shouted.

"I don't know, Mom. I just didn't feel like I should tell the police that."

"Why the hell not? Kyle, they are the only people who can help us!"

"No, they aren't. There's something else. So the leader dude, I heard him tell one of the guys to call their contact at LAPD and tell him the job was done. They have someone working for them in the police department, Mom. I mean, c'mon, this is the Sinners we're talking about it. Of course they would."

"But—" Kendra started to object, but Kyle raised his hand to stop her.

"Let me finish, Mom. So before I really knew what was happening, before I knew they were actually going to *kill* the guy, I started recording it on my phone. I just figured if some guy was getting jumped, then it would go viral or something. It's stupid, I know. But I never meant to record an actual *murder*. Then my phone rang and they saw me. They know I recorded them. And now they know who I am. This is so messed up, I can't believe it," he shouted, punching a pillow.

Kendra was in disbelief over what she was hearing. The gangbangers knew that her son had recorded what she was now certain was a gang assassination. What made it even worse was that someone within the LAPD was somehow linked to it. She was aware that it might not be the investigating officer. But what if it was? Then what? If the police couldn't be trusted to protect them, who else could she turn to?

"So now you're mad at me, right?"

She was. Of course she was.

But Kendra decided to let it drop, because if she didn't, the weight of it would linger heavily between them. And at that moment, they had bigger problems to deal with.

"No. I'm not mad, Kyle. I just really, *really* wish you had mentioned this to me before now. A heads-up would have been nice," she said, trying hard to control the frustration in her voice.

She recognized that he was just a teenager who didn't always make the best choices, but this was a major secret to keep from her. After weighing the options in her mind, she concluded that taking a chance with the police was their only solution. What other choice did she have?

With his hands folded in his lap, Kyle sat on the bed with his head down.

"Kyle, look at me."

He lifted his head and fixed his gaze on Kendra.

"I know you were probably confused about what to do. But if there is anything else I need to know, and I mean *anything,* please tell me now. I can't keep us safe if I don't know what's going on."

"That's it. I swear, Mom."

"Okay, let's try to get a few hours' sleep. I'm going to call Gutierrez in the morning and just see if he has anything new to share with us. Once I talk to him, I'll know whether I feel it's safe to tell him about this or not. Believe me, I am as hesitant as you to let this information get into the wrong hands."

Kendra moved the desk chair under the doorknob to be safe, and they each took a double bed. She believed they were safe for the night, but then remembered their home was found in just a couple of hours. She had no idea what kind of resources the gang had at their disposal. If they had an insider at the LAPD assisting them, they could have access to limitless support.

Kendra stayed up for a long time that night, too worried to sleep. Her life was peaceful until a few hours ago. Tonight, she was in complete turmoil and scared for her and Kyle's well-being. She was off work for the next three days, which meant she could avoid dealing with that. Since tomorrow was Friday, she had the entire weekend to decide what to do.

Kendra drifted off to sleep only to dream of being chased and woke up in a cold sweat at 5:00 a.m. Kyle was up shortly afterward, the first time he had seen that time of day since he was a toddler. Kyle could stay up as late as he wanted, but trying to wake him early usually guaranteed Kendra was in for a fight. She said good morning cautiously, trying to get a read on his mood. He didn't look at her, but grunted a response. She realized he was as scared as she was, and she vowed to herself to do everything possible to prevent the fear from creeping further in.

Kendra decided to swing by a nearby McDonald's for a fast breakfast, hoping that would lend some semblance of normality to their morning. It didn't. Kyle was quiet as they ate back at the motel room. Once they finished, she took out the officer's card and dialed his number.

"Gutierrez," he answered on the second ring.

"Officer Gutierrez, this is Kendra Thompson."

"Yes, Ms. Thompson. I was waiting until it got a bit later to call you this morning. So, we did find a crime scene last night. We recovered a deceased body near the site, and an investigation is now underway."

"Officer, gangbangers came to my home last night looking for us."

"I did get some feedback a few hours ago that your neighbors called in a disturbance last night, right after midnight. I wanted to ask you about that."

Alarm bells went off in Kendra's head. She was unnerved by the officer's nonchalant attitude toward the *disturbance,* as he put it, at her home. Gangbangers went after her and her son at their home, and he had that information for a few hours. Yet his only response was casually inquiring about it, and only after she called him. He was protecting them about as well as a kindergarten teacher would a child being teased. Meaning he wasn't protecting them at all. When she didn't answer him, he proceeded talking as if gangbangers showing up at her home was an everyday occurrence.

"So, the deceased was the nephew and campaign manager for Senator Steven McLeod, visiting Los Angeles during his campaign push. The District Attorney wants this one wrapped up swiftly. Why don't you tell me where you are, and I'll come and get you and bring you in so we can go over the details of what Kyle saw one more time? Oh, and you're sure your son got this on video, right? Does he have his phone with him?"

His words punched a hole right through her chest. Kendra knew she hadn't mentioned the video to officer Gutierrez. She didn't even know that it existed until after they arrived at the motel late last night. Her vision blurred around her, and she felt as though she might pass out. She almost wished she would.

Kendra attempted to keep her voice normal, despite the fact that the first gentle breeze could knock her down. An accurate and likely possibility.

"Officer Gutierrez, I need to call you back," she said, before tapping the end call button on her phone.

"Shit," she said, still looking at her phone.

"What did he say?"

"He asked if I was sure that you got the murder on video and wanted to know if your phone was with us. He didn't react when I told him the Sinners came to our house last night. He already knew they were coming for us. Then he asked where we were so he could come and get us."

"We didn't tell him about the video, Mom! I told you! I knew we shouldn't trust the police. Not after what I heard."

"You're right. We can't trust him. He's obviously involved somehow. He said they found a dead body, and it was the nephew of some senator."

Kendra accessed the local news app on her phone. Her heart began to race as she scrolled down the headline to the article.

Devon McLeod, 26, nephew and senior campaign staffer for Senator Steven McLeod, was found murdered last night in Los Angeles.

"Devon was a bright young man with a promising future. This is a terrible blow not only to our family, but to my campaign as well. Our family is devastated," Senator McLeod was quoted as saying.

According to coworkers, Devon left the Biltmore Hotel alone at around 5:00 p.m. for an early dinner. When he didn't return by 11:00 p.m. and no one could reach him, the police were notified. After receiving a tip, police discovered his partially concealed body in a warehouse garbage bin in the 800 block of Walnut Avenue just after midnight.

Police say the murder appears to be the work of more than one assailant, although they wouldn't say why, and no other details or the cause of death are being released at this time.

Anyone with information is asked to contact Gang Task Force Officer Ramón Gutierrez at 213-555-2000. Or you may remain anonymous by calling Crime Stoppers at 800-888-8000.

Kendra realized with a jolt what that meant. Her son was the sole witness to what promised to become one of the biggest murder investigations in recent Los Angeles history. She didn't know who she could trust in the police department, and a notorious gang wanted them both dead. She realized having the police protect them from the Sinners was an illusion. It would come down to her to keep them safe. At least for the foreseeable future.

"Turn off your phone, Kyle. Take the sim card out and give it to me. No using our phones from this point forward. Grab your things. We're leaving," said Kendra.

SIX

Big Boy wasted no time green-lighting the hit on Kyle Thompson and his mother Kendra upon his return to the trap house last night. Within the South Side Sinners, his captain's position was the minimum rank that could order a hit, and Big Boy made this mission a priority for all the foot soldiers in his chapter. And he made sure his nation, the entire gang, knew it. He was still pissed off that Baby G had betrayed him like he had, but Lil' Loco came through for him. Big Boy's leader put his trust in Big Boy and rarely questioned his orders. But he understood that if the witness wasn't dealt with, his leader's patience would wear thin.

Big Boy's phone rang, and he glanced at the familiar number. He purposely let it ring three times before picking up the call. "Let the *cabrón* wait," he thought.

"Yeah," said Big Boy.

"Have you got this handled yet?" barked the voice on the other end of the line.

"I told you I'm taking care of it. Where the fuck is the intel you promised me?"

"There hasn't been any activity on the mother's credit card, and she called me this morning. I can't get a subpoena for a phone trace. I have no reason to ask a judge for that yet. They aren't missing or impeding an investigation. She'll step out of line soon. She's a fucking nurse, not a double agent. As soon as I have anything, you'll be the first to know. In the meantime, I need a lid put on this thing quickly. So stop dicking around. Get them found and dealt with. Do you hear me?"

"You should remember who you're talking to, *ese*. I don't give a shit who you are, *vato*. Keep it up and you'll wake up to a piece in your face one morning soon."

Big Boy ended the call before the cop could reply. He hated that *culero* and would use any excuse to empty a clip into him one day.

Big Boy's contact at the LAPD gang unit had feelers out everywhere. So what was the holdup? Employees in the city finance office, city works, even the disposal division had workers on the take. They were all eyes and ears for the Sinners. If this kid and his mom so much as sneezed, they should know about it. But it had been nine hours since he called out the hit, and he still had nothing from Gutierrez yet. Kendra and Kyle Thompson could be anywhere by now. That's why he ordered every warrior on the street to find them and their car. Big Boy was eager to advance up the ranks, and he needed a swift resolution to this mission. The fact that the kid was able to record them in the first place didn't bode well for him. He knew his leader had turned a blind eye to it momentarily, but he wouldn't do so for much longer.

A knock on his office door snapped Big Boy out of his thoughts. To call his space an office was a stretch. It was a back bedroom furnished with a desk, laptop, a worn-out office chair, and a mini-refrigerator next to a sagging couch under the window. Above the desk hung a picture of Big Boy and his dad, Frank "Shorty" Delgado, Sr., flashing their gang sign in full gear and colors. The picture was taken right after Big Boy's initiation, when he was jumped into the Sinners. The beating left his left eye swollen shut and his lip bleeding in the picture. Proudly crouched next to his father, he confirmed his allegiance to the South Side Sinners. Frank Sr. was a devout member of the gang and remained so right up until the day he died. A true *veterano*. It was inevitable that Big Boy would follow his lead and pledge to the Sinners.

Most members of the Sinners had family in the gang many generations back. Once you were in, you were in for life because the links were deeply rooted. Death was the only way out, and the Sinners valued loyalty to the gang above all else. When he was twelve years old, Big Boy became a spotter on probation for the Sinners, then a runner at thirteen, and at fifteen, he was initiated as a foot soldier after being jumped in at his dedication. His confirmation came shortly after that when he completed his first mission; a hit on a drug dealer who had doubled-crossed the Sinners. Even as a young boy, Big Boy was fearless and took on every mission with fervor. He moved up the ranks swiftly, and at twenty-one years old, was now a captain. Once he moved up the gang infrastructure, he would be at the higher end of the chain, and he would no longer have contact with street level members.

"Yeah," said Big Boy, giving permission for the visitor to enter.

One of Big Boy's top foot soldiers, Spyder, entered. "Clown found their car. He's following them. She went to a bank on Figueroa. You want him to dump the clip?"

"I want him to follow them. I don't need no more play on this with fuckin' eyes everywhere. Wait till you can do it with no one around. Then bring the kid's phone back to me, and *only* me. Take Joker with you and get out there."

Joker was among the top choices for a back-up shooter, which was a standard procedure on all hits. Joker and Spyder left, leaving Big Boy to wait for word that the mission was completed. It was just a matter of time now. Mother and son were about to get their bedtime story.

Big Boy sent a text to his worthless contact at LAPD. The *pendejo* was a fool. Big Boy's warriors had found the kid and his mother before the police did. At least he wouldn't have to deal with the contact for a while after this. The cop could inform his bosses it was being wrapped up, and Big Boy could tell his leader they were on their way to take the witnesses out. He was relieved it would all be over soon and that he could put an end to it before it spiraled any further out of control. It would be business as usual once Big Boy destroyed the video and the kid's phone. He leaned back, grabbed a beer from the mini fridge, and took a long sip. He sent a text with the latest development to his leader and smiled when he received a positive response. He left the office to move on to other business, thinking the mess was resolved.

SEVEN

Kendra weaved her way through traffic on the crowded 101 Freeway. The traffic in Los Angeles never eased up, not even on the weekends. Although her mind screamed for her to go faster, she drove at a respectable sixty-five miles an hour. Their safest option was to blend in, and she knew it. The strip malls they passed had a mix of fast-food restaurants, gas stations, 7-11s, and grocery stores. The landscape was unremarkable and familiar. But her mind was consumed with worst-case scenarios about their escape plan. Which was nonexistent, really. Her only plan at the moment was just driving away from Lynwood and South Los Angeles. She would figure out a more solid plan later. Right now, she just wanted to put some distance between her and the city. Their first stop had been the bank, where she withdrew as much money as allowed without prior approval from her bank. Which wasn't a significant amount. She didn't understand it. It was *her* money. Why couldn't she withdraw whatever amount she wanted? The teller patiently explained that prior notification was required to withdraw anything over a certain dollar amount. She was sure that it was related to the latest bank regulations for cash deposits and withdrawals. No one dealt in cash anymore. Everyone else had to suffer because of the money launderers. The total sum of her funds, coupled with the cash she took from home, was $10,000.00. To Kyle, it seemed like a substantial amount of money. She knew it wasn't. It would go quickly. Especially since she needed to get rid of her vehicle and buy them a non-descript beater car. If the Sinners knew where she lived, it was likely that they also knew what she drove. Officer Gutierrez could find that information easily.

Kendra didn't know how much information Gutierrez or the Sinners had about her and Kyle, but she couldn't take any chances if she wanted to keep them safe. She chose to be cautious and assume they had access to her entire life. Which meant using credit cards or cell phones was out of the question. But she had to make sure Kyle's phone stayed secure. It was the only bargaining chip they had. That, of course, was assuming the high-profile gang who wanted to kill them were open to negotiations. Which wasn't likely. Kendra wasn't known for her beacon-of-hope demeanor, but she understood the importance of staying positive to prevent herself from breaking down.

"We have to go to the FBI. Since we don't know who to trust at the LAPD, we have to go to another law enforcement agency," said Kendra.

"Okay," said Kyle, nodding.

Kendra put the sim card back in her phone and looked up the nearest FBI field office. Turning the car around, she followed the GPS until they reached their destination. She grabbed a ticket from the automated machine as they entered the parking garage and found a space near the elevator. The sign directed them to the third floor. They exited the lift into a carpeted hallway with glass doors directly across from them.

Department of Justice, Federal Bureau of Investigation
Fidelity, Bravery, Integrity

The logo on the door made Kendra somehow feel better. She felt she could trust the FBI. She needed that to be true. She pulled the heavy door open, and Kyle followed her in. They approached the reception desk and a young man glanced up at them.

"What can I help you with?"

"I need to talk to an agent, I guess. My son saw someone murdered. A gang hit. And we think the LAPD is involved. Gangbangers are after us, and I don't know what to do. We need help."

The young man gave no indication that this wasn't something he heard from walk-ins every day. He calmly picked up the phone and murmured into it. Kendra couldn't hear what he was saying, but he told them to take a seat and an agent would be out soon. They sat in upholstered chairs in the lobby, waiting for someone to come for them. Behind the desk, Kendra saw agents with guns in shoulder holsters and badges attached to their belts, office personnel carrying files, and even some uniformed police officers. She almost closed her eyes for a minute when something, or rather someone, caught her eye. She blinked and sat up straighter in her chair.

It was Gutierrez. What was he doing at the FBI office? She had a hard time reconciling that the officer she suspected of being corrupt was at the agency she had come to for help. She sprang up and walked to the reception desk.

"Excuse me. I think I know that agent. Over there in the black polo shirt and jeans. Do you know his name?"

"He's actually not an FBI agent. He's a gang task force officer with the LAPD assigned to this field office. The LAPD works in conjunction with the FBI gang squad. I think his name is Gutierrez. Maybe Gonzalez? No, it's Gutierrez."

Kendra's pulse quickened as the panic slammed into her chest, almost knocking her off balance. "Wrong person. Thank you."

She spun on her heels without another word and headed straight for Kyle. She grabbed his arm and pulled him out of his chair.

"Come on. We're leaving. Now."

"What? Why? What's wrong?"

"I'll tell you outside. Just move."

Kendra punched the elevator button over and over until she thought she might jam it. Her hands trembled while she waited for the green arrow to appear. She was inside, pulling Kyle in after her before the doors were fully open.

"What is going on, Mom?"

"Wait. We'll talk in the car," she said, glancing up to look for the camera she was sure was there.

The doors opened to the parking garage and Kendra ran to their car, pulling a confused Kyle after her. Once inside, she started the car and pulled out, the tires squealing on the pavement.

"Officer Gutierrez was in the FBI office. He's part of the gang unit assigned to the FBI office. The LAPD and the FBI work together in some kind of co-op squad."

"Seriously? Are you sure it was him?"

"Positive. The guy at the desk confirmed his name for me. Damn it!" Kendra shouted, hitting the steering wheel.

Kyle shot a quick glance her way, but didn't comment. It was rare that he saw his mother this angry. It scared him to know she was worried.

"We have to get out of this car," she said.

"Yeah, I'm hungry. Can we stop for something to eat?"

"No, I mean we have to sell this car and get something that will blend in anywhere. An older car. The Sinners and Gutierrez will be looking for this car. We can eat after that. Keep your eye out for a small car dealership. The seedier, the better."

Kyle looked at Kendra like she had just asked him to jump out of their moving vehicle.

"Seriously, Mom? The seedier the better? You wanna drive an old beater?"

"I want to keep us safe. That's what I want to do. We need to be as anonymous as possible until I can figure out what to do."

Ten miles down the road, she saw the perfect place. Raul's Used Cars.

Exiting the freeway, she pulled into the dirt lot. The door of a small stucco building, which appeared to be on the brink of collapse, was adorned with a large welcome sign. They were greeted by a short Hispanic man with a wrinkled face and a big smile, who approached them before she could bring the car to a full stop. Kendra assumed he was Raul.

"Welcome to Raul's! I am Raul," he said, peeking into the car at Kyle. "We are looking for a first car for this young man today?" he asked.

Kendra got out of the car and leaned against the door. "Actually, I want to get rid of this one and downgrade. To something a bit less expensive."

"Oh, oh, *sí*," he said, walking around Kendra's Kia Optima to check it out.

Kendra left Raul to inspect her car as she made her way to the used cars. Kyle trailed Kendra, looking more and more disheartened with each car they passed. Kendra ignored his attitude and discovered an older silver Toyota Corolla with tinted windows and patches of oxidized paint. The price tag on the windshield showed $5,000.00. Kendra thought Raul was delusional for thinking anyone would pay that much. Opening the door, she settled into the driver's seat. The mileage on the odometer read 188,064 miles. Her confidence in her plan dwindled when she saw the high mileage. She had never owned a car with that many miles on it before.

"Ah, I see you like this beauty," said Raul, leaning his arm against the car door and peering inside at Kendra.

"Well, Raul, I would hardly call it a beauty. But that's not what I care about. Is it in good shape mechanically? I need something reliable."

"Oh yes! I am a certified mechanic. For thirty-five years, I have worked on all kinds of cars. This one drives like a charm. She won't let you down. Very reliable."

"How much will you give me for my Kia?"

"Let's go inside and I'll run the numbers."

Raul led Kendra and Kyle inside, where they sat in two metal folding chairs facing Raul across his desk. The office wasn't pretty, but it was well-kept and organized. Raul pulled his calculator closer and spent several minutes concentrating on the figures.

"I think I buy your car for my wife," he said, smiling. He removed the tape from the calculator, then circled a number and slid it across the desk to Kendra.

Kendra stared at the number. The price was lower than what she knew she could get elsewhere, but she didn't have the luxury of time to shop around.

"This is the cash I give you today. Then you take the Toyota. Fair enough?" asked Raul.

Kendra glanced at Kyle. "Kyle, can you get our things out of the car, please? Make sure you check every inch of the car so we don't leave anything."

Kyle rolled his eyes, but went outside to do as Kendra asked. Raul whistled and a young boy, around Kyle's age, emerged from a back office.

"Mijo, take the Toyota Corolla out back and fill it with gas. Give it a quick rinse and make sure all the paperwork is in there."

The boy nodded and took off at a jog out the front door.

"Your son? asked Kendra.

"Grandson," said Raul. "My daughter, she is no good at motherhood. So her mother and I, we raise him," said Raul, shrugging.

"Listen, Raul. I wanted to talk to you without my son here. I need a favor. I don't want to ask you to do anything that would get you in any kind of trouble, but I need your help."

"I run a legitimate business here, Ms. Thompson. All my paperwork is done just how it's supposed to be done."

"I'm sure it is. I'm just asking you to delay filing the paperwork. Just for a couple of days. I just need to get a head start before someone finds me and my son. That's all I'm asking. Please Raul."

Raul took his time to answer Kendra, staring at her for a long moment. "I see. My daughter, she has a husband, maybe like yours, *si*? Maybe I misplace the contract. I am getting older, and these things happen, yes?"

"Yes. These things happen. Thank you, Raul. I can't let him find us," said Kendra.

Correcting him would have meant telling a long and complicated story to a stranger, so she refrained. It was better for him to think that she was escaping from an abusive partner. Although it had been less than twenty-four hours since her son witnessed a murder, she was certain the weariness had already taken up residence on her face and she looked the part of an abused woman.

After signing the contract, she finalized it by shaking Raul's hand. He held onto her hand for a moment longer than he needed to, then placed his other hand on top of hers. "God bless, Ms. Thompson. You and your boy stay safe."

Kendra put the envelope of cash into her purse, zipped it up, and gave him a smile. Leading her through the back door, Raul led her to the parking lot behind the office, where Kyle and her new car were waiting. As she looked at the dilapidated car, she realized she had never been less excited about a car purchase. Despite her misgivings, she put on a brave face and walked toward them confidently. She gave Raul a wave and a final thank you before getting into the car, starting it, and pulling out onto the street.

Across the street in the U Haul parking lot, Spyder and Joker kept a lookout for Kendra and her son. She had been inside for quite a while, and Joker was eager to empty his clip and finish the mission. But Big Boy wanted things done discreetly. They watched the kid unpack their car, taking backpacks and overnight bags around the back of the building. It looked like they were selling the car, but Joker wasn't worried about it. He would follow her out in whatever car she bought. Joker was getting anxious after a two-hour wait, when an old man moved Kendra's Optima into the gated back lot. After a few minutes, the elderly man left the building and locked the door behind him. They had missed their target leaving the car dealership. Joker stepped on the accelerator after sharing a quick glance with Spyder. Pulling right up to the old man, Spyder jumped out of the car, pointing his 9 mm at him.

"Back inside, old man," said Spyder.

Raul's hands shook as he unlocked the door. He silently prayed that his grandson would stay in the back lot, out of sight.

Joker pushed Raul onto a metal chair and slammed the door after them, while Spyder went to the back.

"Where are the woman and her kid?" asked Joker.

When he didn't respond, Joker stepped closer and leveled his gun at Raul's forehead. Spyder appeared, dragging Raul's grandson after him before Raul had a chance to respond.

"Look what I found, *ese.*"

"No!" yelled Raul.

"I want to know where she was going and what she was driving. Right now, or I'm gonna waste the kid. You understand? I'm not playing, *cabrón,*" said Joker, aiming his gun at Raul's grandson.

"Okay, okay. I don't know where she is going—she didn't tell me anything. Just that she was trying to get away from her husband. She bought a silver Toyota Corolla. Here. Here is the paperwork. Please just don't hurt my grandson," Raul's hands trembled as he handed the contract to Joker. "God forgive me," Raul whispered, as he made the sign of the cross across his chest.

Joker ripped the paper from Raul's hand and pointed the gun at him. The directive from Big Boy was to make sure there were no witnesses. And Joker never failed to finish his missions, which made him one of the best *soldados* in the Sinners. He never disobeyed orders. His target didn't matter, regardless of who or why. He carried out the Sinner's orders without question.

Joker didn't hesitate to pull the trigger twice in a nausea-inducing act of cruelty.

EIGHT

Kendra drove through the unfamiliar streets in her new car, searching for a drugstore. The best she could find was a ninety-nine-cents store. It wasn't ideal, but would have to do for now. She drove into the lot and parked close to the front entrance.

"Let's go get some snacks and supplies. Get whatever you need in the way of toiletries. And a baseball hat too," said Kendra.

Kyle sighed and turned in his seat to face her. "What's the plan, Mom?" he asked, attitude written all over his face.

Kendra shook her head. "I honestly don't know right now, Kyle. I just know we need to keep moving, okay? I know this is frightening. I'm scared too. But I need time to think about what to do, okay? So cut me some slack for the time being. We're safe, so I've done all right so far."

"Yeah, whatever. I guess being alive is a win at this point," he said, rolling his eyes and shaking his head.

Kendra didn't miss the sarcasm in his tone, but ignored it. He was right, but he made it seem as if she deserved to win the world's worst mother award. She didn't get them into this mess. She sighed and attempted to come up with something positive to say, but couldn't.

"Listen, I'm fresh out of motivational speeches at the moment. And I could really do without your attitude right now, okay? I'm doing the best I can."

Kyle didn't reply, instead he opened the squeaky car door and headed toward the entrance of the store.

Kendra counted to ten in her head while trying to tamp down her frustration. The last thing she needed was a knock-down, drag-out fight with him. Following her son, she entered the store. For twenty minutes, they filled the shopping cart with snacks and supplies. She wasn't excited about it, but she knew it was necessary, so she grabbed a box of brown hair dye to cover her very expensive new blonde highlights. Thirty minutes later, they made a quick stop at Taco Bell for lunch and hit the road again.

Kendra headed north and cut over to Highway 99. Compared to Interstate 5, this route had more exits and small towns and was less traveled. By late afternoon, they had been driving most of the day through nondescript farming towns and endless fields of crops and were both eager to stop for the day. After exiting in Tulare, Kendra discovered a Motel 6 less than a mile away. She attempted to use cash, but they wouldn't let her book a room without a credit card. Despite her hesitation, she had to give them one of her cards. She used a Visa card she hadn't charged anything on in months, reasoning that if someone was tracking her, maybe they were only watching her checking account debit card. With any luck, it would take some time for her pursuers to discover her whereabouts.

Kyle went straight for the TV when they got in the room, flopping onto the bed. Kendra decided to dye her hair and get it over with. While the dye set, she watched TV with Kyle, then dried her hair with a towel, and scrutinized herself in the bathroom mirror. She hated the new color. The situation demanded professional help. But that wasn't going to happen, and her hair color was the least of her worries. It didn't even rank in the top twenty. Keeping that in mind, she finished drying her hair and styled it into a loose ponytail.

"What do you think? Is my hair as bad as I think it is?" asked Kendra.

Kyle looked up from the television and frowned. "Well, it's not great."

Kendra sighed and touched her ponytail.

"It's not that bad, Mom."

Not that bad would have to do for now, she thought to herself.

Neither of them was very hungry, so for dinner, they nibbled on the snacks they bought earlier. They had difficulty staying awake due to the stress of their situation and lack of sleep from the previous night, and they were both asleep by 8:00 p.m.

Kendra's body clock woke her up just after five, just like on a workday. She woke Kyle up, packed up their belongings, and they were on the road by 6:00 a.m. They took advantage of the motel's free continental breakfast, though it was only stale cinnamon rolls and what could barely be called coffee. But it was free, and better than having nothing. But only slightly.

Amelia Parker, in the LAPD records department, was tracking Kendra's credit card activity. When she got a hit on Kendra's card at the Motel 6 in Tulare, she called officer Gutierrez to give him Kendra's last known location. She liked Ramón Gutierrez, and she owed him for helping with her brother's tickets. Amelia had no idea that Gutierrez was on the Sinners' payroll and was clueless as to the events she would set in motion by passing along Kendra's information. Gutierrez provided Amelia a legitimate case number, and she had no reason to question him or the validity of his request.

When Kendra and Kyle left the motel, Joker and Spyder were already en route there, but the room was empty by the time they arrived. By discovering the used hair dye box and the information they had on Kendra's new car, they kept the search going, predicting she would continue heading north on Highway 99. They hastily drove out of the hotel parking lot and onto the highway. In under ten minutes, they had the silver Toyota in their sights and Joker hit the gas. They were trailing two car lengths behind Kendra and Kyle. Using Raul's copy of the sales contract, Spyder verified the license plate number.

"Let's empty the clip on them, *ese*. Nothing but farmland and illegals around here. We need these *putos* ten toes down," said Spyder.

With a nod, Joker gave Spyder the go ahead. He didn't care if Spyder was the shooter on this one. The only thing Joker wanted was the hit on the woman and her kid done so he could get back to LA. He pressed harder on the gas pedal and used the emergency lane to pace the Toyota. Drawing his Walther PPK, Spyder lowered the window, but he fired a second too late. The Toyota accelerated hard to try avoiding a minivan that was trying to merge into the lane in front of them, but Kendra wasn't fast enough. The minivan cut them off, and the bullet shattered the back window, forcing Kendra's car to lurch to the right. Kendra had nowhere to go but to squeeze between two big rigs. The eighteen-wheeler she cut off braked hard and blasted the horn at her. When the bullet hit Kendra's car, the driver of the minivan in front of her panicked and slowed down, stopping Joker from reaching the Toyota. As it winds through the California central valley, Highway 99 changes from a two-lane road to a four-lane highway. Luckily for Kendra, they were currently on the two-lane section, so Joker had no way around the minivan blocking him. If he used the emergency lane to go around them, he would be too far ahead of the Toyota to get a good shot. In an attempt to clear their path, Spyder leaned out of the window and fired at the minivan, which sped up to get away. At the same time, the two big rigs took the interchange to Highway 198 west. The Toyota held its position between the two trucks, trailing them onto Highway 198 as Joker and Spyder tried unsuccessfully to cross lanes and follow, but another eighteen-wheeler forced them back into the number two lane. Joker slammed his fist on the dashboard and sped toward the next exit to backtrack.

Kendra's hands trembled as she gripped the steering wheel. Kyle remained on the floor of the passenger seat, where she had pushed him down and yelled at him to stay hidden a few minutes ago. She narrowly avoided the truck in front of her, but almost collided with a fast-moving Hyundai in the lane next to her. The driver swerved and honked at her, flipping her off as she went by. Kendra barely registered it. Her only thought was that the gang had found them. There was no doubt in her mind that it had been the use of her credit card. There was no other way.

"Mom?"

Kyle held out a bloody hand as she turned to him. Touching the back of his neck again, he came back with more blood. He had a terrified look in his eyes.

"Okay, stay calm. It's probably from the glass," said Kendra. Her nursing training taught her to remain calm during emergencies and keep her patients calm too. But this was her son, and her stomach twisted at the thought of him being hurt.

Kendra spotted a sign for a truck stop off the next exit. The large billboard promised the last food and fuel for fifty miles. She pressed the gas pedal and left the highway within two minutes, parking behind a line of trucks in the back of the truck stop café. She was confident her car wasn't visible from the parking lot entrance. After examining Kyle, she discovered a minor cut on his neck, which she cleaned with hand sanitizer and dressed in a bandage she dug out from the bottom of her purse. They sat on the car bumper for a few minutes to calm their nerves, concealed by the trucks.

"Stay in the car and lock the doors. I'm going to leave the keys. If anything happens, lay on the horn and drive to the front of the diner."

"Where are you going?" asked Kyle, looking around nervously.

"I'm going to go inside and get us some food to go and try to find a map. We can't stay here all day."

"What about the gangbangers?"

"They saw us take this highway, but I don't think they will expect us to have stopped right away. So I'm hoping they kept going and are ahead of us now. That will buy us a little time. I'll be back soon."

Kendra handed Kyle the keys and waited until he was inside with the door locked. Jogging to the diner entrance, she stepped inside. The open kitchen was positioned behind a breakfast bar that ran almost the full length of the room. Hustling around the booths and tables were several waitresses wearing jeans, aprons, and t-shirts with the truck stop logo on them.

"Sit anywhere you want to, hon," said a young woman carrying a coffee pot as she passed Kendra.

Kendra found an open stool at the breakfast bar and pulled the menu from between the bottles of ketchup and mustard in front of her. She wasted no time in placing her order for two cheeseburgers and fries once the waitress arrived. There was a small store accessed through a glass door to the left of the restaurant that sold travel items. She was sure she could find a map there.

Glancing around for the bathrooms, she spotted them at the far end of the room. She quickly made her way there, eager to get their food, buy a map, and get back to Kyle. She was washing her hands when a woman came out of the stall furthest from the sinks. She was middle-aged, in faded jeans and a flannel shirt, and nodded a greeting at Kendra. Her wrinkled face showed a life spent outdoors, and her blonde hair was graying and cropped short. She had electric blue eyes that matched her shirt. Kendra nodded briefly and looked away.

"If you don't mind me saying so, you and your son should really stay off the main highways," she said, glancing at Kendra in the mirror.

Kendra froze, her eyes locking on the stranger in the mirror. The bathroom was quiet except for the water that continued to spill from the tap where Kendra left it running. Reaching over her, the woman turned off the faucet.

"Look honey, I don't know what you've got going on, but you look like you could use some help. I was driving the rig you cut in front of when those jackasses shot your car window out."

Kendra released the breath she had been holding in.

"Where are you headed?" asked the woman.

"North," Kendra said, barely above a whisper. She didn't recognize the sound of her own voice.

She sounded terrified. Or crazy. Maybe a little of both.

"Just north? Well, I'm heading up the I-5 into Sacramento. You're gonna have to get that window fixed, but if I were you, I'd ditch that car for now. You and your boy can ride with me if you'd like. I've got plenty of room. I'm not asking for anything in return. Long as you aren't running from the law. But you don't strike me as the fugitive type. I have a buddy near here who can keep your car out of sight, so lover boy doesn't find it. At least until you come back for it. If you want," she said, as she pulled paper towels from the dispenser.

Kendra turned to face her. "Why would you do that for us?"

"Why wouldn't I? It didn't look like whoever those assholes are were playing. What kind of person would I be if I left you and your kid here on your own without offering to help? The truth is, my offer is based solely on selfish reasons. My karma needs some polishing."

Kendra didn't answer her, deep in thought.

"Well, anyway. I'm sitting at a table by the door. If you decide you want to ride with me, let me know. Otherwise, stay safe."

With that, the woman walked out, leaving Kendra alone in the bathroom. She studied her reflection in the mirror. Her newly colored hair was a mess thanks to the wind from the broken car window. She appeared on the verge of a breakdown, with dark circles under her eyes. Their situation was like a house of cards, just one good push away from collapsing, and she knew it. It was becoming clear to Kendra that she couldn't do this alone, however determined she was to save her son. If she knew her last breath would give him another year, a day, even another hour, she would do whatever that took. Without question.

She dried her hands, tossed the towels into the trash can, and headed back to the bar to pick up her food. Turning to the door, she saw the woman sitting by herself at a table. She had a cup of coffee and a piece of pie in front of her as she scrolled through her phone. Kendra laid two twenty-dollar bills on the counter, not waiting for change. Then she walked to the table by the door. She couldn't trust anyone and wasn't sure why she trusted this woman. She had known her all of five minutes. But like it or not, she was all Kendra had at the moment.

The woman glanced up and laid her phone down. Kendra held out her right hand.

"I'm Kendra Thompson. My son and I need help. And if you're willing to help us, I'd be very grateful," she said, her voice shaky.

The woman grasped Kendra's hand in a firm grip. "Pleased to meet you, Kendra. Louella Murphy. But everyone calls me Lou. Let me settle up here and I'll meet you outside."

NINE

Joker took the 198 west at ninety miles per hour. The highway was nearly deserted, so he expected to catch up to the woman and her son quickly. But after driving at high speed for over ten minutes, he had to accept that they had somehow escaped.

"Where the fuck are they?" he asked Spyder. "There's nowhere to get off this fucking freeway. There's nothing but fields in every direction."

"She must have taken that first exit we saw. For that truck stop," said Spyder.

Joker parked the car near the exit after pulling off the highway. He pressed the speed dial for Big Boy, put it on speaker, and laid the cell on the seat between him and Spyder.

"Yeah," answered their captain.

"We had her and some *puto tarado* in a minivan fucked it up and we lost her. We know what detour she took, but we can't find her on the freeway," said Joker.

Big Boy glared at the cell phone on his desk. How did those *caralhos* let her slip through their fingers again? It was beyond belief. He might have had to take action if they weren't two of his most fearless and respected soldiers.

"Where the fuck are you two?"

"Central valley. North of some shithole called Tulare."

"Sit tight. You're too far out of our territory now. Wait to hear from me," said Big Boy, hanging up before Joker could respond.

Big Boy scrolled through his phone for a rarely used number. He had no other option but to call it now, even though he didn't want to. The South Side Sinners and Satans 13 had a long-standing and violent rivalry. But when members of both gangs were in prison in Chino, they joined forces against the white supremacy group, The Aryan Order, to gain control of the prison population. That association remained unbroken, and that cooperation extended to gang life outside of prison walls when needed. If a gang encountered problems on the other's turf, they had the option of asking for support. It was considered an unspoken rule that if soldiers traveled into friendly turf, the other gang leaders would be notified. Big Boy was old school, and it didn't sit well with him, but he knew he couldn't enter Satans 13's area without a courtesy heads-up. He dialed the number and waited for Rodrigo "Monster" Perez to pick up. Monster waited until the fourth ring, right before the call would go to voicemail. Apparently, he was not eager to speak to Big Boy either.

"Big Boy Delgado. What's a Sinners captain from the south side want with a Satans 13 captain? You got yourself in *un lio* you need me to dig you out of, *ese*?"

Big Boy bristled at Monster's cockiness.

"Courtesy call, *ese*. We got a green light on someone who's in your set. Couple of my *soldados* tracked them down outside of Tulare but lost them."

"Okay. I can get behind that. Give me the 411 and I'll see what I can do."

Big Boy told him everything Joker had shared with him, including the route Kendra Thompson and her son Kyle took when they escaped.

"Sounds like your hit is *vato loco*, *ese*. One of my spotters has a sister who works at the truck stop near where your soldiers last saw her. Gotta keep our interests everywhere, man. Give me a few minutes to see if she has anything for us."

As he waited for Monster to call back, Big Boy downed a beer. Fifteen minutes later, Monster's call came through.

"Your woman and her kid left with some *vieja* in an eighteen-wheeler. Left her car there. Got a description of the logo on the truck trailer. I'll put it out to my soldiers. They'll be down for action. Got nothing with the red soldiers, so they're itchin' to get out there."

"Appreciate the co-op, bro. Let me know when you got them."

Big Boy finished the call and texted Joker and Spyder to get back to Sinners territory. He wasn't happy. He knew what Monster was doing. Trying to make him look bad by taking the mission from him. There was nothing Big Boy could do about it though. The targets were on Satan's turf now. Although the mention of red soldiers made Big Boy glad none of his bangers were still hunting the targets. Red soldiers, or Nesters, were members of the *Nuestra Familia* in northern California. It was well known that Satans 13 and *Nuestra Familia* were at war, and the Sinners didn't need to get involved in any Nester business.

TEN

Monster ran a set of the Satans 13, which was a biker gang located in Central California with a territory spanning from Stockton in the north, to the coast in the west, and Bishop in the east. Law enforcement was aware of the well-staffed sets in every city under the Satan's control. The Satans proudly wore their reputation for brutality like a badge.

Monster passed down new orders to his foot soldiers about the Sinners' targets. The gangbangers were excited about a new mission, particularly when it involved a green light. It was irrelevant who the green-lighted targets were or why. That was above their pay grade. The gangbangers savored the thrill of the hunt. The capture and the kill.

The news spread with high speed among the various factions, and before long, Satans 13 soldiers were seen patrolling in force on Highway 198 and Interstate 5, the primary routes that ran north and south through California. Both freeways were well-traveled truck routes, but Monster was confident that even though it would take some time, they could pinpoint the truck they were after. The foot soldiers would inspect every truck stop, rest stop, and weigh station on the freeway until they found the Vanity Fair Foods truck. Vanity Fair Foods was a large distributor, and multiple trucks would often be on the road, traveling between southern and northern California. However, the Satans 13 had enough manpower to monitor the freeways.

Within an hour of his order being sent out, the search began. The combat soldiers cruised the highways, eager to find the truck with their targets. A few Satans had already been detained and questioned about their actions by the California Highway Patrol. Due to the increased activity, the CHP was aware that something was about to happen. They were directed to stop and interrogate any members of the Satans 13 on the road. But the CHP couldn't detain all of them at once, and none of the Satan's members were talking. Word got back to Monster that soldiers were being harassed, but that didn't concern him. He had given the order to ride clean, meaning no drugs. But going strapped, or with weapons, was always a given. Hollowed out handlebars were modified to fire a single shotgun shell. Guns were concealed in seat cushions, and small handguns were hidden in bulky leather gloves. Most bangers had crackers, which were nylon whips on a metal attachment from their handlebars. They were quick to get to and could be used like a ball and chain. Dip sticks with attached knives and tire gauge guns were common weapons. Many Satans had needles, razor blades, and fishhooks sewn into their vests or other clothing. They were ready to go to war if needed.

There was a recent lull in gang activity around Tulare, so the Satans were not only willing but also eager to take on the mission. Monster was confident that an old woman truck driver, a nurse, and a teenager were no match for them. The mission was particularly noteworthy because this was a Sinners' job, and it never looked good for another gang to complete a rival gang's mission. Even if those gangs were on "friendly" terms. The old grudge and rivalry were still a point of contention for many of the Satans, so eliminating a Sinners' target would earn respect and admiration from fellow members. Respect was all-important in the Satans 13, so the prospect of that made them a formidable force.

ELEVEN

Kendra sat on a bench outside the diner door waiting for Lou, wondering what in the world she was thinking, agreeing to catch a ride with a stranger. She was on the verge of changing her mind and sprinting back to her car when Lou appeared. She sat up straighter and looked up at Lou. This was the moment she could change her mind. But Lou smiled at her, and Kendra's fears vanished. Lou wasn't a gangbanger, and that was the best she could hope for.

"Where are you parked?" asked Lou.

"Over there," said Kendra, pointing to a cluster of trucks behind the diner and to the right.

"All right then. Let's go get whatever you need from your car and get this show on the road."

Kendra weaved across the gravel lot, through the maze of trucks, Lou following closely behind. Kyle got out of the car as soon as he saw them coming.

"What took you so long, Mom?" he said, clearly irritated.

"Kyle, this is Lou," said Kendra, giving him a stern look. "She was in one of the trucks on the freeway when we were shot at. We're going to ride with her."

"What about the car?"

Lou stepped forward before Kendra could respond. "Hi, Kyle. I'm Lou," she said, holding out her hand. "I have a friend who can come and get the car and keep it safe until you can pick it up again. Right now, your mom is worried about keeping you both safe. And I think my rig is probably the best way to keep you both out of sight."

Kyle shook her hand begrudgingly and shot a glance at Kendra.

Kendra nodded to show her agreement with Lou. "They obviously know what we drive, and where we have been. They seem to be everywhere. We can't take a chance of moving on with that car. It's not safe."

"So, what's our plan, then? I mean, what, we just keep running forever, Mom? That's your brilliant idea? What the hell! What about my friends? And school? And my job? What about *your* job?" He kicked at the gravel, sending a spray of it into their car.

"Hey! Knock it off, Kyle. I told you before. I don't have all the answers, okay? I'm just trying to keep us alive. Cut me a break. And watch your language."

"Whatever. I'm almost seventeen. It's not like I haven't heard cuss words before." He crossed his arms over his chest and leaned back against the car, glaring at Kendra.

Lou was silent until Kyle was finished. "Okay, Kyle, why don't you grab your bags and whatever else you need from the car? My rig is just on the other side of the diner. The Vanity Fair Foods truck. I've got my name airbrushed on the driver's door in pink. You can't miss it. Your mom and I will be there in a minute or two."

Kyle looked at Lou, then at his mother. When neither of them spoke, he pushed himself off the car with a loud sigh, released the trunk, and walked to the rear of the car. He dropped their bags on the ground, slammed the trunk shut, and stalked off toward the other side of the parking lot in a huff.

"I'm sorry, Lou. He's usually not this rude. Don't get me wrong. He's a teenager and we definitely have our issues. But he's not himself right now."

"I can't imagine why. People shooting at you and all. I can handle a sulky teenager, don't worry about me. And listen, I can't force you to tell me who those morons shooting at you are if you don't want to. But if you're going to be riding with me, it would help if I knew who and what we are up against. Just sayin'."

Kendra hesitated while she weighed the choices in her mind. What other option did she have? She was in a helpless situation with no one else to turn to. With no family, and her recent discovery about officer Gutierrez, she felt lost. Lou was her only ally for now, and for no apparent reason, she trusted her. A woman she met just fifteen minutes ago was her sole ticket to safety. Kendra found it ironic that it took her world falling apart for her to realize just how good things had been. She used to complain that her life was very predictable. Sometimes even lonely and uneventful. Predictability, she now realized, had its advantages.

"Let's get on the road and I'll tell you everything, Lou. I just want to get out of here."

"Fair enough," said Lou. "Leave your car key on the floor under the driver's seat for my friend, Ted."

Kendra followed Lou's instructions, tucking the key under the seat. Kyle was sitting on his backpack and appeared completely bored when they got to Lou's truck. Climbing onto the sideboard, Lou unlocked the truck door and gestured for them to go to the other side.

"I'll let you two decide who's sitting shotgun. The other one can have the bench behind the seats. It's got cushions, so it's not bad."

While Lou contacted her friend about Kendra's car, Kendra and Kyle got into the truck. Kyle decided to take the back bench, next to a sleeping berth behind the driver's seat, equipped with lighting and a cooler. While Lou started the truck, he settled comfortably onto the bench. Kyle had never been in an eighteen-wheeler before, and the engine was louder than he expected. The seat beneath him began to vibrate with the engine's power.

"Okay. Off we go, into the wild blue yonder!" said Lou, raising her voice over the sound of the diesel.

Moving slowly, they left the gravel parking lot behind and entered the street. Kendra only breathed a sigh of relief when Lou turned the truck onto the 198 west. She sank deeper into her seat and gazed out the window as the landscape raced past. Somehow, the truck gave her a sense of security. She felt invincible inside the massive vehicle, as if nothing could harm them. If only that were true, she thought.

Kendra handed the food from the diner to Kyle, and he finished his cheeseburger in record time, but Kendra's appetite had vanished. She closed her eyes and let her head fall back against the seat. She stayed like that for a few minutes, ready to doze off, until Lou spoke.

"You ready to have that talk now, Kendra?" asked Lou, her words dragging Kendra back to the present.

Taking a deep breath, Kendra turned in her seat to face Lou. Then Kendra shared everything with Lou. How Kyle saw the Sinners kill Senator McLeod's nephew. That Kyle had captured the murder on his phone and the gang knew about it. As she told Lou about the Sinners coming to their home, the memory caused tears to well in her eyes. She told Lou about her conversation with Officer Gutierrez, their trip to the FBI field office, and how she didn't know who to trust. Lou remained quiet while listening to the story, and when Kendra had finished speaking, Lou responded with a soft whistle and a head shake.

"Holy cow. That's far worse than I imagined." She turned to glance at Kyle. "How are you doing with all this?"

Kyle shrugged. "Other than my whole life being screwed up, you mean? Yeah. Just great."

"Yeah, I can see why you've got that attitude, kid. I don't blame you. The good news is, I might be able to help you. You picked the right trucker to cut off," she said, laughing, and glancing over at Kendra. "I need to call my brother."

"No!" said Kendra. "I trusted you because you offered to help us get away. But you can't tell anyone else what I told you."

"My brother is a retired cop, of sorts. He was a Senior Special Agent with the DEA for thirty years. He's dealt with his share of gangs, believe me. You can trust him. He'll know what to do. Don't rely on me,

Kendra. I can get you where we're going, but beyond that, I'll be zero help."

"Mom, you need to at least talk to him. Seriously, we have no plan here. We can't just keep running and hiding forever. I have a life to get back to, even if you don't!"

Kendra tamped down the hurt Kyle's statement left, but the truth of his words didn't make the sting any less painful.

"Okay, Lou. Call him. Maybe he has some advice for us. It couldn't hurt at this point."

"Will do. I'll call him when we stop. It's not even 9:00 a.m. yet, so he's probably still out on the lake fishing," she said, glancing at her watch and turning to Kyle. "There are sandwiches in the ice chest there, with some sodas if you get hungry again. You two help yourselves. Might as well get comfortable. We've got a long drive ahead of us."

TWELVE

After a few hours, the trio in the truck pulled over at a rest stop to stretch and walk around. Lou pulled the big rig into the lot but left it running.

"Let's make this quick. We still have a lot of miles to cover today," said Lou.

Kendra followed Lou to the bathroom, while Kyle went around the corner to the men's room. They reconvened at the truck and piled in, where Lou excused herself to call her brother, Sam. Five minutes later, she returned to the truck with a smile.

"So, Sam agreed to meet up with us tomorrow once we get to Lake County."

Kendra nodded at her, still not sure she was comfortable involving Lou's brother. Although as a retired DEA agent, she was hopeful he could, at the very least, offer her some sage advice on what to do next.

The eighteen-wheeler pulled back onto the freeway, headed north on Interstate 5. The landscape was monotonous, providing Kendra with plenty of time to think, and therefore worry. They were near somewhere called Coalinga, which, as far as she could tell, was the back end of nowhere.

Lou kept the truck in the slow lane at a steady sixty miles per hour. Kendra wasn't a fan of the country and western music the radio was tuned to, but she didn't say anything, and she wasn't about to suggest they change the station. Not when Lou had been kind enough to help her and Kyle. Lou hummed along and drummed her fingers on the steering wheel, occasionally singing out loud. As much as Kendra disliked the music, she was sure that Kyle must be going crazy listening to it. She glanced back at him and saw that he was staring straight ahead through the front windshield. He squinted at something up ahead and craned his neck forward.

"Is that a roadblock up there?" he asked.

Lou looked up after placing her soda in the cup holder, just as Kendra turned forward. Lou leaned in and donned glasses she pulled from her shirt pocket.

"It's a bunch of motorcycles," said Lou.

The bikes formed a line that extended along the highway and allowed cars to pass through a gap on the left side, near the dirt divider. The hair on the back of Lou's neck bristled, and she checked her side mirror. About a half a mile behind them, she spotted another line of bikes forming. They were trapped between the two barricades.

"What the hell is going on?" she said to no one in particular. While Kyle sat forward, trying to see what was happening, Kendra peered out the side window mirror.

The truck was now flanked by four motorcycles, two on each side, as it barreled toward the roadblock. The bikers motioned for them to pull over.

"Oh, hell no. Gonna take a hard pass on that suggestion, assholes," said Lou, accelerating the truck.

"What's happening, Mom?" cried Kyle.

"I don't know. They want us to pull over."

"We are not stopping. No way. This reeks of your gang," said Lou, tightening her grip on the steering wheel.

"But look at their vests, they say Satans 13," said Kendra. "The Sinners are after us, not whoever these guys are."

"Oh honey, you really have led a sheltered life, haven't you? Have you never heard of gangs cooperating?"

"Well, I . . . no. I thought all gangs were rivals. How would I know something like that? How do *you* know that?"

"My brother. DEA, remember? I also used to be married to his partner. I've heard the stories. Hang on tight. We are not stopping, and this might get a little bumpy."

"What are you going to do?" said Kyle, gripping the back of Lou's seat.

"We are going to play a little game of chicken. That's what we're going to do. I can't stop now anyway. We'd jackknife this rig into next week."

Lou pulled the air horn and released three long blasts.

Kendra was transfixed on the scene ahead, her hand tightly gripping Kyle's. The bikers attempted to force the truck off the road, but Lou remained steadfast and kept a firm grip on the wheel. She didn't falter, continuing to drive at a consistent speed in their lane. When it became clear that Lou wasn't going to slow down or stop, several bikers hurriedly moved out of the way just seconds before the truck was going to crash into them. One of the bikers was either in a state of panic or couldn't get his bike started. He jumped from his bike and rolled onto the dirt beside the freeway as the truck hit the chopper, causing it to soar into the air and crash to the pavement like a toy. Lou checked her mirror and saw a pile of twisted metal right before it exploded into flames.

Kendra gasped and covered her mouth with her hand. She turned to peer out the back window out of habit. Instead, Kyle was staring back at her from the bunk, eyebrows raised and his mouth hanging open. She turned in her seat to look out the side mirror in time to see a plume of smoke rise from the burning mass of mangled steel. She inhaled sharply as her heart kicked around in her chest.

"How ya like me now, dipshit?" Lou yelled, pumping her fist in the air.

Kendra watched in the mirror, as several CHP cars, lights blazing, raced toward the bikes. Motorcycles scattered in every direction. Some went south by crossing the dirt highway divider, while others took the nearest exit. A few even went into a lettuce field where the patrol cars couldn't pursue them. The CHP was vastly outnumbered. At the first roadblock, some bikers were being held at gunpoint by officers, but the second group, who was forced off the road by Lou's truck, was long gone.

Kendra watched the chaotic scene around her and couldn't help thinking that at least the officers' presence prevented the bikers from chasing after them. So why did this feel so wrong? She was not used to running from law enforcement. They weren't exactly evading the CHP, but leaving the scene of the accident wasn't her usual behavior. Even so, she was happy to have left the bikers behind. She was not thrilled that they had to ditch the CHP to get away, but she'd learn to live with it.

"You okay back there, kiddo?" asked Lou, twisting to glance at Kyle.

"Uh, yeah. That was badass, Lou. You were really gonna run them down if they didn't move, weren't you?"

"Well, I didn't want to, but they really didn't leave me much choice, did they?"

"Guess not."

"Lou, I don't want to make trouble for you. I'll understand if you want to drop us off. Please, just take us somewhere safe where we can get on a bus or something and not use our IDs," said Kendra, on the brink of tears.

"Are you kidding me? This is the most excitement I've had in a long time! I'll get you to Sam in one piece, don't worry. Until then, just trust me."

Kendra was relieved that Lou had no intentions of abandoning them at the first bus stop they came to. Although she wouldn't blame her if she did.

Kyle chose that moment to grab a sandwich from the mini fridge.

"Hand me one too, will ya?" said Lou. "All this drama makes me hungry."

Kendra marveled at how they could eat after what they just experienced. The knot in her stomach was so tight she doubted she could hold anything down.

Kendra took a few minutes to calm down as Kyle and Lou ate sandwiches as if nothing had happened. Her nervous energy was palpable, and she needed to do something to keep busy. Unable to postpone it any longer, Kendra used Lou's phone to call work. She called Human Resources instead of her supervisor. Knowing no one would question it, she told them that she had tested positive for Covid-19 and would be out for a week. It was not unusual for a first responder to contract Covid-19, given the constant exposure, and she had to produce a negative test result before she could resume work as a critical care nurse at the hospital. It would buy her some time while she figured her way out of this mess. Next, she passed the phone to Kyle so he could call his job at the grocery store where he was employed as a bag boy. Kendra instructed him to use the same excuse she had given earlier, as consistency was the key when it came to lies. She felt horrible for telling him to lie, but extreme circumstances called for extreme measures.

After she hung up, she worried her lie might untangle the web of deceit she had woven so carefully. Work believed she was sick. Raul, at the car lot, thought she was escaping from an abusive partner. Who knew what Gutierrez thought? She just hoped he didn't know she was aware of his involvement with the gang hit. And now Lou knew the truth. Kendra stole a quick glance at Lou, who appeared to be completely unruffled after their near miss.

As the sun started to set, Kendra turned back to the window. She considered their journey thus far, which had been lengthy and monotonous, punctuated only by brief moments of intense fear. She giggled to herself, thinking about something her mother used to say. "Cry and move on or stick your head in the oven."

Kyle looked at her like she was crazy when the laugh escaped her. Maybe she was, she thought. She sounded slightly deranged, even to herself. She was too tired to care.

"We are going to have to stop for the night soon. I can only drive so many hours. And we need to get this rig off the road and out of sight. A motel is not going to be safe now. They know what my truck looks like. Plus, it's possible the CHP may have a description of my truck and want to talk to us."

"So what do we do then?" asked Kendra.

"I know somewhere we can park for the night where they won't find us. I've been driving this route for ten years, so I know all the spots. I can sleep up here and you two can take the bunk," she said, lifting her chin to the back.

"What about tomorrow, Lou? Like you said, they know what your truck looks like," said Kendra.

"True. But I also have a lot of trucker friends. There is bound to be chatter about what happened today. I've had the CB radio off, but in the morning I'll get on there and set up a convoy. An escort of eighteen-wheelers. There will be more than a few rigs headed north on Interstate 5 tomorrow, and we long-haulers stick together. Let those assholes try to get through four loaded trailers. It'll be the last thing they try. I guarantee it."

At a deserted exit, Lou pulled off the freeway. The glow of the headlights was the only thing that illuminated the pitch black. They traveled three miles to reach an old barn that looked like it was built a hundred years ago. Lou drove the truck off the road and onto the dirt path behind the barn. The large structure provided enough cover to hide the truck from view of the road. Plus, Kendra was doubtful that anyone could see two feet in front of them without a flashlight, given how dark it was. Lou powered down the truck and switched on the interior light while they rummaged through their bags. Walking the perimeter of the truck, Lou checked for damage from the motorcycle they hit, but found none.

With a bottle of water in hand for brushing her teeth, Kendra ventured out into the cool night. The sound of crickets filled the air as an owl hooted somewhere off in the distance. She and Kyle both made quick pit stops and brushed their teeth before getting back into the truck. They were both sound asleep by the time Lou returned to the truck after taking her turn. They slept a few feet from Lou, unaware she had taken a pump-action shotgun from under her seat, laying it carefully on the floor in front of her. She wouldn't hesitate to use it if she needed to. She made light of the events earlier to keep Kendra and Kyle calm, but it shook her. She knew what the Satans 13 were capable of. And it rocked her to the core.

THIRTEEN

Monster watched the video of his soldier's burning bike, unaware that the trio of targets were settling down for the night only a few miles away. The humiliation burned in his stomach. Who did these women think they were dealing with? They had some *cojones*—he would give them that. But there was no way he could let them get away with what they did. The Satans had been disgraced, and he couldn't let that slide. He planned to make sure the women regretted testing their bravado against his soldiers. Monster was still pissed about it, even though it had happened hours ago. What was supposed to be a simple mission turned out to be a complete clusterfuck. The mistake committed by his soldiers had left Monster feeling embarrassed, especially after receiving a call from Big Boy the night before. The District Attorney was under the gun to prosecute a suspect in the high-profile murder case that was making headlines in Los Angeles and expected the police to make an arrest any day now. As a result, Big Boy was getting increased pressure from his insider at the LAPD to locate and eliminate the kid, his mother, and the video. Monster knew if the video got into the wrong hands, Big Boy's LAPD contact would make sure someone from the Sinners took the fall for the murder, and that could implicate the Satans.

Monster's directive to trail and observe would lead to frustration among the gang members. He knew that. The previous day's scene had left them eager for revenge on the trucker who had pushed through their roadblock. But Monster had to be cautious now that they were entering another gang's turf. And not just any gang. A rival gang—the *Nuestra Familia*. Things had been quiet between the two gangs recently, but it wouldn't take much to bring tensions to the surface. Playing it right was crucial, or he'd have to deal with a war. However, the hit was no longer just a matter of business. The women had made it personal. But as long as he was careful, the mission could be completed without anyone knowing that Satans 13 members were involved.

Unlike Big Boy, Monster was solely focused on his reputation. He didn't care about what had gone down in Los Angeles. He refused to be made a fool of by the *gringa* and her son, and he had no intention of being humiliated or losing a rival gang's respect because of them. He intended to win the vendetta at any cost.

He put in a call to Chewy "Ghost" Cordero, his top combat soldier.

"I want this motherfucking woman and her kid found and taken care of. Do you hear me? And that *culero* truck driver too. I don't care what it takes, but no more fuckups. This is the Satan's mission now, you understand? Fuck the Sinners. Those *putos* came for us. They're ours now. Put soldiers and spotters on the roads, but out of sight. I don't want them to know they are being trailed. I want to catch them by surprise."

He didn't wait for a response before ending the call and putting his phone in his front vest pocket. He started his bike, revved the engine loudly, and burned rubber out of the bar parking lot.

FOURTEEN

Lou's face was illuminated by the early morning sun streaming through the truck windows. Looking away, she let out a yawn. She sat up, peered out the window, and then checked her watch. Six o'clock. Time to get up and on the CB radio to round up some escorts. She leaned over the seat and caught Kendra's eye.

"Morning," said Kendra sleepily.

"Good morning, sunshine. I'm going to put out a call to some friends for help. Then we can get a quick breakfast and hit the trail. I'm guessing we'll be ahead of the gangbangers this early. I assume they have either been partying all night or planning our swift demise," she said, chuckling.

Kendra's expression told Lou she was worried that Lou might be right. That the gang could be formulating a new plan to take them out.

"Hey, I was only joking. They won't stand a chance in hell against a convoy of truckers. I don't have a death wish. If I didn't think we'd be okay, I wouldn't get back on the road."

"Okay. I hope you're right, Lou. I'll get Kyle up."

"Let him sleep. If he can sleep over the engine noise and me on the CB, more power to him."

"He's a teenager. He could probably sleep through a nuclear explosion," deadpanned Kendra.

Lou laughed. "Oh, to be young again."

Kendra grabbed her pack of tissues, a bottle of water, and her toothbrush then stepped out into the morning chill. She zipped her hoodie up and walked around the side of the barn for some privacy.

Firing up the CB radio, Lou tuned to channel nineteen. After a brief moment of listening to the chatter, she broke into the conversation by using the standard CB code.

"Break nineteen. Sweet Peach doing a radio check."

"Come back Sweet Peach, Gentle Giant here."

"Morning, Gentle Giant. 10-17. Coming in from shaky city and picked up a couple of bumper stickers yesterday looking for a visitor I have on board. I need a convoy to do a rocking chair into sack of tomatoes. Anyone heading that way?"

Lou heard Kyle stir behind her. Sitting upright in the bunk, he leaned forward between the seats.

"What the heck?"

"Morning, sunshine. Sorry if I woke you. Your mom thought you'd sleep through it."

"What are you even saying to that guy?" said Kyle, frowning.

"I told him we had unwanted visitors yesterday, and I asked for a few other truckers to escort us to Sacramento. A rocking chair means my truck would ride in the middle of three other trucks. One in front, one in back, and the other in the lane beside us. They'd surround us and keep any *undesirables* from getting near us."

"And they'd do that?"

"Sure they will. Lots of truckers drive the same route all the time. We all know one another. And we look out for each other."

"Oh. Well, that's cool, I guess."

"Sweet Peach, Midnight Cowboy here. Was that your kerfuffle with the scooters and the bears yesterday?"

"Affirmative, Midnight Cowboy. Bears and scooters were present."

"We can rustle up a convoy for you. I'll take the lead, Gentle Giant at your back door, Mad Dog at your side. You stay in the granny lane, and we'll get you north safely."

"Roger that Midnight Cowboy. I appreciate ya'll being good neighbors."

"Sweet Peach, Gentle Giant here. You looking to go through the woods?"

"Not unless we have to, Gentle Giant. I need to get my passengers up to Lake County ASAP."

Kyle climbed into the front seat, interested in Lou's conversation.

"Midnight Cowboy asked me if the motorcycles and CHP issue was our deal yesterday. Then Gentle Giant asked if we wanted to go off the freeway and travel on secondary roads. But I said no. That would take us too long."

Kyle nodded.

"Mad Dog here Sweet Peach. What's your 10-20?"

"I'll be entering again at on-ramp fifty-two, in about twenty."

"Roger that Sweet Peach. We'll see you at the chicken coop."

"Roger that. I owe you all."

Lou turned to Kyle. "I need to fuel up, then we'll meet them at the next weigh station. We can use the bathroom there to wash up and get something to eat. But we need to get on the move, so we don't keep them waiting. They have loads to deliver and escorting us will already slow them down some."

"Where's my mom?"

"Nature called. Oh, here she comes," said Lou, as Kendra came into view from around the barn.

Kyle climbed over the seat into the back as Kendra got into the truck, and Lou powered up the diesel engine once Kendra was inside. "I've got a convoy worked out for us. I'll tell you about it on the way," she said, glancing at Kendra.

"Okay. Do you need to step outside before we take off, Kyle?" asked Kendra.

"No, I'll go to the bathroom when we stop for gas. Lou says we can get some food then too."

"Oh, good. I'm starving this morning."

"We can pick up some sandwiches and drinks for later while we're there," said Lou, maneuvering the truck onto the road.

Lou filled Kendra in on the plan during the ride. Kendra looked unsure, so Lou did her best to reassure her.

"We'll be surrounded by about one-hundred-twenty tons of steel. Those bikers are no match for that."

"Well, no offense to your friends, Lou, but color me skeptical. I'm not optimistic, given the lengths the gang has gone to so far."

"Yes, and yet here you are, safe and sound in my truck. You'll see. This will be the most secure you two have been since you left Los Angeles."

Kendra merely grunted and turned to face the window.

They arrived at the truck stop in Tracy, where Lou pumped diesel for the truck and went inside to get them egg sandwiches for breakfast and turkey and cheese sandwiches with chips for later. Kendra and Kyle went to the bathroom to freshen up, where Kendra waited for Kyle to finish and made sure he was back in the truck before entering the restroom herself. Kyle made it clear that he was unhappy with her following him around like a toddler, but she didn't feel it was safe for either of them to be out of the truck. Everything felt risky. She kept her eyes glued to the parking lot, searching for any sign of a motorcycle.

Once Lou stashed the food in the truck, she joined Kendra to wash her face and use the facilities. Anxious to get back to the truck, Kendra hurried through cleaning up.

"Don't worry, he's safe in the truck. The doors are locked, and no one can see him back in the bunk area. My friends will get us to my brother's place safely," said Lou, leaning against the sink, watching Kendra brush her hair.

"Thank you, Lou. It's not that I'm ungrateful for your help. I appreciate it more than you know. I just don't know what good going to your brother's is going to do for us. They keep coming, this gang. And now, apparently, they've incorporated the help of another gang, which I didn't even know was a *thing*," she said, dropping the brush in the sink and covering her eyes with her hands as she sobbed.

"Hey, look at me," said Lou, touching Kendra's shoulder gently.

Kendra's eyes were red and swollen as she looked up, burdened by the weight of the world on her shoulders.

"My brother may be a lot of things, but one thing I know about him is he's smart. And he was a damned good agent. He can help you. Just trust me. And the way I see it, he's the only person you can trust to do so right now. So, chin up, okay? You need to be strong for your son, no matter how you feel right now. It's okay to lose your shit in front of me. I get it. But when you walk out of this bathroom, you'd better be the pillar of strength that kid out there needs. Because as frightened as you are, think about how he must feel."

Inhaling deeply, Kendra steeled herself. She knew Lou was right. Her son needed reassurance that she was capable of protecting him. After splashing her face with cool water, Kendra stood tall and examined her reflection in the mirror. It was still a shock to see her new hair color at times, although nothing else felt like herself right now either. After putting the brush back in her purse, she drew Lou in for a hug.

"Thank you for everything, Lou. You're an angel."

"Let's not get crazy now, Kendra. That was just a come-to-Jesus lecture to snap you back into shape."

Kendra laughed and pulled away from Lou. "You were right. What you said back at the truck stop when we first met, Lou. I truly did pick the right trucker to cut off."

Lou smiled and indicated the door with a lift of her chin. Singing Willie Nelson's *On the Road Again*, she pulled the door open and followed Kendra outside.

Lou took the wheel again, and they settled back into the truck, cruising onto Interstate 5. They didn't have to travel far before reaching the weigh station, which Lou immediately entered. After going through the scales, Kendra spotted three other trucks parked on the side of the road with their engines running. Lou waved at a trucker, and then followed behind as they pulled out. Kendra was amazed at how skillfully the other rigs positioned themselves around Lou's truck when they were back on the freeway. With this formation, motorcycles didn't stand a chance of getting near them. It would be suicidal for them to try to squeeze between the eighteen-wheelers.

Kendra felt safe as they headed up the freeway toward Sacramento, despite her earlier misgivings. She hummed along to a familiar old Waylon Jennings tune on the radio, completely oblivious to the Satans 13 members who were monitoring their travel from overpasses and other viewpoints.

FIFTEEN

The miles flew by as Lou's truck traveled north. Bathroom breaks were limited to just two, and the other trucks remained glued to them throughout the journey. The highway signs told Kendra they were just sixty miles outside of Sacramento. Kendra was hopeful that either the gangs had given up or they had lost them, as they had seen no sign of them.

"Tell me about your brother, Lou," said Kendra.

Lou sighed. "Well, there isn't a whole bunch to tell. Sam is a very private person. He doesn't share a lot. I know he was a brilliant agent and had an illustrious career with the DEA. Then something happened. His partner set him up, Sam got divorced, and his partner married Sam's ex. And the next thing I know, Sam is retiring suddenly. Now he lives alone, tucked away in the hills just outside Lake County. I was never close to Sadie—that's Sam's ex—and he doesn't talk about her, so I can only guess as to what happened with the marriage. Now he spends a lot of time on his boat, fishing on Clearlake."

"Hmmmm. Well, we haven't had any trouble since yesterday, and no sign of the gang, so maybe it isn't necessary to meet him after all. I can rent a car, and Kyle and I can contact the local FBI. I'm sure they can do something to help us."

"Well, you are obviously welcome to do whatever you think is best, Kendra, but I don't reckon that's such a great idea. First of all, the local FBI is going to contact LAPD immediately, and if there is a dirty cop involved, you'll be right back to square one. Second, I think you're kidding yourself if you believe those gangs have lost interest in you. You have a video recording of them murdering a prominent senator's nephew. That's not the kind of thing they are going to let you walk away from. After the debacle on the freeway yesterday, I'm sure they are lying low. But don't delude yourself into thinking that means it's over. I would say I'm not trying to scare you, but maybe I am, just a little. Now is not the time to let your guard down, Kendra."

"Lou's right, Mom. We should go meet her brother. It's not like talking to him will hurt anything. And you already said we can't trust the cops in LA. So what else are we going to do? I mean, Lou brought us this far. We might as well see it through."

Kendra glanced back at Kyle. "Okay, Kyle. We're going to see him. I was just thinking out loud."

"I am only going as far as Williams and Highway 20, which is on the other side of Sacto. My rig can't make it all the way to Sam's place. The roads get too narrow and dangerous. I told him I would drop you at a local restaurant and he'll meet you there. Don't worry, he will be there waiting for us."

"Okay. How long before we get there, do you think?" asked Kendra.

"Couple of hours, max. Our escorts will leave us and go their own way once we get to Highway 20."

Each mile they put behind them made Kendra feel a little better, and the drive to reach Highway 20 to Williams was uneventful. By the time they reached the parking lot of Dolly's Café, Kendra was more than ready to get out of the truck. The diesel engine's noise and the constant rumble under her seat were starting to grate on her nerves. She and Kyle gathered their bags as Lou hopped down from the truck cab and stretched.

Kendra walked to the other side of the truck, where Lou leaned against the door.

"Lou, I want to—" Kendra became emotional as she stepped closer. Lou interrupted her before she could finish.

"Don't go getting all emotional on me, Kendra. No crying, remember? Stay strong for that son of yours."

"I don't know what would have happened to us without your help, Lou."

"I just did what anyone in the same situation would have done. It wasn't a big deal."

Kendra scoffed. "That is not true, and you know it. Thank you. From the bottom of my heart. I don't know how I will ever repay you."

"Stay safe. Listen to Sam. That's how you repay me," said Lou, turning and wiping her eyes. "Damn allergies. They always start when I get to this area."

Kendra smiled and hugged Lou, surprised when she returned the embrace. "Get on in here, Kyle," Lou motioned to him.

Kyle walked over, wrapping his arms around his mom and Lou. "You're pretty cool, Lou."

"Well, that, young man, is the nicest compliment I've received in a very long time. Shall we go in and you can meet Sam? That's his truck there," said Lou, pointing to a blue Dodge Ram.

Kendra inhaled a deep breath and followed Lou toward the café entrance, while Kyle trailed behind with the bags. Their arrival was announced by a bell over the door. Red and white checkered tablecloths covered a dozen or so tables that were scattered around the room, all with mismatched chairs. The place had a homey feel, and Kendra's stomach growled from the delicious smells emanating from the kitchen. Lou waved to a man in a cowboy hat, who was sitting in the corner alone with his back to the wall. He got up with a grin as they approached. He stood at an impressive height. Kendra estimated him to be six foot three. He was dressed in a blue plaid button-down shirt tucked into blue jeans, complete with a western style buckle. His hair was gray and brushed the top of his neck, and he had a mustache to match. Kendra's first impression of him was that he looked like Sam Elliott. He took off his hat and smoothed down his hair with his hand.

He certainly wasn't what Kendra pictured a federal agent to look like. He wasn't very intimidating. In fact, he appeared very approachable and friendly. Kendra's optimism waned with each passing minute.

"Howdy, sis," he said, pulling Lou into a bear hug. His voice was deep and confident.

Lou kissed his cheek and held him at arm's length for a moment. "Good to see you, little brother. This is Kendra and Kyle Thompson," she said, turning to face them.

"Pleased to meet you, Kendra. Kyle, thanks for getting these two here in one piece. I know my sister can be a bit much at times, so well done for not bailing at the first pit stop," he said, extending his hand to Kendra and then Kyle.

Kyle smirked at him and nodded his head as Lou punched Sam's arm playfully.

"Thank you for agreeing to talk to us, Sam. I'm at a loss as to what I should do at this point," said Kendra.

"I guess you should wait to thank me until you hear what I have to say, ma'am," he said, smiling. "Why don't you two take a seat and order something to eat? I'm going to walk Lou out and have a little chat with her. You're safe in here, and I'll just be right outside," said Sam.

"Sure, okay. Thank you," said Kendra.

"I'm not big on goodbyes. So, I'll just say until we meet again," said Lou. She grinned at them, and with a final wave, followed Sam outside.

The waitress motioned she'd be right over as Kendra and Kyle sat at the table. The waitress was a young girl with pink hair styled in a high ponytail and long nails to match. After laying down two menus, she took their drink order—an iced tea for Kendra and a Sprite for Kyle.

The bell jingled when two men walked in, and Kendra stiffened at the sight. Kyle turned in his chair to see who it was. It seemed unlikely that they were gangbangers. Both of them were in jeans and western shirts, just like Sam. Seated a few tables away, she could sense one of them gazing at her. She was aware he was watching them, though she avoided looking his way. She peered out the window behind Kyle and saw that Sam was still talking to Lou. She wished he would come back inside. The two men gave her an uneasy feeling. She didn't think she was making something out of nothing, even though she remained on high alert. When their drinks arrived, Kendra took the opportunity to glance at their table. As suspected, the man facing her was looking directly at her. He lifted his chin at her and grinned. Ignoring him, Kendra looked away and busied herself by opening a sugar packet for her tea as the waitress took their lunch order. Her heart started to race when she saw movement out of the corner of her eye. Seconds later, the man stood at their table, looking down at Kendra.

"Hey, beautiful. You know, when a man tries to be friendly, you should give him the respect he deserves."

Kendra ignored him and didn't look up. She knew the type of man he was. He believed that anyone without a Y chromosome was beneath him, and therefore thought he was superior because he was a man. Kendra attempted to keep her composure, but she was convinced she appeared anything but composed. Her nerves had been on edge for the past few days, and she felt her patience start to crack like a thin layer of ice.

"Hey, I'm talking to you. Don't ignore me. I might take that as an insult."

"I'm not interested, thanks."

"Well, I don't remember asking if you were interested. I'm just trying to be friendly and get to know you. Why don't you come party with my friend and me on my boat today? We can have a real good time. I've got the best boat on the lake and we've got plenty of party favors, if you know what I mean," he said, chuckling.

Kendra felt the last of her patience slip away. As she looked at the man, she spoke before she could even think to stop herself.

"Well, that's a lot of words to say no one will sleep with you."

Kyle snorted and spat out some of the soda in his mouth.

The man's face contorted, but he got himself under control again quickly. "I like a woman with a little fire in her," he said, ogling Kendra like she was catnip. "I'm gonna chalk that one up to you having a rough day, sweetheart. But just so we're clear, don't ever talk to me like that again."

Kendra chuckled out loud. Rough day? *Rough day*? That would be a welcome upgrade to her last few days, she thought. "Listen, I am not going to any lake with you today, tomorrow, or *ever*. To be honest, I would rather put out a fire with my tongue than go anywhere with you."

He glared at Kendra. "What did you just say? No bitch talks to me like that."

She didn't flinch. She was on the run from gangbangers, who had something even more terrible than a quick death planned for her and Kyle. Did the backward country piece of crap in front of her really think she was going to pretend he didn't just say that? A week ago, she might have. Correction. She probably would have. But now? Now he was an unwelcome piece of gum on her shoe she needed to scrape off.

"I could be wrong, but I don't think the lady is interested."

Sam had appeared behind the man. The stranger redirected his attention to Sam as his friend rose and started toward them.

"This ain't none of your concern, Grandpa. You her bodyguard or something?" he said, snickering.

Sam peered around him. "Something like that. Think of me as her faithful sidekick. Kendra, why don't you and Kyle go get in the truck," he said, tossing her the keys.

"Hey, I just told you to stay out of this!" the man shouted at Sam.

"Yeah, I heard that. The thing is, you're just such a fucking idiot, it's hard for me to take you seriously. And honestly, you killed my appetite with all your pseudo-macho talk, so we're going to leave now," said Sam.

Kyle's head swiveled from one man to the other, his eyes widening as he watched their exchange.

The man swung for Sam, who countered the man's swing, twisting his arm behind his back and taking him down to the floor in one swift motion. The man's friend rushed forward, ready to attack Sam. But Sam was faster and drew a gun from his ankle holster and aimed it at his approaching attacker. Raising his hands in surrender, the man came to an abrupt stop.

"Son, am I going to have to shoot one of you to teach you two some manners? No means no. The lady isn't interested. Now go on. Get on outta here before the waitress calls the sheriff's office and you spend the next three days in county lock-up."

Sam released the man on the ground, who glared at him as he and his friend left the café. Their truck tires sprayed gravel as they sped out of the parking lot.

Kendra let out a sigh.

"Mom, OMG. What's got into you?"

Kendra shook her head, unable to give him a good answer.

"Well, I see you're already making new friends. I like the initiative, but I wouldn't recommend any more encounters like that since we're trying to stay under the radar here. Let's get going before Billy Bob and Jethro out there call for back up and I really *do* have to shoot someone," said Sam.

The waitress appeared, holding a bag of food. "Taking these to go then, Sam?"

"Yep. Thanks, Candi."

"See you next time, handsome," said Candi, winking at Sam.

"You bet. Put it on my tab."

They had only been on the run for a few days, and apparently this lanky Sam Elliot look-alike was their best hope for survival. Kendra wasn't at all sure this was going to work out for them.

Kyle, on the other hand, was grinning from ear to ear. "Badass runs in the family, I guess," he said.

Kendra didn't utter another word. Instead, she took hold of a beaming Kyle's wrist and pulled him outside after Sam toward the blue Dodge.

SIXTEEN

The truck chirped in response to Sam pressing the unlock icon on the key fob.

"Sorry for the mess. Just toss anything in your way into the back," he said, crumpling a few fast-food wrappers and launching them into the back seat.

Kendra and Kyle gathered unopened mail, empty water bottles and a thermos, putting them on the seat behind them. Sam had Kyle slide in next to him, while Kendra occupied the seat next to the passenger door. Pulling out of the parking lot, Sam headed west on Highway 20. The scenery was breathtaking, with a stream on their left side and pine trees on the right. Sunlight filtered through the trees, dappling the pavement with shadows where a doe and her fawn sprinted across the road. After driving a few miles, Sam slowed down and turned right, stopping at a dirt road with a gate. He stepped out, opened the gate, and pulled it back to give them enough space to drive through. He locked the gate after them, and they drove along the path surrounded by trees. A mile down the road, a log cabin came into view. Pots of bright flowers and hanging ferns on the eaves added charm to the wrap-around porch. A bench and two rocking chairs were positioned at the far end. The setting was lovely and welcoming. Although Kendra had half-expected a borderline hoarder situation based on the interior of Sam's truck, it appeared to be a quaint, charming home from the outside. It didn't need to be perfect; anywhere with walls and a roof other than a semi-truck was a victory at that point.

A large yellow lab raced toward the truck from around the back of the house, startling Kendra. Jumping and yelping excitedly, the dog didn't wait for Sam to stop the truck.

"Hey, Buddy, get down. Mind your manners, we have company," said Sam, ruffling the dog's ears.

Kyle was more than happy to give Buddy some attention after the dog made a beeline for him. Sam grabbed their bags from the truck bed and headed for the porch. Kyle and Buddy were content playing fetch outside while Kendra followed Sam inside. Although small, the house was tidy. Two chairs were placed in front of a large fireplace dominating one wall. The opposite side of the room was set up with a couch, coffee table, and desk. To Kendra's left, the living room provided a view of the kitchen. Despite the need for an update, it appeared in good shape. The bedrooms, she assumed, were located at the end of the hall straight ahead.

"The place is small, only two bedrooms, which means you'll have to share with Kyle, or he can bunk out here on the couch," said Sam, leading her down the hall.

Sam led Kendra to a bedroom on the right. "My room is at the end of the hall. The bathroom is right across the hall. Why don't we eat our lunch before it gets cold and then after that we can talk?"

He set Kendra's bags on the bed before heading off to set the table for lunch. Kendra poked her head out the screen door to call Kyle in for lunch and was greeted by the scent of pine. Looking around the yard, she took a moment to appreciate how peaceful and serene it was.

"Kyle, lunch is ready."

Kyle glanced up and bolted for the porch, Buddy in hot pursuit. The dog trailed Kyle into the house and settled at his feet beneath the table.

"Looks like you've got a new friend," said Sam, laughing.

"Yeah. He's a great dog. How long have you had Buddy?"

"Eight years now. He was at a crack house I was at for a raid, and he was just a pup then. I didn't have the heart to turn him over to animal control. He looked so pathetic. So I took him home with me and we've been together ever since."

Kyle reached down to pet Buddy's head and the dog licked his hand in response.

"So, Kyle, why don't you walk me through what happened the night you saw the gang? Don't leave anything out, no matter how insignificant you may think it is," said Sam.

Between bites of his burger, Kyle recounted everything he could remember from that night.

"You're certain you lost your school ID in the parking lot?"

"Yes. I felt it leave my t-shirt pocket. But I just couldn't find it again. It was too dark."

"Okay. And Kendra, tell me exactly what happened and what you heard when you were hiding in the house later that night."

Kendra repeated the gang's conversation word for word. It was something that would stay with her forever.

"And the phone call with the task force officer? You're absolutely certain you have that conversation correct?"

"Yes," said Kendra. "I'm one hundred percent sure. He knew about the video, and neither one of us told him about it."

"Okay," said Sam, rising. "I'm going to make a few calls, so just make yourself at home. The TV remote is on the coffee table," said Sam, walking out the back door and away from the house.

Kendra was drained of all energy. The combination of days spent driving for hours and the stress had taken a toll on her. She eyed the couch with longing. When Kyle took Buddy outside again, she gave in to temptation. Settling into the couch pillows, she turned on the TV. She flipped through the channels randomly, searching for a mindless program to doze off to. The news caught her eye when she stopped on a local channel.

It has been reported by LAPD sources that there is a witness to the brutal slaying of Devon McLeod, the nephew of Senator Steven McLeod.

The source declined to comment further, except to say that they are actively searching for the witness. According to confidential sources, the South Side Sinners gang is speculated to have played a role in Mr. McLeod's death. However, that information cannot be confirmed at this time. This is Kelly McGrath reporting live from Los Angeles. Back to you in the studio, Don.

Thank you, Kelly. I can understand why that witness would want to keep a low profile. The South Side Sinners have a well-known history of violence and brutality. Next up, how to keep your summer grass from burning in the upcoming heatwave.

Kendra turned off the TV and tossed the remote onto the coffee table as if it had burned her hand. Her worry resurfaced like an unwelcome friend. The situation was escalating, not dying down as she had hoped. She sat silently on the couch for a long time, listening to the birds chirping and Kyle praising Buddy for being a good boy. Her only hope was that Sam had some kind of plan to get them out of this mess.

Kendra was jolted back to reality when the back screen door slammed shut. Sam repositioned one of the chairs by the fireplace to face the couch and took a seat.

"I have some news. Not sure you're going to like it, but you need to hear it."

"Okay."

"The gang officer working your case has a colorful background. Rumor has it he is in thick with the Sinners, but nothing has ever been proven, and no official investigation has ever been opened, due to lack of evidence. There are also some allegations that Senator McLeod may have somehow been involved with the hit on his nephew. There were some campaign contribution irregularities and embezzlement claims brought to the attention of the feds by Devon McLeod just a few weeks before his death. It seems the Senator and his nephew weren't seeing eye to eye on how to run things at camp McLeod."

"So, that's good, right? If the feds already know about McLeod, then they can help us."

"Sure. If they have a joint task force and we're talking about a corrupt officer, the FBI will investigate him. So will LAPD internal affairs."

"But we went to the FBI, and Gutierrez was there. And he's assigned to that field office. So it's possible that maybe someone else there is in on it with him."

"Sure, anything's possible. There's another way, but you probably aren't going to like it."

"Let's call Kyle in here for this. It affects him too."

"Okay. If that's what you're comfortable doing, I'll go get him."

Kendra didn't say it, but they had left her comfort zone behind in the dust days ago.

Following Sam, Kyle came through the front screen door with Buddy, who was panting and jumping behind him.

"What's up, Mom?" said Kyle, scratching Buddy behind the ears.

"Sam was going to offer some suggestions for us moving forward, and I thought you should hear what he has to say."

"Okay. So, what is it?" asked Kyle.

"Not a lot of options in your situation, I'm sorry to say. You can go back to the FBI, and they will investigate Gutierrez. That won't happen overnight. They would need to gather evidence and build a case against him. But eventually, if what you say about him is correct, the Assistant US Attorney would press charges and prosecute him. LAPD Internal Affairs would investigate and also the Department of Justice's Office of Professional Responsibility, since he is attached to the FBI field office in LA."

"But I don't trust them. I have no way of knowing who might be involved with Gutierrez," said Kendra.

"I don't trust them either," said Kyle.

"Okay. Sit down, Kyle," said Sam, taking a seat in the chair again. "I've learned some things about the situation which I've shared with your mom. It's a bit more complicated than we originally thought. There are some things in play here that make it impossible for the gang to let your video ever go public. Not just because it implicates them and at least one law enforcement officer, but someone else as well. A public figure that has a lot more to lose. What that means is they cannot risk any witnesses ever coming to light."

"So, I'm screwed basically. Is that what you're saying?" asked Kyle.

"Yeah, Kyle. I'm not going to lie to you. You and your mom both, unfortunately."

"Well, there has to be some way to get us some protection, somehow," said Kendra.

"The only other way is to cut all ties to your previous life," said Sam.

Kendra sprung up from the couch. "What? You can't be serious!"

"Calm down and hear me out," said Sam, holding his hands up like he was dealing with a crazy person.

Telling Kendra to calm down probably wasn't the best strategy, as she promptly pointed out.

"Calm down? You're suggesting that my son and I either take our chances with corrupt cops and play right into their hands, or give up our entire lives and get new identities and you want me to calm down? You want us to never speak to anyone we know or love again. What about Kyle's father? What about my job? Um, excuse me, but back here on planet earth, clear heads prevail."

"Yeah! What about school and all my friends? This is total bullshit!" said Kyle, rising to stand next to his mom.

Sam continued, unruffled. "Well, listen. I can't tell you what to do. My advice is you go to the FBI. Let them handle it. They would probably get you into the Federal Witness Protection Program pretty rapidly. You asked for my help and my professional opinion. That's my advice. I understand you were probably hoping for a miracle, but I can't make chicken salad out of chicken shit. Those are your two options. What happened that night is going to change your lives forever. It's as simple as that. If you don't want my help, that's up to you. But you have to realize that disappearing on your own as you've done for the past few days is risky. No offense, but you certainly aren't prepared to survive that."

"What are you even talking about, making chicken salad out of chicken shit? What does that even mean? This is all easy for you to say, Sam. Your entire existence isn't being flipped upside down, is it? I don't even know if you know what you're talking about. You could have been a shit agent, for all I know," said Kendra.

Kendra stopped talking as soon as she saw Sam's face. She suddenly wished she had said something—anything other than what had just come out of her mouth. She didn't think it was possible to feel any worse than she already did, but the hurt in his eyes made her want to cry. He was the only person helping them right now, and she might as well have just spit on him.

"I'm sorry, Sam. I didn't mean that. I appreciate that you're trying to help us. But there has to be another way. Isn't there?" she asked, tears pricking at her eyes.

Kyle slumped onto the sofa, his head buried in his hands.

"No need to apologize. I get it, Kendra. I really do. I admire your unyielding determination and obviously fierce instinct to protect your son. But I'm telling you, there is no other way. They won't stop coming for you. Ever. This is better than the alternative. Which would be you and Kyle dead. I can make a call to the FBI if you'd like me to, and I can keep you safe here until you're transported back to Los Angeles."

Kendra sat next to Kyle on the couch, wrapping her arms around him.

"If you insist on remaining on the run on your own, while I highly discourage that, I can help you make it work. I know people from my prior career in the area who can get you identification. I can train you both to protect yourselves, and how to shoot. But I honestly can't say this enough. I think that's a colossally bad idea."

"You mean like a confidential informant who could get us IDs?" asked Kendra.

"No. Any confidential sources I ever worked with would have been assigned to other agents. If I put my ass on the line to get IDs and commit a felony, it sure as hell won't be with someone who has ties to the DEA. With my prior experience in the city, I know plenty of good document forgers that have never been arrested."

"I just don't feel safe going to the FBI. Not after what I saw there. This gang is never going to stop. And if they have LAPD helping them, which they clearly do, then I don't even trust the FBI to put us into Witness Protection. If Gutierrez is assigned to the FBI field office, how do I know he won't find a way to access our records? Or pay someone for them. I have no idea how many people are involved in this."

"I don't want to be scared for the rest of my life, Mom. Or worried about you. And I sure as hell don't want to die. I'm only sixteen! Why would the Sinners ever stop looking for us? As long as we're out here, we're a threat. And with the police helping them, it's not like they wouldn't find us. At least with new identities that even the cops don't know about, we have half a freaking chance."

Kendra looked at Kyle and then at Sam. "What would we need to do?"

"You sure about this?"

Kendra nodded, although she wasn't sure about anything, least of all this decision.

Sam slapped his hands on his knees and stood. "Relax today. We start tomorrow. I'm going to cram a month's worth of training into a week. It won't be fun, but it's necessary. I need to take a picture of both of you for your new IDs. Stand in front of the white wall over there," he said, pointing to the far wall. "I'll be right back with my camera. Oh, and get your old IDs and anything else in your wallets with your legal names on it. I need to shred them."

A shiver slipped down Kendra's spine as she rubbed the goosebumps on her arms. Was she doing the right thing? She didn't know. But Sam's words wouldn't stop playing on repeat in her head. "This is better than the alternative. Which would be you and Kyle dead."

SEVENTEEN

Steven McLeod found it difficult to concentrate on the paperwork in front of him. He eventually surrendered and grabbed his phone, where he dialed a number and put in on speakerphone.

"What?"

"What? Are you kidding me? What the fuck do you think I want, Gutierrez? Where is the witness you told me would be dispatched without a problem? Where is the video the kid took? I've got the goddamn feds with one fist down my throat and the other up my ass until they meet in the middle!" he screamed into the phone.

"I'm working on it. You're not the only one who wants the kid found, you know. The DA wants him brought in too. Not to mention my contacts who took care of your little problem for you. Let me remind you, Steven, I have my ass on the line here too."

"Yeah, well, I'm looking at federal prison if they connect me to Devon's murder. With the amount of money I'm paying you, I expect some goddamn results! You'd better find the kid and his mother before they're gone in the wind if you know what's good for you. Because I promise you, it will be the last mistake you make if that happens."

"Are you threatening me, McLeod? You'd be wise to—"

Senator McLeod hit the disconnect button and launched his cell at the office door before Gutierrez finished his sentence. What a worthless waste of space the man had proved to be. The only thing Senator McLeod required of Gutierrez was to eliminate his nephew and make it look like a random murder. They were in Los Angeles for the love of God, where every day, people were killed for no other reason than making eye contact with the wrong person. But even a simple task like that was too much for Gutierrez to handle without screwing it to high heaven. Now, thanks to the officer, things had gone from bad to worse. The campaign contribution and embezzlement charges didn't worry the senator. He had hired the best defense attorney money could buy, even though no charges had been brought yet. He doubted the matter would ever see the inside of a courtroom. His attorney would quash it before it left the ground. However, if anyone linked him to Devon's death, it would be a different story. Steven never wanted to take such extreme measures with his nephew. The kid was family, and Steven was quite fond of him before he became a liability. Devon was his sister's only child, and his death left her devastated. But Devon's refusal to listen and his threat to expose Steven led to his nephews' downfall. Steven had worked too hard for thirty years to build his political career, and he wasn't going to let a smart-mouthed, do-gooder, millennial destroy it.

The senator rose from his desk and picked up his phone. When it landed, the back cover had popped off and ended up several feet away. Luckily, that was all the damage done to the phone. He was willing to admit that impulse control was sometimes problematic for him. Having to replace the device and have his assistant input all the numbers again would be a major inconvenience. The worst part was that there were several numbers she didn't have. Private numbers, such as the one he was about to call. He snapped the cover into place and went back to his desk.

Listening to the number ring three times, Steven thought the man might not answer, but he picked up on the fourth ring.

"Yeah?"

What was it about people these days? Did no one answer their phone and say hello anymore? He found it not only incredibly rude, but in bad taste as well.

"I have a little problem I may need your help with."

"Yeah, so I've read. The *LA Times* is covering it nicely."

"I need the witness found and disposed of. That idiot at the PD has been zero help."

"Send me everything you have on it," said the man, then he hung up abruptly.

Steven pulled the phone from his ear and stared at it, shocked that the man had hung up on him. He was an odd character, that guy. But the quality of his work wasn't something Steven could complain about. He had utilized his services in the past on confidential assignments and had never been let down. If Gutierrez couldn't get things handled, Steven would be left with no choice but to have the exterminator take matters into his own hands.

An hour later, he had put together a dossier and forwarded it to the assassin. He felt better the instant he hit send. At least now he was certain things would go as planned and not run further off the rails. Just then, his assistant knocked and entered, reminding him about an interview with a local reporter. Hopefully, this reporter would remain focused on Steven's political campaign agenda, as instructed. Every reporter wanted to stray off subject and steer the conversation to Devon's death. Frankly, he didn't think he could feign the anguish and put on another Oscar-worthy performance. His head just wasn't in the game today. Senator McLeod was focused on taking down the woman and teenager who had dropped the match and set his world on fire.

EIGHTEEN

Kendra woke to the sound of birds chirping and bright sunlight. Her stomach growled as the aroma of bacon and coffee drifted into her room, and the sound of laughter was followed by Buddy's bark. She tossed the blanket aside and quickly put on her robe, feeling the coolness of the hardwood floor beneath her feet. She rifled through her bag to find a t-shirt, jeans, and her favorite sneakers. She wanted to be prepared for anything, since she had no idea what Sam had planned for them today. Yesterday, he said they would start training this morning, which could mean any number of things to Kendra.

Creeping into the bathroom in the hall, she locked the door after herself and stepped into the shower. Taking a proper shower, instead of just washing up in a truck stop bathroom, was just what she needed to feel human again. Kendra dried off and wiped the towel across the bathroom mirror. She had to do something about her hair. Initially, her homemade dye job was not great, and it had only worsened over the past few days. After drying her hair by hand she eventually gave up and twisted it into a ponytail. That seemed to be her new go-to look. Sam and Kyle had finished breakfast by the time she reached the kitchen.

"Why didn't you wake me up?" she asked.

"I figured you needed the rest. Today wasn't the norm. Moving forward, we get up at 6:00 a.m. for training every day. I'm going to walk you through some basics today," said Sam.

"Sam made you a plate, Mom," said Kyle, pointing to a plate on the counter covered with a pan lid.

"Thank you, Sam. I can make my own breakfast though. You don't have to do all the cooking."

"I like to cook. Coffee is in the pot. Cream and sugar next to that. I've got to make a call, so you two hang out in here and I'll be back shortly."

Kendra took her plate to the table after pouring herself a cup of coffee. As she lifted the lid, her jaw dropped in amazement. Sam had prepared a spinach and bacon frittata and served it with a side of hash browns and sausage. The food was as good as that of any restaurant, and the meal was a welcome change after days of eating fast food on the go. Kendra cleaned her plate and could have eaten more.

"It was good, right?" said Kyle.

Kendra nodded, sipping her coffee. "It sure was. Who knew he could cook? He's full of surprises."

Kyle leaned down to pet Buddy, who was his constant companion now. "So, are we really doing this, Mom?"

Kendra looked at her son, guilt coursing through her. "I don't want to, but I don't know what else to do."

"Yeah, me neither. I was up thinking about it last night. It's totally screwed up. But I don't want to keep running forever, either. Can I at least tell Brendan what's happening? He'll think something bad happened to me by now. Especially when I don't go back to school. Does this mean I don't have to go to school anymore?"

Before Kendra could answer, Sam appeared out of nowhere. Somehow, he had snuck back inside without either of them hearing him.

"No. You can't tell anyone what your new names will be, or where you're going. Don't even tell me where you're going. I'll know your new names, but only because I have to secure your IDs from my source," said Sam.

"So everyone will just wonder what happened to us?"

"I'm afraid so," said Sam, putting a hand on Kyle's shoulder.

Kyle got up and headed for the door. "I'll be outside when you're ready to start training."

Kendra sighed. "He's taking this better than I thought he would."

"For now, maybe. I reckon that'll change the closer we get to your leave day. Come with me. I want to show you something. We need Kyle for this too."

Kendra called Kyle inside and they followed Sam to the walk-in pantry, where he headed toward the back to open another door.

"The basement. Come on," he said, flipping on a light switch next to the door.

Kendra hesitated. She had never been fond of basements. They were creepy, and most had a musty, dark atmosphere that made her uneasy. Sam was half-way down the stairs and Kyle was close behind, leaving her with no other option but to follow them. Sam's was a typical basement. The walls were lined with stacked boxes, plastic-covered furniture, and a washer and dryer in one corner. With a single push, Sam moved a pile of boxes to the side, and they moved in unison as a single unit.

"They're empty and glued together," said Sam. "They're here to hide this."

He stepped aside to reveal a door with a single handle on one side. Sam swung the door inward, then turned back to face them.

"This is my escape route. If something ever goes wrong and I need to get out of here undetected, this is how I'll do it. Sort of like a panic room, but with an exit. This may seem like overkill, but I worked deep undercover for many years. There are more than a few people who have a reason to come after me. This will be your escape path now if needed. You are going to have to learn to trust me, both of you. If I tell you to take the panic room out, don't question me, just do it."

Kendra and Kyle looked at Sam like he was crazy. The door opened, revealing a seemingly endless corridor. Dirt was visible between the wooden plank walls.

"Do you really think this is necessary?" asked Kendra, peering around the strange hallway.

"I'd rather have you prepared than caught unaware. Hopefully, it will not come to this. But it's best if you know how to get out in case it's needed later. The door to the pantry, the basement door at the top of the stairs, and this door are all reinforced with steel. They are heavy and hard to get through. Not impossible, mind you, but it will slow someone down. If you ever have to use this exit, you need to pull the barrier down after each door," he said, pointing to the basement door.

Kendra looked at the door and noticed a long wooden plank attached to the wall used to barricade the door in place.

"My go bag is here," he said, pointing to a duffle bag just inside the corridor on the dirt floor. "As of tomorrow, you will each have your own go bag here as well. After you barricade both doors behind you, step into the tunnel here and barricade this door as well. Take the flashlight and the gun," he opened the door further to reveal a handgun and a large Maglite hanging on the inside of the door. "And you follow the tunnel until it ends. We'll walk it together now, so you know where it goes."

"Wow, this is so dope. Like, seriously, Sam," said Kyle, looking around the tunnel in awe.

Kendra still didn't have words to describe her feelings. Claustrophobia came over her in waves as she entered the tunnel. She couldn't believe this was her life now–secret tunnels, barricaded doors, and guns. Her profession was nursing, not espionage. Everything about this felt wrong. As if she was living a nightmare that didn't belong to her.

"You ready to go?" asked Sam, ushering them inside. "I'm not going to barricade the door since we want to leave it open for access, obviously. But try it while we're here, so you know what to do."

Sam turned on the flashlight, illuminating the door. Kyle managed to get the barricade into position across the door, although it was a struggle.

"It's so heavy," said Kyle.

"Reinforced with steel," said Sam, lifting the barricade back into the open position. "Good job, Kyle. You ready to walk the tunnel?"

"Yeah!" said Kyle enthusiastically.

Kendra would really rather not, but she had a feeling she wasn't going to get out of it. So she reluctantly nodded and followed behind Kyle as they began the trek into the dark tunnel. The large flashlight lit up the narrow tunnel for several feet ahead, although there was nothing to see. The tunnel appeared to stretch on endlessly. With each step they took, Kendra became more anxious, eager to get out of the confined space. She glanced over her shoulder, but the tunnel was completely dark behind her. Sam came to a halt just as she thought she couldn't bear it any longer, and she caught sight of a ladder.

"This is the exit. It's about three quarters of a mile away from the house," he said, starting the climb up the ladder. "No one knows about this exit except me, Lou, and the person who built it. And now both of you. This wasn't permitted or anything, so it doesn't appear in the original house plans."

Kyle scrambled up the ladder after Sam, and Kendra was relieved to see daylight as Sam pushed open the top of the shelter. They exited in what seemed like the middle of nowhere. All Kendra could see was a sea of pine trees. Sam reached out to her and offered his hand to help her up.

"Now we go a half mile straight due west. Look for the trees with green paint on the trunk." He pointed to a large pine tree with a swash of green paint across the trunk. It was so well disguised that it would be impossible to detect unless someone knew what to look for.

They walked single file into the forest with Sam in the lead, Kyle behind him, and Kendra bringing up the rear. Sam showed them other trees marked with green paint to help them navigate. They quickly arrived at their destination, where Sam stopped at an older model brown truck parked at the head of a trail.

"From here you take the truck onto the trail until you hit the highway," said Sam. "Keys are on the front left tire." He reached under the wheel well and grabbed a set of keys.

Opening the door, he motioned them over. "The front seat lifts up," he said, pulling the bench seat up. "When you get in, put your go bags and the flashlight in here for safekeeping. Depending on the situation, the gun either goes in here or stays up top with you."

"We don't even know how to use a gun though," said Kyle.

"Well, you will by the end of the week," said Sam.

"Sick!" said Kyle, grinning.

Kyle's words rang true for Kendra, but not in the way he meant them. She felt unmistakably sick, her stomach churning at the prospect of having to use a firearm for protection. The thought was too much to handle, leaving her feeling helpless and frightened.

"One thing you will need to remember. There is a map in the glove box with two routes marked. One is Highway 20, that will take you straight past Clear Lake and into Lake Mendocino. That's where the 101 Freeway intersects. The other route is Highway 29 through Lake County, to Hopland pass. Hopland is a mountain road with some hairpin turns, but if you're being chased, they won't find you on that route. They will assume you are going west to the 101, or east back to Williams and Interstate 5. The Hopland pass will dump you on the 101 in Hopland, just north of Cloverdale. What that means is, you'd be several miles ahead of anyone tracking you via the 101 Freeway."

"None of those cities mean anything to me. I've never been in this area before," said Kendra.

"There's a map, like I said. The important thing to remember is if you think someone is on your trail, take the Hopland route. I come out here every week and start the truck up, check the tires and make sure she's in good running order. Anyway, we can walk back to the house from here. I've got to check my informant's drop point. Your new IDs should be here this morning."

Kendra nodded absentmindedly, her mind already elsewhere.

NINETEEN

"Katherine Sorensen? I couldn't have chosen my own new name?" asked Kendra.

"Nope. These are legitimate names and social security numbers of deceased persons. They aren't just plucked from the sky. There's a method the forger follows to ensure they pass muster," replied Sam.

"Ewww. Dead people's names. Gross. But I don't mind my new name. Jared isn't so bad. I can live with that," said Kyle.

Kendra studied the paperwork in front of her. She gave credit where credit was due to the forger. Her new driver's license and social security card were on point, and the birth certificate was complete with an embossment stamp from the county. The passport contained stamps from Mexico, Canada, and Denmark. Although she found the Denmark stamp to be unusual, the fact that Sorensen was a Scandinavian surname led her to believe that the first Katherine Sorensen may have had family ties there. The face staring back at Kendra from her new driver's license was hardly recognizable to her. The new Katherine Sorensen was unsmiling, her dull brown hair listless, and dark circles lining her deep green eyes. Kendra seemed to have aged beyond her thirty-eight years. She *felt* older than her age. She studied her new VISA card that had a $5,000.00 credit limit. She was unsure how Sam managed to do it, but he assured her it was legitimate and told her to update the card with her new mailing address after settling in. He told her to use the card for travel expenses to their new destination. Wherever that was. Kendra had no idea where she and Kyle would go. Limited funds made her anxious about their ability to survive without a steady income. Getting a nursing job would be impossible for her without obtaining a degree and passing the NCLEX tests again as Katherine Sorensen, as her nursing license was under the name Kendra Thompson. Unfortunately, all of that new education came at a price. And she lacked the necessary funds. The future was full of unknowns for them.

"Okay, break's over. Let's get back to it," said Sam, standing and snapping Kendra out of her daydream.

They spent the remainder of the day in Sam's version of a self-defense training class. One of many to come. She fell into bed each night exhausted.

On day three, Kendra woke up completely spent. For the past two days, Sam had been training them almost non-stop for ten hours a day. She wanted a break, but he was insistent on continuing. Sam had an inexhaustible supply of energy for a man of his age, and Kyle was undaunted by the strenuous schedule. Kendra glared at Sam behind his back and resisted the urge to vent at him. Instead, she watched him walk outside without a snappy retort to her credit. She bit her tongue, feeling like she had been doing nothing but complaining for the past two days.

She reluctantly followed Sam, Kyle, and Buddy outside after a quick breakfast. A few hours of training had Kendra feeling cranky, but she pushed on.

"Okay, right now we are going to learn how to escape if someone grabs you from behind. Your situational awareness will not be great when you don't see them coming. So, you need to think fast. Kyle, grab me from behind and let me show you a few ways to get loose."

Kyle approached Sam from behind, wrapping his arms around him and pinning Sam's arms to his side.

"Method number one. You can duck and spin if the grip isn't too tight." Sam lowered his body and twisted around to face Kyle in a matter of seconds. "You want to stun them by going for soft tissue somewhere around this area," he said, indicating Kyle's side between his ribs and hip. "Kyle, you try next."

Kyle executed the move flawlessly. Kendra tried several times before she got it right.

"That was the most difficult way to release yourself. Now we'll move on to some easier methods. If your attacker has you in a tight grip, head-butt him. Draw your head forward as far as possible and slam it back into them with everything you've got." Sam demonstrated the movement on Kyle in slow motion.

"You can also use your foot to stomp on theirs and grind it into the soft part of the top of their foot. The moment they loosen their grip or let go, you turn toward them. Use the hard heel of your palm and smash it into the underside of their nose as hard as you can. You are trying to drive the nose bone upward. Don't try to pull hands away from your neck. It won't work. Focus on one finger. The pinky finger. Pull it back and break it. They will loosen their grip for a second, and that's all you need. Then knee them in the groin as hard as possible immediately afterward. Then you run like hell. Remember, you are trying to stun them with shock and awe. Chances are you won't be able to outfight your attacker. We have to assume they will be stronger than you. But they won't expect you to fight back. You can take them by surprise."

Sam made them practice the techniques repeatedly until they became almost like reflexes. Wiping the sweat off her forehead, Kendra muttered curses under her breath at him.

"I heard that, Kendra. Use that anger and frustration. Channel it into strength," said Sam, coming at her from behind again.

Yesterday, Sam pushed Kendra to go beyond her limits and think outside the box. Yesterday she had appreciated that. Today, she simply wanted him to stop talking and leave her alone. Her throat burned with a snarky response, but she managed to swallow it and was proud of herself for doing so. Kendra's foot came down hard on top of Sam's as he grabbed her. He let her go immediately and took a step back.

"Mom! What are you doing? We aren't supposed to hurt Sam for real. It's just practice!" yelled Kyle.

"I'm channeling my frustration," said Kendra, panting with exertion.

With a laugh, Sam nodded in agreement. "Yes, you are. Well done, Kendra."

Bent over with hands on her knees, Kendra relaxed and took a deep breath. "Sorry, Sam. I just reacted."

"Don't be sorry. That's what I've been trying to teach you to do—react to a threat without over-thinking it. We have just one more release technique, then we can call it a day. You've both been working so hard. You deserve a break."

Kendra stood up with a groan. Eager to learn more, Kyle stood in front of Sam.

"This method is used as a last resort, because it can put you in a vulnerable position if you aren't careful. Go completely limp. I mean absolutely slack. Let your attacker believe you've passed out. This will force them to support your weight for a moment and they will be focused on that. Use that to your advantage. Once again, they won't expect you to come at them."

Sam ended the session for the day after an additional twenty minutes of training. Kendra limped her way to the porch, where she collapsed into a chair. They sat next to each other in silence for several minutes. Resting her head on the back of the chair, Kendra closed her eyes. It was so peaceful and serene. For the first time in days, she felt safe and at ease as a sliver of sun touched her face.

"When did you retire from the DEA, Sam?"

"Is that what Lou told you? That I retired?"

His response took Kendra by surprise, and the tranquil music playing in her head stopped suddenly, like a record screeching to a halt.

"Well, yes. Is that not the truth?"

"It's a half truth, I suppose. I was accused of planting evidence, tampering with evidence, and the willful neglect of duty, among other misconducts. No official investigation or charges were ever brought.

Once word got around, it tarnished my reputation with fellow agents. Not that I was big on making friends at work to begin with. Because of my exemplary record up to that point, my supervisor gave me a choice. Take early retirement or take my chances with internal affairs and the Office of Professional Responsibility building a case against me. The truth is, they didn't want the bad press. So I took the path of least resistance."

"I see," Kendra said, cautiously.

"I don't think you do. I didn't do any of the things they accused me of. My partner did. But proving that was going to be almost impossible. He did a stellar job of setting me up. And to complicate things further, he was still my brother-in-law at the time. He and Lou were at the start of a nasty divorce. Then my ex-wife divorced me and married him."

Kendra's gaze shifted to Sam, who remained fixated on staring straight ahead. Kendra thought she was the only one with problems, but Sam was a walking dumpster fire.

"So, he was Lou's soon to be ex-husband? And then your ex-wife's new husband? Who set you up? And you let him just get away with it?"

"No choice, really. It would have hurt Lou in the long run, not only financially, but her reputation as well. The publicity would have destroyed her. She told me to go after him, but I couldn't do that and hurt her. And my partner knew I would never do anything to jeopardize Lou. And by that time, I was pretty much done with being undercover and chasing hypes anyway. So I took retirement. And that was the end of that. The agency started an investigation, but I knew they wouldn't find anything. I hadn't done anything."

"Wow. I'm sorry, Sam. I had no idea."

"No need to apologize. It was five years ago. I'm over it. Mostly."

They sat in silence for a few minutes while Kendra studied Sam's features. "You remind me of Daniel Taylor."

He turned to face her. "I'm almost afraid to ask, but is that a good thing?"

"Well, I thought he was the love of my life at one time."

"And now you don't?" asked Sam, smiling.

"No, not anymore."

"So, what happened?"

"He tried to hold Shelly Hallmark's hand in the lunch line."

Sam grinned. "The lunch line, huh?"

"Yep. My eighth-grade crush was over before it ever began."

"Well, if you ask me, Daniel Taylor sounds like an idiot. Then again, having never met Shelly Hallmark, who's to say he didn't make the best choice?"

Kendra chuckled. "Well, given my current circumstances, I'd say Daniel probably made the right decision. Although it's possible I may be romanticizing him now, as my memories have taken on a rosy glow over the years. Except for Shelley Hallmark, that is."

"Ah, the rosy glow. Memories often do that with former loves. Don't be so hard on yourself, Kendra. This situation isn't your fault. Or Kyle's fault. Your boy was just in the wrong place at the wrong time."

Kendra started to say something, but Sam was off the porch before she had a chance to reply. It sounded so simple. Yet being in the wrong place at the wrong time had changed the trajectory of their lives forever.

TWENTY

Officer Ramón Gutierrez stared at his monitor, scrolling through pages of public property records. He despised the monotony of what he considered grunt work, but the records department was backlogged. Even Amelia, the head of the records department who owed him for fixing tickets for her brother, couldn't escalate his request.

Three days ago, Big Boy told Gutierrez the trucker who helped Kendra Thompson and her son took westbound Highway 20 after leaving Interstate 5 at Williams, but the lack of traffic on the route had made it impossible for the spotters to keep track of them without being detected. That made Gutierrez shift his focus to a different angle. He trusted his intuition when he sensed that the truck driver was taking them somewhere she knew well. She had to have a place in mind where she thought they would be safe. When he ran the truck's license plate, Louella Murphy-Jonas came up as the registered owner. It made sense because he knew the trucker was a female. When conducting a background check, he learned that she was divorced, and her ex-spouse was a DEA agent. Gutierrez thought Louella must have ties to the area. Her, her ex-husband, or her brother might have a place close by. She had no family except for her brother Sam, who also happened to be a retired narc squad agent. The DEA angle caught his attention. She would feel comfortable entrusting Kendra and Kyle's protection to her ex or her brother, given their law enforcement backgrounds. Gutierrez had been searching through property records for days, hoping to find a house in the area where Kendra and her son might be hiding.

As he was about to end his three-hour computer session, he scrolled past a name he recognized. Tapping the page up key, he grinned. Samuel Jonathan Murphy's property deed was displayed on his screen. He rapped his knuckles on his desk. "Gotcha!"

With his cell phone pressed to his ear, Gutierrez walked out of the station. "I know where they are," he said into the phone.

"It's about fucking time, *ese*. Glad to hear you're done playing keystone cop and got your shit together," said Big Boy.

"Watch your mouth, asshole. We're in this bind because your soldiers fucked up," Gutierrez said.

Big Boy laughed. "Fuck you, *caralho*. Don't worry about my soldiers. It's been taken care of. One day you're going to go too far with me, and there'll be pieces of you spread from here to Tijuana."

Gutierrez hung up abruptly. He hated that Big Boy got to him. He knew the Sinners captain was capable of delivering on his promise, and it unsettled him. He had learned years ago not to push things too far with him. Big Boy could say whatever he wanted about his gang, but Gutierrez wasn't afforded the same privilege. He let it go and sent Big Boy a text containing Sam Murphy's address and instructions to handle it by the following day.

His next move was to dial Senator McLeod's number. His dislike for Steven McLeod surpassed even that of Big Boy. The man's own arrogance would be his undoing one day. Like most politicians, he was adept at maintaining his public persona, but Gutierrez knew him for what he truly was—a self-serving prick who only cared about his own interests.

"Hello, officer. Calling to discuss the weather, or have you actually done something to earn some of the money I've paid you?"

The senator's cockiness always rubbed Gutierrez the wrong way. "I know where they are. It will be handled by tomorrow."

"Well, that's delightful to hear, Ramón. And just where are the elusive nurse and her teenager hiding that they've managed to elude not only you, but a gang hit?"

"It doesn't matter. I found them, and they'll be taken care of."

"That's where you're wrong, Gutierrez. It matters to me, and since I'm paying you, I want the address."

"Don't do something stupid, McLeod. You'll only jeopardize the operation."

"I think you've done a fine job of that yourself thus far. What do you think I'm going to do, Gutierrez? Jet off to parts unknown with a gun in hand and take them down myself? Hardly. I don't need to get my hands any dirtier than they already are. I'm just curious as to where they are. Send me the address. I have more important things to do than waste any more time chatting with you, Gutierrez. I'll be waiting for your text. Goodbye."

Gutierrez sighed heavily before sending the text to McLeod. He didn't care if the asshole had Sam Murphy's address, as long as it got the guy off his back. He knew the senator was telling the truth. He had no intention of intervening. McLeod was a white-collar pansy who paid other people to do his dirty work. And if he sent someone after Kendra and Kyle Thompson, then so be it. It made no difference to Gutierrez if the senator's henchman and the gang fought to the death among themselves. He didn't care about other casualties, only that the targets were eliminated. If Kendra and her son were under the protection of a DEA agent, retired or otherwise, then that was the hitter's problem, not his.

Meanwhile, from a South Los Angeles trap house, Big Boy called Monster to inform him that the targets had been found. A smile crept onto Monster's face. After what that bitch did, he planned to go on this hit himself to ensure it went down as planned. He enlisted Ghost for the mission, along with a new member, Diego "Young G" Navarro, to serve as backup shooter. He instructed them to be ready to leave immediately since the drive north would take them about four hours.

Several miles away from Big Boy and the Los Angeles trap house, Senator McLeod stepped into his plush office and closed the door to call the hitman.

"Talk to me," said the man, as a way of greeting.

"I have the address where they are hiding. I want you to get there immediately. The gang task force officer is going to dispatch his gangbangers, although I don't have much faith in them getting this handled. I need you to beat them there and take out the targets. I need this thing finished."

"Rush jobs require extra funds."

"I don't care how much it costs. I just need it done!" he said, struggling to control his temper.

"Duly noted. Send me the information."

After sending the text, the senator sat back in his office chair. He felt that he could at last move on and leave the entire mess behind him. The hitman would handle things. The inquiry into Devon's death would reach a standstill and eventually be classified as yet another unresolved homicide in Los Angeles. He might even be able to squeeze some more publicity from it. That's precisely what he would do. He would publicly criticize the LAPD, and officer Gutierrez in particular, for their inadequate progress. The prick deserved it.

A few hours later, the hitman sent senator McLeod a text that he was driving northbound, on his way to the Lake County house where Kendra and her son were hiding, and would arrive that evening. Steven McLeod smiled to himself and celebrated by making dinner reservations at Spago in Beverly Hills. He couldn't think of any reason he shouldn't enjoy a nice meal with his wife.

TWENTY-ONE

Kendra flinched at the sound of the gunshot, despite anticipating it and wearing earplugs. Kyle successfully hit his target and exchanged a high-five with Sam as Kendra positioned herself at the mark and aimed. With nerves running high, she grasped the gun tightly. She took a deep breath, exhaled, and squeezed the trigger. At least this time, she was able to hit the target. That made a total of three times she had managed to hit it somewhere on the paper outline. She let her arm fall to her side, feeling disappointed about her lack of progress despite practicing for two days.

"You'll get better," said Sam, gently taking the gun from her.

"I wouldn't bet on it, Sam."

"Tomorrow is another day. You're doing better with a rifle, so you should be proud of that progress."

"Right. So if someone comes after us and I'm loaded for bear, we'll be fine," she said.

Sam chuckled. "Be prepared for any situation, that's what I always say."

"Which reminds me, Sam. Is there any place around here I can get my hair done? I really need to have my attempt at dying it myself fixed. Plus, I need to get out, even for just a while."

"I reckon Patti's place can probably squeeze you in."

"I'm not picky. Anyone with a cosmetologist's license would be a win for me."

"All right. Let's get these guns cleaned and we can head out. Kyle, I bet you're ready for some fast-food by now," said Sam, glancing over at Kyle.

"You're a great cook, Sam, but yeah. I could do with a greasy burger or a couple of tacos."

Gathering the firearms, ammunition, and targets, they carried the weapons into the house, where Sam opened the gun case and pulled out the cleaning supplies. The trio chatted and cleaned the guns while Buddy slept at their feet. An hour later, Kendra grabbed her wallet from her purse and they piled into Sam's truck, heading down Highway 20. They drove onto Highway 53 toward Clearlake, with Sam telling them they could take it to Highway 29 in a loop around the lake.

"We might as well take the long way back and give you a tour of the lake," said Sam.

"Fine with me," said Kendra. "Anything that gets me out of more of your training is good."

"Better the devil you know than the devil you don't," said Sam, grinning at her.

Sam pulled into a parking lot and stopped in front of Hair We Are, an unremarkable gray stucco building off Highway 29. Kendra leaped from the truck to stretch and contemplated whether she should put her hair in the hands of this Patti person. As soon as she stepped inside the storefront, she had second thoughts. The entire space was pink, except for the floor, which was black tile. The walls, the chairs, even the sinks, were various shades of pink.

"Howdy, Sam! Didn't I just see you a couple of weeks ago? You ready for a trim so soon?"

A woman with black hair piled high and a robust physique walked up to Sam and hugged him tightly. As Kendra scrutinized Patti's hair, her doubts grew stronger.

"Hello, Patti. Not for me this time. This is my friend, Sharon. She needs some time with you if you can squeeze her in?"

Kendra looked at Sam quizzically when he referred to her as Sharon. Patti approached Kendra and tilted her head to the side while studying her.

"Oh, honey. Let's get you fixed up. Take a seat and I'll be with you in a jiff."

Sam guided Kendra to the waiting area, where Kyle was already thumbing through a Popular Mechanics magazine.

"Why did you tell her my name was Sharon?"

"Because I don't want to use your real name for obvious reasons. And you shouldn't use your new name until you leave here. Once you drive away from my house on your own, then you become Katherine and Jared Sorensen. No need for anyone to associate that name with Lake County."

"And when do you think that will be? Leaving here, I mean," asked Kendra.

"I think by Sunday you should be ready to leave the nest," said Sam, picking up a Reader's Digest.

"But that's only two days from now," said Kendra.

"Yep."

"I'm not ready yet, Sam."

"You'll be as ready as you ever will be. You can't stay here much longer. Even two more days is pushing it, in my opinion. Either the bangers or the task force is going to make the connection between Lou and me. When they do, you'll be sitting ducks here. You need to get on the move with your new identities. Get on a plane and put some distance between you and them."

Kendra bit her bottom lip, deep in thought. Kyle stopped reading and glanced between her and Sam.

Sam put the magazine down to focus on Kendra. "Look, you are more prepared for this than you know. Follow my instructions. Get a burner phone. Once you get settled, open an account with a wireless provider under your new name. Keep the sim card out of Kyle's phone and put it in a safe deposit box. Your new identities are clean. They cannot be traced to your real identities. Just don't go getting your picture in the paper. Kyle, I know it's unrealistic to say you can't open new social media accounts at some point. But you cannot have your picture on any of those accounts. You can create profiles under your new name, but no photos of yourself. And no mention of LA, your old school, your old friends, or anything else related to your old life. Don't add old friends to your new profiles. Got it?"

Kyle nodded while gazing out the window.

Patti appeared from around the corner, drying her hands on her apron. "Okay, Sharon, let's get you in a chair and see what we can do to save what you've got going on here," she said, grimacing at Kendra's hair.

After a fifteen-minute consultation, Patti was mixing a new color for Kendra. It took two and a half hours, but Kendra emerged looking and feeling like a new woman. Her chestnut hair was cut to frame her face and hung down her back in soft waves. Patti was a miracle worker, in Kendra's opinion. Her green eyes were accentuated by the color, which also looked great with her skin tone. Kyle's eyebrows raised in surprise as Sam whistled at the sight of her returning to the reception area.

"Wow, Mom. You look great."

Kendra smiled at Kyle, feeling more like herself than she had in a week.

"Thank you, Patti. You don't know how much I needed this," said Kendra, turning to give her a quick hug goodbye.

"Oh, sweetie, it was my pleasure. Now, you go out there and rock this cut and color. And when anyone asks, you tell them Patti at Hair We Are is responsible for this gorgeous creation."

"I sure will."

"Sam, I'll see you in another week or so," said Patti, winking at him.

"You bet, Patti," he said, nodding at her.

Back on the road, Sam lowered the windows, allowing a bit of fresh air to circulate through the truck cab. The beauty of the day was matched only by the spectacular views of Clear Lake, and if the circumstances were different, Kendra would have opted for a local winery for lunch rather than a fast-food restaurant.

They passed a few stoplights on the highway as they approached the city of Lakeport. At one of the signals, Sam pointed out the sign for Highway 175.

"That's the Hopland grade shortcut I mentioned to you a few days ago."

They left the highway at the upcoming exit and found themselves at a roundabout with several fast-food establishments.

"Take your pick, Kyle. Kentucky Fried Chicken, Burger King, Taco Bell, or Mickey D's," said Sam, entering the roundabout.

"Taco Bell sounds awesome."

"Tacos it is, then."

Sam parked the truck, and they piled out. Kyle got inside first and was already placing an order when Sam and Kendra walked through the door. Kendra was taken aback by the amount of food Kyle ordered, and even more so when he polished off everything.

"Oh my God, that was so good," said Kyle, leaning back in the booth sipping his soda.

Sam sighed and shook his head. "I could have made you tacos at home that would put those to shame."

"Yeah, but sometimes I just need a little junk food."

"Well, when you get to be my age, you have to be picky about your junk food. I feel like I'll have to diet for a week to make up for this," said Sam, patting his stomach. "Shall we get on the road and take a drive around the lake?"

Kendra nodded and left their trays on the trash bin on the way out. The drive back to Sam's house was breathtaking. The lake was beautiful. The scenery and towns they passed through were quaint, with an old-fashioned feel to them. Just before sunset, they pulled up to Sam's house feeling tired, but happy. They were all anticipating an evening of TV, followed by an early night to bed. Kendra made it through one movie before she excused herself for the night, and Kyle and Sam assured her they were not far behind. She tumbled into bed exhausted and was asleep within minutes.

TWENTY-TWO

The TV's light shone through the front window, creating a flickering effect. Concealed in the darkness, the assassin rested against a tree trunk. His plan was to wait until the occupants of the house had been asleep for several hours before making a move. When he arrived earlier that day, they were out, which was lucky. He picked the lock to enter through the back door and went inside to get acquainted with the layout. He planned to eliminate the man first, then the woman, and finally the teenager. He didn't enjoy killing children, but that was part of the job sometimes. He justified it by telling himself the target wasn't actually a child. He was sixteen. Almost an adult. He knew the Labrador would become aware of him through hearing and scent long before any human in the house would. He always anticipated the unpredictable and had a small piece of meat infused with a sedative to prevent having to take down the dog—he had limits, and harming an innocent animal wasn't something he wanted to do. He liked animals more than most people he knew.

He was certain the kid's phone was in the house, and he was confident he could retrieve it and be gone in under fifteen minutes. He had every reason to believe that would happen, as he was highly skilled at his job. His services were in high demand all over the country because of his uniquely varied skill set and excellent reputation.

The hitman got up to stretch his muscles every thirty minutes. His eagerness to start the job made him twitchy, and he had to release his extra energy. Despite his restlessness, he remained patient. He had waited in far more uncomfortable hiding spots for much longer, many times. As soon as the TV light disappeared and the front room lights turned off, he felt an electrifying sensation. He had to wait just a few more hours until he was positive that the targets were sound asleep, and then he could re-enter the house. Sticking to the shadows, he took a reconnaissance walk around the house's perimeter. He was nothing short of thorough. He had made sure to pick the lock on the gun case, remove all the ammo, and relock it while in the house earlier as a safety measure. In addition, he searched all the common spots for a concealed gun, including the nightstand, under the bed, and the top of the closet. He was convinced that the man inside would not pose a threat and would die tonight without ever waking up.

Time dragged as one hour stretched into two. It was cold outside among the trees, and the hitman shivered and pulled his collar further up. As he stretched, he caught wind of a sound from a distance. He was sure it was a motorcycle engine. As he listened closely, he came to the realization that it was not just one chopper he heard, but possibly two or three. He was surprised when the noise stopped. Instead of fading into the distance as they moved farther away, the sound was suddenly gone. The motorcycles had come to a stop. The hitman stood and was immediately on high alert, with the hair on his arms standing up. They were three miles away from the nearest house, in the middle of nowhere, in the middle of the night. There was no reason for motorcycles to stop anywhere near his location. He sprang into action as soon as he sensed something was off. He grabbed his backpack, swung it onto his shoulder, and crept deeper into the woods. Crouching behind a large boulder, he waited. He suspected the gangbangers had arrived, and he planned to take them down individually before they ever got close to the house. The noise from their bikes told him they were inexperienced in surveillance and tracking and lacked discretion.

The assassin remained completely still as the first footsteps approached. He heard whispered voices coming from a short distance away and became increasingly angry. He had to silence them before the targets realized they were there. Just as the first man was closing in, he leaned out from behind the boulder and pulled the trigger. The gun's silencer produced nothing more than a quiet *swish* of air. The gangbanger went down quickly and stayed down as soon as the bullet hit his brain. He was dead before hitting the ground. The second man arrived moments later and upon seeing his cohort on the ground with a bullet hole in his head, he yelled out for the third man. The hitman appeared from around the boulder and seized the gangbanger from behind where he brought him down with a choke hold. The executioner's jaw muscles twitched as he strangled the man. Unsure if he had silenced him fast enough to go unnoticed by the targets, he now knew there were at least three of them.

He dropped the limp body onto the forest floor next to the man he had shot moments earlier. He turned the strangled gangbanger over and fired a round into his head to make sure he was dead, then grabbed his bag before advancing toward the house. He stood at the edge of the clearing and waited for his eyes to adapt. Though no lights were on in the house, he couldn't be sure they were still asleep. Scanning the area around the house, he wasted no time in locating the third man. His white t-shirt was like a homing beacon. The hitman raised his arm and took aim, but the man retreated deeper into the forest as he fired, causing the bullet to hit a tree instead of its intended target. The gang member returned fired multiple times, the sound cutting through the stillness of the night. The noise resembled light machine gun fire, suggesting that he was carrying an assault rifle. He would have woken the entire neighborhood had there been any houses nearby.

The hitman cursed under his breath. It was impossible that the occupants of the house slept through that. He moved silently through the woods, following the other man. He had to neutralize him fast and enter the house before the targets had a chance to escape.

When he reached the other side of the clearing, he saw the gangbanger hiding behind a large bush, his assault rifle aimed in the opposite direction. Without making a sound, the hitman approached him, having spent years perfecting his technique. With one shot to the back of his head, the gangbanger fell over without a sound.

The executioner made his way to the house, which remained still and lifeless.

TWENTY-THREE

Sam woke up immediately at the sound of rapid gunfire and realized that his house guests had been found. He reached behind the headboard and snatched his SIG Sauer from the holster secured there and racked the slide. As he inched toward the closet, his years of training took over. He hurriedly pulled on jeans and slipped into black sneakers to match his black t-shirt before heading into the hall. Opening the guest bedroom door, he expected to see Kendra on the bed, only to find she wasn't there.

"Kendra?" he whisper-shouted.

The closet door opened a crack and Kendra peeked out, with Kyle looking over her shoulder.

"Where is Kyle's phone?"

"I hid it in the pocket of a pair of jeans. What's happening, Sam? Did they find us?"

"Yes. Get your purse and the phone and let's get you both to the panic room. There are three go bags there. Take all three of them and get to the truck. Now!"

Kendra scrambled out of the closet with Kyle right behind her and rummaged through the dresser for her jeans with the cell phone tucked into the front pocket. She grabbed the phone and tossed it into her purse. Clutching her bag tightly, she followed closely behind Sam as they made their way to the pantry door.

"Barricade the doors behind you and get out of here," said Sam, keeping his back to them and covering the back door with his gun.

"How are you going to get in if I do that?" asked Kendra nervously.

"I'm not. I'll hold them off here as long as possible. If I don't get all of them, they'll eventually figure out you've gone through the basement. Then I'm fucked, anyway, because I'm no longer useful to them. Just go, Kendra. You're wasting time!"

"I'm not leaving you here alone! I can shoot. I can help and Kyle can hide in the tunnel," she said, desperately.

"Kyle, get your mother in that goddamn panic room before I have to pick her up and put her there myself," said Sam, a hard edge to his voice that Kendra had not heard from him before.

Kyle pulled the door open and pushed Kendra through before she could protest. He slammed the door shut behind them and turned the lock.

"Mom, help me get this barricade in place."

Kendra remained motionless, staring at the door. "Mom! Come on! Snap out of it!"

Kyle's voice pulled her back to the present. Her son needed her, and she had to do everything in her power to protect him and keep him safe. Sam's training as a federal agent meant that she had to have faith in his abilities. She had to focus and not let her concern for Sam get in the way of doing what needed to be done.

With their combined effort, she and Kyle pushed the heavy bar into place and did the same after entering the basement door, where they descended the stairs. Pushing the stack of boxes aside, Kyle opened the tunnel door. He picked up the three duffel bags, slinging one over each shoulder and grasping the third in his hand, as Kendra grabbed the gun and Maglite from the back of the door. Kendra was about to close the door when the sound of close-range rapid gunfire made her freeze. As Kyle slammed the heavy door, she glanced nervously at him. She hit the power button for the flashlight, and they pulled the bar down over the last door between them and the gunfire. They jogged the entire way through the tunnel and reached the exit within minutes. They paused to catch their breath before Kendra continued up the ladder. Leaves and twigs fell into the tunnel as she pushed the heavy metal lid aside. She shook the leaves from her hair and peered out of the opening into the dark forest. With nothing but trees in sight, she climbed out of the tunnel and had Kyle hand her the duffle bags. She grabbed the bags with shaking hands as Kyle emerged from the tunnel and replaced the lid, concealing it with leaves and moss. Kendra shone the flashlight on the trees in search of the trunk with the green paint markings. Being there at night was disorienting. The view appeared vastly different in the daylight. It took her several seconds, but she eventually found the tree.

"There!" she said, shining the light on the trunk.

Kyle grabbed the duffel bags, and they started on the path to the truck. Kendra felt an almost physical need to run, the adrenaline rushing through her veins. But confirming the correct path meant she needed to look for tree trunks with the distinctive green paint mark. Twice they got lost and had to retrace their steps, so that when they finally got to the truck, it had taken them nearly fifteen minutes. Kendra dropped the keys while attempting to retrieve them from the top of the front tire due to her trembling hands. With the flashlight in hand, Kyle crawled under the truck to find them, then opened the truck door. He lifted the seat bench and tossed the bags inside. Kendra flipped off the flashlight and threw it on top of the bags. Examining the gun in her hand, she decided it would be best to keep it within her reach inside the truck.

"Put this in the glove box, behind whatever else is in there," she said. "And grab that map. It's dark and I don't know where I'm going."

Kyle reached into the hidden seat compartment and removed the flashlight. "I don't think we should turn on the interior light."

"Right. Put that baseball cap on," she said, pointing to a hat Sam had hung from the rear-view mirror.

Kendra grabbed a hair tie from her back pocket and twisted her hair into a bun. They got into the truck, and she turned the key in the ignition. The quiet was shattered by the sound of the engine, worrying her that it would give away their position and they would be discovered. After switching on the headlights, she turned onto the path that led to the highway. Kendra drove the truck through the narrow lane, half expecting for someone to jump out of the woods and block their path. A little less than thirty minutes after entering the basement, Kendra and Kyle reached the deserted highway. The darkness was complete, and the silence was unsettling.

Kendra didn't feel good leaving Sam behind, especially after hearing so much gunfire. She was terrified now that she and Kyle were left truly on their own after so many days spent with Lou and Sam. Without any help, they had to begin again with brand-new lives and identities.

TWENTY-FOUR

The hitman turned his gaze to the injured man on the kitchen floor and knew he had to get information from him quickly, as he was bleeding out. But the man's dog was distracting him. It was snarling and throwing itself at the back door, making it impossible for him to hear his own thoughts. The dog's loyalty was evident when he showed no interest in the treat that was laced with narcotics. The hitman found that loyalty an admirable trait. It was a pity that he was going to have to shoot such a beautiful creature to shut it up. As he headed toward the back door, the man on the floor warned the dog to run, suggesting he knew what was coming. The dog ran off like a bat out of hell.

Walking back to the man on the floor, the hitman smiled down at him. "We both know you'll be dead in ten minutes, tops. Where are they? All you have to do is tell me and I'll shoot you now and save you the agony of a slow, painful death."

"Why don't you go fuck yourself instead?" replied Sam, his voice raspy as he fought through the pain.

The hitman sighed and shook his head. "That's a no, then? Not a very fast learner, are you?"

Sam winced in pain as a second bullet tore through his knee. The man crouched down and spoke softly to Sam. "I can go on like this until the end. There are many parts of the body I can shoot to ensure you bleed out slowly."

Sam didn't reply, firm in his belief that the man wouldn't be able to extract information from him. Whoever this was, he obviously wasn't a gangbanger. His behavior resembled that of a professional assassin. So who hired him? The gang officer? The gangbangers? Neither made any sense. Before Sam could complete the thought, the man stood and walked to the pantry door. Turning the knob, he pushed on the door. When it didn't move, he attempted again, applying more pressure.

"Well, well. Isn't that interesting? A pantry door that locks from the inside. Now why do you suppose you'd need that? Unless that's where our mutual friends are hiding away?"

He stepped back and kicked the door. It didn't budge at all. The man moved closer to the door.

"Kendra, come on out or I will be forced to finish off your friend here."

There was no response from the other side of the door, and his frustration grew as he banged and yelled louder. "You have five seconds to get out here with the kid, or your friend is dead!"

When he still got no response, he started counting. "Five, four, three, two, one. Times up, Kendra. Say goodbye."

The man turned to Sam, and without hesitation, he fired a single bullet into his forehead. He wasn't one to issue idle threats. Say what you mean and mean what you say. Words to live by, in his opinion.

Sam had already resigned himself to dying, and his eyes were closed in anticipation. He was aware that he was bleeding out, and without proper medical attention, his life would end in a matter of minutes. The first bullet had hit Sam's femoral artery, and he realized he had roughly five minutes to live, three of which had already passed.

Convinced that Kendra and her son were hiding in the basement, the man set to work getting the door open. Ten minutes into it, he came to the realization that the door was barricaded from inside and wouldn't swing inward. He grabbed an axe from beside the woodpile outside and started chipping away at the sides of the door. Due to the reinforced steel, there was only six inches of unsupported space on each side, requiring thirty minutes of hard physical labor to remove enough wood to bring the door down in one piece. Entering the pantry, he tried the basement door and found the same level of resistance as the pantry door. He began work on taking down the basement door, his anger increasing with every swing of the axe. By the time he entered the basement, he was consumed with fury. He descended the stairs and quickly searched the room. The tunnel door was still partially hidden behind the stack of boxes, but he spotted it. Battering the boxes aside, he tried to push the door open, but it was as solid as the upstairs doors.

"Fuck! Un-fucking-believable!" he shouted, kicking the door. "Okay, okay," he whispered to himself, while taking deep breaths.

He took the stairs up two at a time and grabbed the ax. He hurried back to the panic room door and began hacking at it, just as he had with the pantry and basement doors. He stepped into the tunnel after removing the door and turned on his cell flashlight. Upon realizing it was an escape tunnel, he let out a loud curse.

"Son of a bitch!"

He ran through the tunnel, reaching the ladder and climbing up quickly. Emerging from the tunnel, he found himself in complete darkness. He was unsure of his location relative to the house, but had a general sense of the direction he had come from. Retracing the tunnel path as best he could, he walked through the woods. Before long, he saw light coming from the house. He entered through the back door, stepped over the lifeless body on the kitchen floor, and collected his things. He took the man's wallet and cell phone after emptying his pockets. The federal badge inside caught him off guard when he opened the wallet, but recognizing it might come in handy someday, he kept it. In hindsight, it made sense the man would have an escape room and an abundance of guns in the house. He had no doubts that McLeod would have revealed the man's DEA affiliation if he had known. The senator would regret that indiscretion if he had known and kept it a secret.

He sat on the couch and pulled up a familiar tracking app on his iPhone. Tapping in his password, he waited for the dot to appear that would reveal where Kendra and her son were. He placed the tracker in Kendra's purse during his house recon, but hadn't bothered to check it since he thought they were hiding in the basement. Just south of Santa Rosa, the blinking dot on the screen moved steadily along the 101 Freeway.

On impulse, he grabbed the dog's leash from the hook next to the back door and went to the doghouse. Knowing the dog would be hungry and scared by now, he threw the spiked meat inside. He watched as the animal inched forward, whimpering with excitement at the treat. The dog was fast asleep within five minutes. He scooped up the animal and brought him to his van. After placing the harness over him, he grabbed a muzzle from the center console. He learned firsthand years ago that animals can be unpredictable, so he made sure to have sedatives, muzzles, and leashes with him at all times. But he had a liking for this dog. While traveling, he would have a well-trained companion to keep him company. He could always get rid of him if he became too troublesome.

Satisfied he would soon have Kendra and her son in his sights, he entered Santa Rosa on his GPS, turned the van around, and set off after his targets.

TWENTY-FIVE

Kendra kept the truck at a steady sixty-five miles per hour on the freeway. She planned to rest somewhere soon before heading to San Francisco, where they would decide on a more concrete plan. Sam's words repeated over and over in her head, telling her to get to the panic room and get away.

She shot a quick glance in Kyle's direction. His head rested on the window, the baseball cap pulled down over his eyes. She turned back to the dashboard where the fuel gauge caught her attention. They needed gas. She couldn't decide if it was best to stop at a large, busy station where people would be less likely to remember them, or a smaller mom and pop place where there would be less foot traffic. Either way felt unsafe. A large chain would probably have security cameras, but the clerk at a smaller station would be more likely to remember them if questioned by someone later.

The truck decided for Kendra when the fuel light begin to flash. She refueled at a small Rotten Robbie's station in Novato as the sun rose. After filling the tank, she woke Kyle up so they could go inside together and get coffee and pastries.

Back in the truck, they ate their snack before hitting the road again.

"We should stop and get some rest, then we'll go into the city and figure out what we want to do from there," said Kendra.

"Okay," said Kyle, yawning. He pulled his cap down and slumped further into the seat.

Kendra left the 101 Freeway to take Highway 37 east, as it was a seemingly random route that someone following her might not predict they'd take. Her thoughts kept wandering back to Sam. If he had not outgunned the intruders, she had no doubt that by now their pursuers had uncovered the basement and the escape tunnel. She had no way of knowing if Sam had defeated the gangbangers, and the alternative was not something she wanted to consider. She shouldn't have been surprised the gang had found them, yet she still was. It was beyond her how she thought she could outrun a group of gangbangers who had set their sights on killing them. Yet somehow, she had deluded herself into thinking they had a shot at it. She had been so naïve. Before Kyle witnessed the Sinners murder Devon McLeod in cold blood, she thought nothing evil could ever touch their lives. If only he hadn't cut through the abandoned warehouses that night. Maybe their lives would have continued on as they always had. But that wasn't how things had worked out, and now she had to deal with it.

Their new identities were the only advantage she had left. It would be challenging, if not impossible, for someone to track her and Kyle with their new names. That knowledge gave her a slight sense of safety, and she allowed herself a tentative moment of relief.

Kendra spotted a motel after driving for a while, right before the connection to Highway 29 north that led back to Lake County. She wanted to follow that route right back to Lake County and Sam's house to make sure he was all right. But she knew that was impossible. It wouldn't be safe, and Kyle remained her priority.

She circled the area surrounding the motel in search of a parking spot. Not willing to take any risks, she had to assume her hunters had seen the truck in the woods. When she spotted a diner that was adjacent to a small patch of forest behind the motel, she pulled in and parked. She let Kyle grab the duffle bags from under the seat, but decided to leave the gun hidden in the truck, thinking it was unnecessary. She was just checking into the motel, and despite her training with Sam she still wasn't comfortable with firearms.

She looked around to see a small lake situated on the other side of the diner. The water was peaceful and calm under the shimmering morning sunlight. It was a stark contrast to her thoughts. Kendra began walking toward the motel and stumbled over a small rock, only saving herself from falling by grabbing onto the truck hood. Kyle's snicker made her erupt into giggles with him. It felt good to laugh again. Although it wasn't a conversation, it was a nice, stress-free moment with her son. Those had been few and far between lately.

She checked them into the motel using her new name, stored their bags in the room, and then returned to the diner for a proper meal. It was early afternoon by that time, and they were both exhausted from being awakened in the middle of the night and under such stressful circumstances. Following a quick lunch, they walked to a nearby convenience store to purchase toiletries. The only items Kendra gave Sam for their go bags were clothes and shoes, and she wasn't sure if he had added anything else. After returning to the motel, they spent the remainder of the day watching TV and napping.

Before taking a shower that evening, Kyle picked up one of the duffel bags to search for a t-shirt to wear. Unzipping the bag, he stepped back in shock, mouth wide open.

"Uh, Mom? You need to come and see this."

"What is it?" asked Kendra, walking out of the bathroom.

Kyle's eyes widened as he pointed at the bag on the bed. Kendra took a step forward and gasped. The bag was full of cash. Hundred-dollar bills wrapped in bundles of one thousand dollars stared back at her. She lifted a few rows to find neatly bundled packages of twenty, ten, and five-dollar bills. On top was a handwritten note. Kendra took the note and sat down on the bed, Kyle taking a seat next to her.

Kendra,

If you have my go bag, it's because I told you to take Kyle and run. I've been stashing this money away for a long time with the idea I might need a fast exit one day. But you're going to need this more than me when you and Kyle start over. I know what you're thinking. But I want you to have it. I have no one to leave it to. I never had children, and I certainly don't want my ex-wife to get her greedy hands on it. My retirement money is more than enough for me to live on, and don't worry about Lou. She will be well taken care of financially if anything ever happens to me.

Do not think that because you've made it this far, they won't keep looking for you. They will. There's too much at stake for Senator McLeod if he's involved. And I'm certain that he is. So don't let your guard down. Stay vigilant and be safe. Kyle is a good kid. I know how fond you are of my favorite saying, so I'll just say it. You're knee-deep in a pile of chicken shit, Kendra. Use this money to make chicken salad out of it.

I am not a man who is great at goodbyes, so I will just say that it was a privilege to protect you both, and hopefully teach you a few things about protecting yourselves along the way.

Please do not attempt to contact me or Lou again. That could endanger not only you, but Lou as well.

All my best,

Sam

Kendra's tears spilled onto the paper, blurring the ink.

"Sam gave us all this money? But why?" whispered Kyle.

"Because he's a good man, Kyle. He wants us to be safe, and he knew I'd never accept it if he told me about it first."

"Wow. He really is a good guy. I'm gonna miss him."

Kendra reached over and hugged Kyle tightly. "Me too. Sam and Lou are phenomenal people."

Kendra wiped her eyes and zipped the bag up. Never before had she seen such a large amount of money. Although she didn't know the precise amount, she was aware it was substantial. And she was grateful for it. They sat there for several moments, both lost in their own thoughts, before a motorcycle pulled up outside, causing Kyle to stiffen. Kendra rushed to the window and peered out. A young man parked his bike, clutching a fast-food bag. Relief washed over her as she realized it wasn't a member of the Satans 13 gang.

"It was just a guy getting some food," she said, looking back at Kyle. "We're safe here," she promised, sounding far more confident than she felt.

Was it true, Kendra wondered? Were they safe anywhere? Only time would tell. But it was what Kyle needed to hear. And she desperately wanted to believe it.

Kendra's nerves were rattled after that, so while Kyle showered she busied herself by emptying her purse and consolidating what she wanted to keep in the duffel bag with her clothes. She hid their cell phones on the bottom of her bag and tucked their sim cards into her make-up bag. Kyle's sim card was the key to everything. Their only leverage was the video of the Sinners hit, and she was acutely aware of that. She got rid of the things she wanted to toss in the wastebasket next to the bed, and then stumbled upon something she didn't recognize among the miscellaneous items in her purse. The object was a small, silver disc that looked like a button cell battery. She examined it in her hand, but there were none of the usual battery markings. She hadn't bought a burner cell yet, so googling it wasn't an option. She made a mental note to buy a phone first thing the next day, then after examining the disc again, shrugged and threw it away without a second thought.

They walked back to the diner for dinner to go, then settled in for the night back at the motel. Sleep did not come easy for Kendra. She tossed and turned for an hour, thinking about Sam. Sam's safety and the cash in the duffel bag were all she could think about, her thoughts stuck in a constant loop of fear and worry. The money would be a game-changer for her and Kyle. She glanced over at her son nestled under a mound of blankets in the bed next to hers. If they were at home and not in some anonymous, crappy motel, it could be any other night.

Except it wasn't.

It was tonight.

And they were on the run.

Despite the gift of money from Sam, Kendra could almost picture their lives crumbling right in front of her very eyes as she drifted off to sleep.

TWENTY-SIX

Kendra was jolted awake by a sudden sound. She couldn't determine if the sound was real or something from her dreams. She remained still, listening for anything unusual. The only sound she could hear was the distant rumble of a car, while Kyle snored softly in the bed next to hers.

She closed her eyes and let her head fall back against the headboard. Her anxiety was getting the best of her.

That's when she heard it again. The doorknob shook as the chair wedged beneath it wiggled. It was the confirmation she needed to know she hadn't imagined it. Someone was outside their room, attempting to break in. She dropped to the floor and grabbed the duffel bag of cash beside her bed. Kyle stirred, and she quickly crawled to his bedside, where she shook him awake and covered his mouth with her hand. He struggled against her, but she pinned him down to avoid alerting anyone outside.

"It's me, Kyle! We need to leave. Grab the bags. Now!" she whispered.

In an instant, Kyle was wide awake and on the floor, grabbing their other two bags. She motioned for him to follow her to the bathroom. His brow furrowed as he slung one of the bags over his shoulder. His fearful expression made Kendra's stomach lurch. She too, was frightened, but she remained composed as they crawled to the small motel bathroom. Kyle needed her to be strong and guide them to safety.

"It's all right, we'll be fine. Let's just go as fast as we can," she whispered, trying to project some confidence.

They reached the bathroom in seconds and Kendra locked the door, jamming a rubber doorstop beneath it.

Moonlight streaming through the tiny window allowed them just enough light to maneuver their way through the small opening. Kendra pushed the screen out of its track and tossed the bags out. Kyle crawled through first and she followed, landing hard on the dirt underneath. She swiveled her head from side to side, searching for anyone coming after them. They were alone on the pathway behind the motel, so they wasted no time running for the cover of the trees across the dirt divide.

Kendra led them through the forested area toward the parking lot of the diner where their truck was parked. The silence was shattered by a loud *CRACK*, and she knew their pursuers had breached their motel room. It was just a matter of time before the gangbangers caught up to them.

Kendra picked up speed and glanced over her shoulder to make sure Kyle was keeping pace with her. She pushed past a low-hanging branch that scraped across her face as they raced to the parking lot. After a couple of minutes, she saw light from the diner's neon sign, and hope bloomed in her chest.

Her hand reached out to stop Kyle as she scanned the parking lot. When she saw no one nearby, she gestured for him to follow her. They sprinted across the lot to their truck. Unlocking the door with trembling hands, she threw the bags inside and turned the key in the ignition.

Kyle clamored into the truck and reached for the baseball cap and the gun in the glove box, while Kendra adjusted the rearview mirror and drove out of the parking lot.

"They're going to be looking for two people, so you need to get down, out of sight," she said.

Kyle crouched down into the footwell of the passenger side as Kendra pulled onto the highway headed west. She used all her self-control not to push the accelerator to the floor, despite her every instinct screaming at her to get away as quickly as possible.

After a few miles, Kendra glanced over at Kyle. "You can sit up now," she said, breaking the silence.

Kyle climbed back into his seat without saying anything. She was disappointed, but not surprised. He was coping with the aftermath of a traumatic week in his own way, and although Kendra wanted nothing more than to ease his burden, she was clueless about how to do it.

"Do you want to pick something to listen to? You can have complete control of the radio, and I promise I won't complain," she asked, hoping to lighten the tension.

Kyle continued to stare out the window without answering her, and she didn't force the issue. He had more than enough on his plate without her lecturing him.

The miles rushed by as they drove in silence, Kyle staring out the window at nothing but the dark landscape, and Kendra questioning her every decision over the last week.

Would they be better off going back to the FBI office instead of running on their own? Could she trust them to protect her and Kyle? Was taking that chance even an option for her?

She didn't have the answers. It was impossible for her to speak to Sam, even though she desperately wanted to. His instructions were clear; she was not to contact him or Lou. The last thing she wanted to do was to risk their safety. Like it or not, she and Kyle were on their own. As frightening as that was.

Kendra's mind raced with questions about how they had been found. Even if their pursuers had seen the brown truck in the woods and connected it to Sam, she had driven off the main highway and down a lesser traveled road, making it more challenging for someone to find them. How did the gang manage to locate their motel and the exact room they were in? She had taken every precaution by parking the truck at the diner and registering at the motel under her new name.

They should have been safe. She ran through the possibilities over and over, but kept coming up empty. She thought about everything they did that evening right up until they went to bed, when she had a sudden memory of the small silver disc she found in her purse. She was puzzled by the strange-looking device, wondering how it got into her bag. Was it possible it was a bug or some sort of tracking device? The more she thought about it, the more it began to make sense. And the thought terrified her. Either someone had slipped it into her purse without her knowledge, or it was placed there during the only time she didn't have her purse with her—which was when she grabbed her wallet from Sam's house to go to her hair appointment. That same evening, their pursuers found them. That couldn't be a coincidence.

Considering this new information, Kendra was torn between seeking help from law enforcement or following her gut instinct to keep running. Her ultimate goal was to protect her son at all costs, and she was willing to do whatever was necessary to make sure that happened. But she also felt as if she was being driven to unimaginable heights by her desperation. With so many uncertainties, she let her intuition guide her decision, and her gut won out.

She continued to drive aimlessly, putting more distance between them and the motel without a clear goal in mind. The feeling of being lost and alone completely consumed her. Their pursuers were coming after them, she knew, so they had to get out of sight before the gangbangers found them again. She continued driving, searching for a safe place to hide, even though a little voice in her head told her such a place didn't exist.

TWENTY-SEVEN

Across the street from the motel, the hitman sat, watching and waiting. He observed Kendra and her son enter the room with bags from the diner. After the room lights went out just after 11:00 p.m., he waited for two more hours before eventually giving the dog another sedative and getting out of his van. The small town was deserted, with no sign of life, cars, or people.

Walking across the street, he kept close to the shadows. His target's room was situated at the end of a row of standard rooms. There was only one other means of exit, a window to the right of the entry door. While driving around the back of the place earlier, he noticed that the rooms had small bathroom windows set up high, but it seemed unlikely that Kendra would escape that way. He had to hope that wasn't the case, because he couldn't be in two places at the same time.

Out of sight from the street, he stood at the edge of the building and listened. Kendra's room was completely quiet. Silently, he made his way around the corner and tested the motel door. It was locked, but he had expected it to be. He took out his lock pick and inserted it into the keyhole. The door refused to move, despite the knob turning easily. He realized then that Kendra had something jammed beneath the door handle. That was a minor setback. It meant he had to create more noise than he wanted to, but by the time the police were called by another guest, Kendra and Kyle would be dead and he would be gone.

After a couple of shoulder rams, the door came off its hinges. As the quiet night was interrupted by the sound, he quickly made his way inside. The room was empty, and the unmade beds were still warm. He turned his focus to the closed bathroom door. Time had ultimately run out for Kendra and her son, he thought to himself. He grabbed the doorknob and pushed, but it would only open a crack. He pushed harder and then looked down to see a rubber doorstop stuck under the door. She was really going to make him work for this. Doing a job usually didn't stir any emotion within him. But this time, he felt a surge of anger. He wanted this woman and her kid dead after all the trouble they had caused him. He stepped back and swung his foot at the door. It snapped off the hinges after two vicious kicks. He stormed into the small bathroom, expecting to see Kendra and her son cowering in the bathtub, tears streaming down their faces as they begged for mercy. Instead, the window was open, and the screen was missing. The bathroom filled with cool air as a gentle breeze blew in. Anger churned inside of him as he realized they had escaped again. He jogged across the street to his van, made a U-turn and parked in the diner parking lot just in time to see a police car pass with lights flashing and sirens blaring.

"God damnit!" he shouted, punching the dashboard. The sleeping dog whimpered in response.

He impatiently tapped the tracker app on his iPhone, willing it to load faster. The dot finally appeared, but it remained stationary, its location no more than a few hundred feet away. He couldn't believe it. The tracker was in the motel room. Kendra had obviously found it and left it there. But why wouldn't she destroy it? Leaving it active made no sense, yet she did. Unless she didn't recognize what it was. There was no other explanation. That had to be it. He pulled out and raced toward the highway. They had to be close by. Kendra hadn't had enough time to get very far. He would need to inspect every car, but at this time of night, traffic was minimal. It was manageable. He headed west toward the 101 Freeway, which seemed the most logical route for Kendra to take.

His fingers flexed with anxiety on the steering wheel when he spotted red taillights up ahead. This bitch was going to pay. He had reached his breaking point with her. Underestimating her was not a mistake he would make again. Not now that it had become personal.

TWENTY-EIGHT

Kendra drove with trembling hands as she scoured the area for a place to hide. Spotting rows of apple trees ahead, she knew that there had to be a road that led further into the orchard. To gather apples during picking season, trucks needed to drive between the rows of trees. She remembered that from when Kyle was young. She and Trent took him to Julian, where apple-picking was a well-known attraction in the area. The event stood out to her as it was one of the few times they did something together as a family, despite Trent's constant complaints about the tour cost. Weaving through the apple trees, they collected the fruit Kyle had picked in a bucket. She recalled that the tour guide told them that apple orchards usually consist of numerous acres and require several days to fill the truck beds during the picking season.

As Kendra drove into the dirt lane beside the orchard, she switched off the headlights. With the moon as her guide, she drove for about a mile, then switched the lights back on and strayed from the path, driving between the rows of trees. She continued deeper into the orchard, wondering if she could find her way out again. She parked the truck under a large tree after she was satisfied with their hiding spot.

"We're going to have to stay here for the night and let them get ahead of us," said Kendra.

"We need to get out of California, Mom."

"I know. I was thinking somewhere in the Midwest would be good. We could stretch the money for a long time there, because it's so much less expensive than California."

"Seriously? I was thinking of New York City or something like that."

"Oh no. That's even more expensive than here."

"Well, Sam left us all that money. It's not like we can't afford it," said Kyle.

"That money has to last us. I can't get a job as a nurse without a license under my new name. Working at a grocery store or as a home health aide isn't going to get us any kind of decent salary. We have to be smart about the money."

"We won't be on the run forever, Mom. I mean, how long do you think it'll be before it's safe for us to go back home?"

Kendra couldn't bring herself to look Kyle in the eye. Now she understood why he was taking this so well. He thought of them on the run as a temporary situation. Kendra knew better, but she didn't have the heart to have that talk with Kyle just then. She would leave that for another time. Although she couldn't shake the feeling that it would be sooner than she hoped.

"I don't know, Kyle. We are just going to have to deal with things as they come and figure it out as we go."

She was thankful that he seemed satisfied with her generic answer.

"Okay, so define Midwest," he said, using air quotes on the last word.

"I don't know. Oklahoma, Kansas, Missouri?"

Kyle couldn't hide his revulsion. His face screwed into a half grimace, half scowl.

"Please tell me you're joking, Mom. Things aren't bad enough? Now you want to move us to Kansas?"

"No, I'm not joking. I'll get a cell in the morning, and we can do some research. You can pick where we go, as long as it's several states from here and somewhere cheap," she said, stifling a yawn. "Let's get some rest for now."

Kyle slipped further down into the seat and took a comfortable position. Kendra was certain he was sulking, but she had more pressing things to figure out. Once Kyle was asleep, she searched their duffle bags to be sure there were no more silver discs hidden anywhere. Satisfied that there weren't, she settled back in her seat and began to formulate a plan in her head.

Kendra was greeted the next morning by sunlight magnified through the front windshield when she woke up. She winced when a sharp pain traveled through her neck as she sat up. There was movement next to her as Kyle stirred. Her thoughts last night were focused on what their next move would be. An idea had occurred to her, but it required Kyle's expertise.

"Good morning. I guess it would be pointless to ask how you slept?" Kendra asked.

Kyle responded with a grunt.

"So I have a question. If I want to send an email but I want it to deliver hours later or even the following day, is that possible?"

Frowning, he turned to face her. "Yeah, of course. You just schedule it for whenever."

"And you know how to do that, right?"

"Duh, Mom. Of course, I do. Because I live in this century."

"No need to get snippy with me. Do you wanna pick an apple and go water a tree before we take off?" Kendra asked.

"Water a tree? Seriously, don't ever say that out loud again, please."

Laughing, Kendra opened her door. "Whatever. Pick us a couple of apples for the road and let's get going."

"Um, okay. Where are we going?"

"We're still going to San Francisco to get a burner phone, find an internet café, buy a safe deposit box, get a map of the US, and get a decent breakfast. Not necessarily in that order. Get moving. We have a lot to do today."

Kyle groaned and flung open the passenger door to search for a suitable tree.

Ten minutes later, they were driving through the apple orchard, the truck kicking up a dust trail behind them as they made their way to the highway. A surge of power coursed through Kendra. She drove away from the orchard with a sense of purpose, as if she knew exactly where she was headed and what she intended to do once she arrived. She finally felt in control of their lives with a semi-solid plan after days of uncertainty. Not like a puppet, with someone else pulling the strings.

Traffic slowed to a crawl as they reached the 101 Freeway. Kendra tried to remember what day it was. It had to be a weekday, judging from the traffic, with commuters making their way into the city. Then she remembered it was Saturday. The traffic made her already heightened nerves worse. She switched on the radio and landed on a rock station that both she and Kyle could agree on, and she hummed along to a Journey song. Seeing the Golden Gate Bridge, Kyle straightened up in his seat. The sight of it was truly spectacular. The bridge rose into the sky like a majestic, mythical creature as the sun reflected off the ocean surrounding it. As they crossed the bridge, Kyle opened his window and let the smell of sea air fill the truck. Although the morning was cool, with patches of fog still visible, the view was unlike anything she had ever seen. The city of San Francisco stretched out before them, its skyline a stunning sight across the bay. Despite being unsure of where to begin, Kendra knew that a city that size would have everything they needed.

When they reached the end of the bridge, Kendra kept her head down as she inserted money into the toll booth receptacle. She stayed on the freeway and merged back into traffic before taking the first exit into the city. Turning left on Lombard brought them to a bustling street lined with bars, restaurants, motels, and shops. She pulled into a fast-food restaurant and parked behind the building. Due to the large glass windows, Kendra felt too exposed to eat inside, so they took their breakfast sandwiches back to the truck. Following their meal, she pulled across the street to a gas station and topped off the gas tank while Kyle went inside to get maps of the United States and San Francisco.

They continued down Lombard, traveling west. As they approached Van Ness, Kendra recalled that it was a major street leading to the heart of the city, even though it had been many years since she had been to San Francisco. She took a right turn and followed it for a couple of blocks before she saw what she was looking for. On one corner was a T-Mobile store, and across the street was a Bank of America. When she turned onto Jackson Street, she miraculously found an open parking spot. She grabbed the duffel bag full of cash and her own emergency bag. She fished through her bag for their phones and her make-up bag that held the SIM cards and tucked it all into the cash bag. Then they walked to the wireless store, where she acquired a cell phone and service with her credit card, using her new name.

"What about me?" Kyle asked.

"What about you? Who are you going to call?"

He shot her a look of disapproval before quickly turning away. Kendra felt a pang of guilt. She realized his former life was gone and reminding him of that probably made her the worst mother on earth. Her fears were confirmed when he shook her hand off his shoulder.

Crossing the street to the bank, she leased a safe deposit box. She opened the duffel once they were alone in the room with the box. She inserted Kyle's SIM card into his phone. Using her new charger, she plugged it in.

"What are you doing, Mom? I thought you said no cells, or they could track us!"

"I did. But I need the video. This won't take long."

Kendra opened her new cell and went to Google, where she set up a new email address. She turned the screen to Kyle. "Email it to this address."

Kyle tapped open his email icon and created a draft addressed to Kendra's new email. He tapped the body of the email and inserted the video, then hit send.

"Perfect," said Kendra.

Carefully, she removed the SIM card from his phone and placed their old cells and the cards inside the safe deposit box, locking it in place.

"This is what keeps us safe." She said to Kyle.

Kyle looked doubtful, but Kendra refused to accept that there could be any other outcome. They had made it this far and survived, and she believed they were on the verge of reaching safety.

"Mom, what about all our stuff? Like at home, I mean. Our clothes, my PlayStation, photo albums. Stuff like that. And what about my dad?"

Kendra leaned against the table. "I guess we leave everything. I don't see where we have a choice. Sam said we had to just disappear. It's only stuff. We can get you a new PlayStation. I have your baby pictures on a disc that I brought with us. We'll work out what to do about your dad."

"You took our pictures?"

"Yep. I guess when I threw my stuff into my bag, I was subconsciously packing like I was evacuating for a fire or something. I grabbed our passports and the picture discs. I was in a slight state of panic."

"So we just move somewhere new and make new friends and start over? What are we going to tell people?"

"We can figure that out. If we stick to some version of the truth about our pasts, it will be easier to remember. Remember what Sam told us? We reinvent our former lives, but don't stray too far from the truth. Let's go find a motel and look at the maps. We can shower and get some rest and figure out where we go next."

"I really wish I had my old life back," said Kyle.

Kendra watched Kyle walk to the door, thinking she had never felt worse in her life.

The best she could hope for them now was to be invisible.

TWENTY-NINE

Senator Steven McLeod was stunned as he watched the late-night news. It was hard for him to believe what he was hearing. The bodies of a former DEA agent and three known gang members were discovered on a property in Lake County in northern California. There was no way that was just a coincidence. He stood and reached for his cell phone on the end table.

"Where are you going, dear?" asked his wife, Marilyn.

"I'll be back soon. I have a couple of calls I just remembered I need to make. I'll just be in my study. Don't wait up for me if you're tired."

"Steven, it's eleven thirty, for heaven's sake."

He plastered a smile on his face before turning to face her. "I'm aware of that, honey. But you know how it goes. As a senator, I must make sacrifices from time to time."

Marilyn McLeod matched the senator's forced smile with one of her own.

"Of course, dear."

She muttered "Jackass" under her breath to her husband's retreating back.

Steven sat in his office chair and tapped the number for the hitman. "Yes?"

"Oh, for God's sake. When were you going to tell me about this fuck up? What the hell happened?" he shouted, then gained control and lowered his voice again. "What is the problem with getting this job handled, huh? Tell me that. Because I personally do not understand it!"

"I don't check in with a daily account of what I'm doing. You'll be notified when the job is done."

"You'll notify me when the job is done? Are you telling me that woman and her kid are still alive?"

"Ding, ding, ding. Give the man a prize."

"This is unbelievable. The bodies are piling up, but they aren't the two bodies I need to have eliminated. Never in my fifty-five years have I witnessed such incompetency!"

"Careful, Senator. I know about all your skeletons. Don't piss me off or maybe one night when you least expect it, I might let something slip in mixed company. Or perhaps I'll pay you a late-night visit. Capisce?"

"Save your threats for someone who gives a shit. This is one woman and a teenager, for fuck's sake."

"Calm down. I have the guy's phone. The phone from the DEA agent who was hiding them. Were you aware he was DEA? I'm pretty sure he got them new identities. It's just a matter of time before your cop runs down his contact, and then I can find out what name she is going under now. I'm going to text you the number. Get it to your contact at the PD."

"Of course I didn't know he was DEA. How would I know that? This had better be the last time I have to make a call like this to you." McLeod hung up without waiting for a response.

Hired killers appreciated a show of strength and leadership. Steven McLeod believed at least this much. The senator possessed those qualities abundantly. Leading and inspiring people was something he was used to, but this situation was spiraling out of control and becoming less manageable by the day. Gutierrez was the next person he called.

He sounded like he was asleep when he answered. "Gutierrez."

"Have you seen the news?"

"Do you know what time it is?"

"I don't give two shits what time it is. Have you seen the news tonight?"

"No. I pulled a double shift and was sleeping until now. No thanks to you."

"Well, we have a problem. There's a DEA agent and three gangbangers with bullets in them at a house in northern California."

Wide awake, Gutierrez sat up in bed. "What?"

"You heard me. Why didn't you tell me he was DEA?"

"Why would I? What have you done, McLeod?"

"I hired someone to take care of things, since you and your gangbangers can't seem to find your own faces in a mirror."

"What? Why the hell would you do that without telling me? You have no idea of the shitstorm you just stirred up, McLeod. And obviously, your guy did a shit job. Sounds like he left a trail of bodies everywhere." Gutierrez sighed heavily. "So, it's done then?"

"No! It's *not* done. And right now, you and I are the only two with our bare asses hanging out to dry. So we'd better come up with a plan to put out this fire before the entire thing comes crashing down on us. My guy has the dead DEA guy's cell. He thinks he had someone get them new identities, and we'll find evidence of who that was on his phone. I'm sending you the number now."

"Okay. I'll run that lead down. I'll try to get cell records for all his calls for the last two weeks, incoming and outgoing."

"Do more than try, Gutierrez. I don't give a flying fuck what you have to do to get the information. Once you have that, I'll give it to my guy and let him deal with it. There's no sense in getting our hands any dirtier."

"Fine. Send me the number. I'll be in touch," said Gutierrez.

"See that you do, officer. I don't think I need to remind you that we've got to get this reined in before someone makes a connection to us."

"I know that! I'll have something for you as soon as I can. I'll run down the activity on his cell. If his contact is on there, I'll find it. Tell your guy to hang tight until then."

"I'll wait to hear from you."

Giving up any further hope of sleep, Gutierrez swung his legs over the side of the bed. He scrolled through his phone to find the news about the deceased DEA agent. He then made a call to the sheriff's station in charge of the case, leaving a message for the detective. His plan was to ask for interdepartmental courtesy to acquire the dead agent's phone records. He was certain the detective working the case would have been issued a warrant for phone records on all the deceased. It would take Gutierrez too long to get a warrant, and he couldn't think of a judge who would grant him one based on no direct connection to the case. At least no evidence that he could tell anyone about. It was possible he could convince the other detective that the Sinners were involved with the bangers' deaths. That would be reason enough for the Sheriff's detective to share his evidence.

A bad feeling churned in his stomach. He feared the situation was about to blow up, and he would be the one to take the fall. He couldn't let that happen. This needed to end quickly.

He knew a call from Big Boy was imminent, and that was never a positive thing. Big Boy was a banger with anger issues, and that made him dangerous. With every minute that went by, his anxiety increased until he was nauseous. He couldn't turn evidence on the Sinners. Anyone who spoke out against them suffered the consequences. He couldn't go to prison, either. He knew what happened to cops in there. The fact that he was a gang intelligence officer would make it even worse for him. He had no other choice but to find the DEA agent's informant, get Kendra Thompson's new identity, and guarantee that she, her kid, and the video were never uncovered.

THIRTY

Kendra turned the truck around and drove back to Lombard Street to search for a motel she had seen earlier. She preferred an upper floor location for added security and wasn't interested in anything too extravagant. They settled on the Coventry Motor Inn as their choice. The hotel wasn't the most luxurious, but it was secure and clean and had covered parking away from the street. Which meant she could conceal the truck from anyone who might be searching for them.

Using her new driver's license and credit card, Kendra checked them in. As soon as they got to the room, she dropped onto the bed in exhaustion while Kyle showered. She was almost asleep when Kyle emerged from the bathroom, telling her it was all hers. She decided to shower while she still had the energy.

When Kendra came out of the bathroom twenty minutes later, Kyle was on his stomach on the bed with the map of the United States spread out in front of him.

"Find anything interesting?" she asked, while towel drying her hair.

"Kind of. How about Tennessee? Nashville has the whole music scene there, and it has a chill vibe. There are tons of smaller cities around Nashville too. Brendan went there last year with his parents and said it was pretty cool."

Kendra took a moment to consider before replying. "I don't see any reason why we can't go there. We've never been to Tennessee, we have no ties there, so it's not as if it would be an obvious place for anyone to search for us."

Kendra finished drying her hair with the wall-mounted blow dryer while Kyle remained focused on the map. The idea of Tennessee grew on her the more she thought about it. The beauty of the area was matched by the convenience of having a major city like Nashville nearby, making it easier to find work when needed.

She took a seat next to Kyle on the bed and studied the map. Moving from California to Tennessee would be a significant adjustment. But that was precisely the objective, right? To go somewhere no one would expect them to be. Plus, she was happy to let Kyle make the decision and have control over at least one thing in his life. Despite everything, she was surprised at how well he was coping with their situation, although she suspected his cooperation was driven by fear of retribution from the Sinners. Witnessing a murder was traumatizing enough, but being hunted by the killers took it to another level.

"So, I think we should leave tonight. Take a red-eye flight to Nashville and put some distance between us and California as soon as possible. How do you feel about that?" Kendra asked, glancing at Kyle.

"Tonight? Really?"

"Sure. Why wait?"

"I guess so. Yeah. Okay. What are we gonna do with Sam's truck? Just leave it here?"

"I have an idea about that. First, I need to find an internet café or somewhere we can use a computer to send an email."

"What email?"

"I want Gutierrez to know exactly what and who he's dealing with. He needs to know I'm not playing anymore."

Kendra checked her new phone for the closest public internet service and discovered a FedEx store close by on Van Ness. Following that, she went online and booked two tickets to Nashville using their new identities. They were set to depart from San Francisco International Airport just after 11:00 p.m. that evening.

Kendra replayed her plan in her mind during the drive to the FedEx store. She couldn't decide if it was a brilliant way to escape their predicament, or if her adrenaline rush prevented her from realizing just how terrible an idea it actually was.

They arrived at the copy store and paid cash for thirty minutes of computer time, but Kendra doubted she'd need that long. As she opened her new email, Kyle pulled up a chair beside her.

This was no time to be diplomatic. Kendra knew she had to play hardball. She narrowed her eyes, channeled the anger and terror of the past week, and started typing.

Officer Gutierrez,

I'm sure by now you realize my son and I are not only still alive and well, but have no intention of ever being captured by you or the Sinners. We are going into hiding and I have taken every precaution so you won't find us. While I think what the Sinners did is reprehensible, the most important thing to me is keeping my son safe. So if that's the trade-off, if I have to keep quiet to save him, then that's what I'll do. But know this—if anyone comes after us, if one hair on my son's head is harmed, the attached video goes to the district attorney and the Los Angeles Times. The original is under safekeeping somewhere you will never find it, with instructions that if I don't check in once every two weeks with the person holding it, the video goes out. No questions asked. There is also a letter detailing your involvement and Senator McLeod's participation. Let me be very clear. This ends now. We go our separate ways. Call off the Sinners and the video will never see the light of day. Continue to hunt us and take your chances with the DA and the public exposure. Make no mistake—I will not go down without a fight. It's your choice.

Kendra Thompson

Kendra attached the video to the email and turned to Kyle.

"I need you to schedule this so it delivers to him tomorrow at noon," said Kendra, handing Kyle the officer's business card.

"Okay, but we don't have anyone to check in with, like you said."

"Yeah, but he doesn't have to know that."

They switched chairs, and within minutes, Kyle had scheduled the email for the next day. He looked at Kendra for a final confirmation as the cursor hovered over the send icon. She had reached a crossroads. They had two options: go back home and take their chances with the FBI or go deeper on the run. She made her decision, nodding at Kyle and holding her breath as he sent the email into cyberspace. She said a silent prayer, hoping this strategy wouldn't backfire.

Kendra glanced at the clock and saw they had time for an early dinner on their way to their final errand before the airport. They chose a restaurant designed as a 1950s diner to grab some burgers, fries, and shakes. After dinner, they collected their meager belongings from the hotel room, then headed back down to the parking garage to the truck. Making sure they were alone, Kendra grabbed the gun from the glove box. She disassembled the firearm like Sam had demonstrated for cleaning, removing the bullets first. She handed Kyle a couple of the parts.

"Go throw these in the trash bin over there," she said, pointing to the far end of the garage.

She made her way to the other end, where another bin was located. Stuffing the remaining part of the gun as far down as she could, she was satisfied it would stay hidden. Inside the truck again, she searched her purse for the envelope of cash Raul had given her when selling her car. After counting out two thousand dollars, she stuffed it in her pocket with the room key card. They pulled out onto Lombard Street and drove toward Van Ness. The buildings started to look run-down the farther they traveled down Van Ness. There was a homeless encampment under the 101 Freeway overpass that caught Kendra's attention. She turned and followed the street lined with tents and box shelters. After traveling a half mile, she found what she was searching for. A young man in his early twenties held a sign at a stoplight, asking for food. The car in front of them threw some coins into his hand and quickly drove off. Stopping at the red light, Kendra rolled down the truck window.

The young man acknowledged her with a nod and a smile. "Do you take drugs?" asked Kendra.

"Mom, what the heck?" Kyle whispered.

"No, ma'am. I can't help you with that," said the man, moving a few feet away from the truck.

Kendra smiled. "No, I don't want to buy drugs. I want to help you. But I wanted to make sure I wasn't wasting it on someone who just wants to get high."

"No, I just want to eat."

"Can you meet us over at the Starbucks there? We'll get you something to eat," said Kendra pointing ahead to the coffeeshop on the corner.

"Sure! I'll be there," he said, smiling.

When the traffic light turned green, the car behind Kendra honked. She drove through the intersection and immediately pulled into the Starbucks parking lot. The homeless man was already waiting on the sidewalk for them.

Kendra and Kyle stepped out of the truck, and Kendra motioned for him to come over. "Do you know what you like here?"

"Not really. I don't eat here very often. Never, actually," he said.

"Okay. Do you like breakfast sandwiches?"

"Yeah. Very much."

"All right, wait here. We'll be right back."

Kendra grabbed the duffel bag with the cash and then locked the truck. She didn't mind leaving their go bags in the truck, but she never let the bag with cash out of her sight. Their future was entirely dependent on that bag. She ordered two sandwiches and a large vanilla latte for the young man.

"Mom, what are you doing?" asked Kyle as they waited for their order.

"You'll see. Something nice that I hope the universe will recognize and repay to us down the line."

Standing by the truck, the man shifted his feet anxiously. The sight of his shoes almost brought Kendra to tears, where the soles flapped open at the ends. Leaning against the truck, she handed him the sandwiches and drink.

"I'm Katherine and this is my son, Jared."

"I'm Brian. Thanks so much for getting this for me."

"How old are you, Brian?"

"I'm twenty-one. No, wait, my birthday was a couple of weeks ago. I'm twenty-two now."

"How did you end up here?" asked Kendra. "I hope it doesn't offend you, me asking you that so bluntly."

Brian replied after swallowing a bite of sandwich. "Nah, not much offends me. I was in the foster system. Then I aged out and had nowhere to go. It's a common story around here," he said, shrugging.

"Well, Brian, today I'm going to give you the break someone should have given you a long time ago."

Kendra motioned for him to hold out his hand while she pulled something out of her front pocket. She laid the cash and the hotel key card in his hand. She dropped the truck keys on top of the cash. Brian's expression was one of disbelief as he gazed back at her.

"This is a key to room 305 at the Coventry Inn Hotel on Lombard Street. The room is paid for the next two days. I saw a Goodwill store on the corner back there. Get some clean clothes and shoes and stay in the room. The hotel is hiring for a bell boy position. I'm sure it doesn't pay much, but it's a start. The truck is yours. I hope this gives you a boost and gets you back on your feet. You know how to drive, right? Do you have a driver's license?"

"Uh, yeah. I know how to drive, and I have a license. It's expired, but I can take care of that. Why are you doing this for me? You don't even know me," he said, his eyes glistening with unshed tears.

"Because, Brian, sometimes life gives you chicken shit. And I want you to be able to make chicken salad out of it, okay?"

He appeared confused as Kendra and Kyle laughed. "Someone very important to us used to use that reference a lot," said Kendra, picturing Sam's face.

She smiled at Brian and left him in the parking lot as she and Kyle walked into the Starbucks to order an Uber ride to the airport.

THIRTY-ONE

The rideshare driver glanced at Kendra in the rearview mirror. "You sure you don't have any other luggage? I've been driving people to the airport for a few years now, and I find that women always take way more than they need. My wife packs three bags for an overnight at our daughter's house," he said, chuckling.

"Nope, this is it," she said, tightening her grip on the duffel bag of cash.

"So where you folks going, anyway?"

Kendra concealed her mounting frustration behind a composed expression. Why did they have to get a chatty Uber driver who wanted to play twenty questions? Her nerves were already on edge, considering what they were about to do.

"Just going to Washington to see my sister," she said, glancing out the window and hoping he would take the hint.

"Really? My wife is from Washington. What area are you traveling to?" he asked, beaming at her in the mirror.

Of course she was, Kendra thought to herself. "Seattle."

"Oh, she's from Spokane. That's a fair bit east of Seattle. Probably wouldn't know your sister then."

Kyle cleared his throat. "Mom, can you show me that Wikipedia site on your phone again?"

Saved by the bell, thought Kendra as she tapped her phone to life. She opened the Nashville website, and they scrolled through it together. The driver eventually stopped talking as they focused on Kendra's cell phone, and they were at the exit for the airport before she knew it.

San Francisco International Airport was a vast and thriving hub of activity. She reminded the driver of the airline they were flying with, and he pulled up outside the terminal where Kendra tipped him generously before joining Kyle on the sidewalk. Kendra had gone online and looked into carrying large sums of cash on domestic flights. The amount of cash you could carry was not limited, but if TSA suspected any criminal activity, such as drug trafficking or money laundering, they could refer it to a law enforcement agency. Obviously, she didn't want that to happen. She had the right to request a private screening, and that was her plan. She had confidence in her ability to sell her story to a TSA agent but was less optimistic about her chances of convincing a law enforcement officer.

Glancing at her new phone, she checked the time. They had a couple of hours before their flight, so she checked them in online, then headed for the security line. She told Kyle to follow her lead, explaining what they had to do. She requested a private screening from the TSA agent manning the scanner, citing unusual circumstances. Without a second glance, he called for a supervisor and instructed them to step aside and wait.

After ten minutes, the supervising agent arrived, and the man at the scanner pointed to Kendra and Kyle. They followed the supervisor to a small room where she instructed them to place the three duffle bags on a table. When the agent unzipped the cash bag, Kendra spoke.

"You see why I didn't want anyone to know what I'm carrying. It's a lot of money, and my son and I are traveling alone."

"Ms. Sorensen, where did you obtain this cash from?"

"My father passed recently," said Kendra. She sniffled and pretended to wipe away a tear. "This is my sister's half of our inheritance. It was in my dad's safe deposit box. He'd saved his entire life, working as an Oakland police detective to make sure we were taken care of when he passed."

"Where are you traveling today?" The agent appeared to be incredibly uninterested.

"To Nashville, to my sister Carolyn's place. As you can imagine, I'm not comfortable carrying so much cash, but she's disabled since her accident, so it's very hard for her to make the trip out here. I thought about converting the money to a cashier's check, but that would take a while because of the amount. So my son and I are going to stay there for a week so I can give Carolyn her share of the inheritance. It's quite expensive for her in-home care and she could really use the money. I want to get this to her as soon as possible."

The TSA supervisor scrutinized Kendra, deciding whether to believe her story. Kendra stayed silent and maintained eye contact, understanding that too much nervous talk would only make her appear dishonest. The agent averted her gaze and gestured them toward the door.

"Please follow me back to the scanner."

Kendra and Kyle cleared security quickly and were in the departure area in minutes. Her confidence in airport security diminished rapidly after getting through screening so easily.

They found seats in a secluded corner near their departure gate. The TV mounted in the corner broadcast the local news, but Kendra wasn't paying attention to the TV. Instead, to pass the time, she looked up more information on Nashville and its surrounding area on her phone. As she scanned an article about healthcare employment in Tennessee, Kyle elbowed her.

"Ow. What was that for?" Kendra asked, frowning at him.

"Look. Doesn't that look like Sam's house on the news?"

Kendra's gaze followed Kyle's to the television screen. As the camera zoomed out and revealed Sam's property, her jaw dropped open in recognition. Bold, red lettering displayed the news headline at the bottom of the screen.

Lake County murder victims include former DEA agent and three Satans 13 gang members.

"Oh my God," whispered Kendra.

"Did they kill Sam, Mom?" asked Kyle, in a state of shock.

"Oh my God," Kendra repeated. "Sam's dead." As she spoke, the bitterness of the words lingered on her tongue as if they were never meant to be uttered. Sam had been murdered two days ago when they fled his house. He died protecting them.

Kendra's vision swam as time continued on, despite the fact that the world had stopped for her. She leaned forward in her chair, gasping as she slid dangerously close to a full-blown panic attack. As the news story unfolded, she couldn't control the tears that slid down her cheeks. The screen flickered to an earlier scene where a newswoman confronted an obviously grieving Lou, shoving a microphone at her as she walked out of the Sheriff's office. Kendra gasped at the sight of Lou, while soft sobs wracked Kyle's body as Kendra hugged him tightly. It took them several minutes to gain control as they sat next to each other in the terminal, both at a loss for words. Kendra bore the responsibility for Sam's death, and she knew it. The gang came after him because of her and Kyle, and she would never be able to forgive herself. She looked down at the duffle bag filled with cash. Despite being strangers, Sam and Lou had both done so much to help them. And she had repaid them by bringing the evil directly to Sam's doorstep. She was determined to protect her son and ensure Sam's death was not meaningless. She knew that's what he would want, but she was aware of the long road ahead of her, always looking over her shoulder. Would the gang go as far as Tennessee to come after them? She didn't know. Kendra was clueless about how a gang's infrastructure worked. But she was aware that she couldn't drop her guard, not even for a moment.

As the announcement for their flight was called, they were still grappling with the news of Sam's death. They stood at the back of the queue until everyone ahead of them had checked in. Erich, the ticket agent with a nametag stating his name and *They/Them* greeted Kendra and Kyle as they approached the check-in counter.

Kendra turned her cell toward Erich to allow him to scan their boarding passes.

"Good evening, Ms. Sorensen," said Erich, tapping away on a keyboard.

"Hi," said Kendra, without any enthusiasm.

"I'm sorry, but you can each bring only one bag on board. The third bag will have to be checked. I can do that here for you if you'd like," he said, smiling.

Kendra looked down at the duffel bags at her feet. She definitely wasn't going to risk checking a bag full of cash, and she wasn't fond of the idea of entrusting all her worldly possessions to the airline's baggage handling system, either.

"I can fit them all in the overhead bin. All three bags are coming with us," Kendra said firmly, fixing her gaze on him.

"I'm so sorry, but it's airline regulations," Erich said, wrinkling his nose like he agreed it was a stupid rule and shrugging. "Only one bag per person is allowed on board as a carry-on."

Kendra felt something inside her snap. The news of Sam's murder was the tipping point for her.

"I really don't care about the regulations. All three bags are coming on the plane with us."

Kendra felt guilty as Erich withered like a dead weed under her glare. He had nothing to do with why she was so unsettled, and this would hardly be a fair fight, considering her current state of mind.

Kendra shook her head, wondering when she had become *that* person. She instantly wished the ground would open and just swallow her whole. She never behaved like a typical *Karen,* causing trouble or complaining about service providers. With no other choice, she reluctantly placed her bag of clothes on the counter and sighed. The last thing she wanted was for her new name to end up on a no-fly watchlist somewhere.

"I'm sorry. That was very rude of me. It's been a very long day. You can check this bag."

Erich smiled graciously and checked Kendra's bag of clothes, secured a tag on the bag's handle, and placed it on the cart behind the podium. Kendra hoped he wouldn't hold a grudge and her clothes would make it to Nashville.

Despite blaming it on the stress of the last week, she felt the burn of Erich's stare as they walked onto the air bridge to board the plane. They settled into their seats, and Kendra immediately ordered a glass of wine once they were airborne. Although the wine helped her nerves a bit, the news of Sam's death continued to haunt her all the way to Tennessee. She was devastated that they wouldn't even be able to attend his funeral, but she was sure Lou wouldn't want them there, anyway.

Kendra closed her eyes and settled into her seat as they began the five-hour, non-stop flight to Nashville, while Kyle withdrew into himself, watching the in-flight movie. Kendra grew more relaxed with each passing mile from California. She had never been a huge fan of flying, but at that moment, she felt safer than she had in days. Relatively certain there were no gangbangers on flight 1632 to Nashville, she'd never felt more relaxed at 35,000 feet in the air. She was asleep before they crossed the airspace into Arizona.

THIRTY-TWO

Four days after the murders in Lake County, Gutierrez obtained Sam Murphy's phone records. He received a text from the sheriff's detective saying the records were on their way over via email. Cross-referencing numbers and names, Gutierrez ran the names through NCIC, the National Crime Information Center. Gutierrez was convinced that Sam Murphy knew plenty of document forgers that could help Kendra Thompson and her son obtain new identities, and the criminal records database would aid in identifying anyone with a criminal history. Even if they hadn't been incarcerated for forgery, they would have some criminal history. He would bet his next paycheck on that. The agent's cell records showed very few outgoing calls. While the majority of calls were to his sister, Louella, Gutierrez uncovered two calls made to a local number within a day of each other. By cross-referencing the number with the name, he discovered that James Edward Frazier was the owner of the phone. And, upon running the name through NCIC, he was certain that he had found the forger. James Frazier spent a short stint in state prison for his role in a counterfeit operation, following a lengthy history of criminal activities.

"Gotcha, asshole," Gutierrez said to himself.

The sound of his cell phone ringing broke his concentration. He recognized the number, and although he didn't want to answer it, he knew he couldn't postpone it any further.

"Yeah, what's up?"

"What's up? That's rich, even coming from a *chavalo* like you," Big Boy barked into the phone. "I don't know what the fuck happened up there, but three dead bangers are a real problem. My leader got a call from a Satan's leader up north, and shit is about to go down, *ese*."

"I didn't have anything to do with that. That asshole McLeod hired a hit on the woman and her kid when your guys weren't getting the job done," Gutierrez said, after walking to an empty interview room for privacy.

"Well, he fucked up, big time. Word is the Satans are coming to our turf. The Sinners are prepping for a war, homie, and the LAPD is gonna be right in the middle of it."

Big Boy hung up, leaving Gutierrez uneasy. He didn't need the Sinners and Satan 13 throwing down in his city. The gang detail would undoubtedly want to know what triggered the fighting, and chatter about the Satans 13 murders would likely be a part of the investigation. Gutierrez couldn't risk anything being traced back to him. He returned to his desk in a hurry and scribbled James Frazier's information onto a piece of notebook paper.

Gutierrez sent his partner a text saying he was out running down a lead on the McLeod murder. He decided to scroll through his emails before lunch, when he noticed an email address that stopped him in his tracks.

DevonMcLeodsmurdervideo@gmail.com

"What the hell?" whispered Gutierrez.

When he opened the email, it was from Kendra Thompson. He glanced behind him to ensure he was alone before pulling his laptop closer and opening the video attachment. After watching it for less than a minute, he knew it was legitimate and incriminating. He slammed his laptop shut, picked up his phone and the scrap of paper with James Frazier's information, and went straight to the parking garage.

He let out a loud curse and slammed his palm against the steering wheel once he was in his car. With every passing day, the situation deteriorated and his fear of being associated with Devon McLeod's murder weighed heavily on him. Taking a few deep breaths, he called the senator.

"Now is not a good time to speak, officer. Do you have any new information on my nephew's murder?" asked McLeod, answering on the first ring.

"Are you not alone?"

"That's right, I'm in a staff meeting at the moment," the senator responded.

"Well, get the hell out of your staff meeting and call me right back. We need to talk."

"Fine. Give me five minutes."

Gutierrez waited for a call back from Steven McLeod while sitting in his car in the underground parking lot of the LAPD. He wasted no time in picking up the phone when he recognized McLeod's number on the screen.

"What is so important that you had to pull me out of a staff meeting? I sincerely hope it's to tell me that you found the CI we're looking for. My guy is itching to get out there before that woman has run too far."

"I found him."

"Well, at long last, you're doing something to earn your fee. It's about time."

"Don't give me that bullshit, McLeod. Your nephew is dead. That's what I was paid to arrange. This current mess is your own doing. I didn't hire a third party to muddy the waters. That was all you."

"I wouldn't have had to do that if your people hadn't been careless enough to allow a random teenager to record the murder in progress! Just give me the information so I can get it to my guy. Clearly, your gangbangers have bigger fish to fry right now."

"Exactly my point. The Sinners and Satans 13 are about to go to war, and if that happens, it's just one more avenue to lead this entire clusterfuck to me. You'd better pray that doesn't happen, because if I go down, I'm taking you with me. No way am I assuming all the liability."

"Calm down, Gutierrez. My guy will handle it. Without the kid's testimony or the video, the DA can spout all the theories he wants to. He'll have nothing on us without that."

"Yeah, well, there's more," Gutierrez said.

"Spare me the dramatics. I'm listening."

"Kendra Thompson sent me an email with a copy of the video."

Gutierrez shared the email specifics and video details with McLeod. When he was done, McLeod remained quiet.

"Did you hear me, McLeod?"

"Of course I did. I'm not deaf. My guy will have it handled by the end of the week."

"See that he does. This is heating up way too much. Let me know once it's done."

Senator McLeod immediately called the hitman after ending the call with Gutierrez. Handing the information on James Frazier over to the assassin brought him a sense of relief. The hitman had always been dependable, but this assignment was pushing him to the brink of failure. The nurse and her teenager had managed to elude the gang and a hired assassin, leaving McLeod baffled. It was true that they had some help along the way, but even so, either he hadn't given Kendra Thompson enough credit, or she was incredibly lucky. However, there was no doubt in McLeod's mind that Kendra and her son were on their own now and that would be their downfall.

THIRTY-THREE

Positioned down the street from James Frazier's house, the hitman waited. It was a middle-class bungalow, probably forty years old, and in need of some TLC. A tricycle lay on its side in the yard, with a basketball hoop listing to one side in the driveway. From the outside, it looked just like any other slightly run-down family home. Looking at the house, no one would ever suspect that a professional forger lived there.

There had been no activity at the house since the family returned home at 6:00 p.m., carrying large bags from Kentucky Fried Chicken. The hitman ate a protein bar while he waited in the van and split it with the dog. Maybe he would bring some chicken back to the dog in the van later. He had not yet thought of a new name for his recently acquired pet, so he continued to call him the dog. The hitman considered the name Buddy on the dog's tag to be lacking in originality. With a new owner would come a new name for the dog. Swallowing the snack whole, the dog turned his head back to the door and ignored him. It was evident that the animal had not warmed up to him yet. Most of the time, he would growl and snarl at him. But the hitman knew the dog would see things differently once he surrendered to his new circumstances. If there was one trait the hitman possessed, it was patience.

At midnight, the hitman made his move. James Frazier, being a family man with children, would be asleep early, so the hitman felt no need to wait until later. He donned a ski mask, tucked his gun in his waistband, and jogged across the street to the side gate of Frazier's home. He picked the lock to the sliding door and entered the family room. He climbed the stairs cautiously, testing for squeaks before putting his weight on each step. The hall had two doors on one side, one linen closet cabinet and a bathroom on the other side, and double doors at the end. He guessed the master bedroom was behind the double doors. The first door on the left had a wooden name plate painted in pink with the name "Hayley". He walked into the room, where the nightlight created star-shaped shadows on the ceiling. Silently, he made his way to the bed and placed a gloved hand over the little girl's mouth. After gagging and binding her, he carried her to the family room couch downstairs. Placing a finger to his mouth, he signaled for her to stay quiet. Every inch of the girl's body trembled.

He bent down to whisper in her ear. "If you move from this couch, I will kill you. Do you understand, Hayley?"

Tear-filled, terrified blue eyes stared back at him. "Do you understand me?" he asked her again.

She nodded and sunk deeper into the couch. "Okay, good. I'll be right back with your brother and mom and dad."

Then, he proceeded to the room next to Hayley's. The boy inside had kicked off his covers and was lying facing the wall. The hitman acted swiftly, gagging him and binding the victim's hands behind his back. The boy, aged around twelve or thirteen, was in a fight for his life. After subduing him, the hitman leaned in closely.

"I have your sister downstairs. If you fight me, I will kill her. Do you believe me?"

The boy nodded, eyes widening. "Good boy. Now, we are going to walk downstairs quietly, and you will sit next to your sister while I get your parents. If you try to run, I will kill them. If I get back downstairs and you or Hayley are gone, I will kill both of your parents. Am I clear? Do you understand?"

The boy maintained a wide-eyed gaze at him. "I need you to let me know that you understand what I just said."

The boy nodded vigorously, his head bobbing up and down.

"Excellent. This will be over before you know it if you do what I tell you to."

The hitman guided the boy downstairs by his shoulder to sit next to his sister. He reminded them both to keep quiet and then headed up the stairs to the master bedroom.

He opened the door without a sound and carefully moved toward the king-size bed. He moved swiftly, subduing James first, and then his wife. James stopped fighting when the hitman pulled out his gun and aimed it at Mrs. Frazier's head.

"Both of your children are already downstairs. You will both walk ahead of me down to the family room and join them. Don't make me shoot one of them because you try to be a hero. Am I making myself clear?"

They nodded in unison as Mrs. Frazier struggled to speak through the tape covering her mouth.

"Stop talking. I do the talking here until I ask you a question. Got it?"

She immediately stopped trying to speak and hung her head.

"Let's go," he said, motioning toward the door with his gun.

Once downstairs, the hitman turned on a table lamp. He instructed Mrs. Frazier to sit next to her children, who both immediately slid closer to her. He directed James to take a seat in the chair across the room.

"James, I am going to remove the tape from your face and ask you a series of questions. If you shout or otherwise try to garner attention, or if you refuse to answer any of my questions, you will force me to shoot one of your family members for every unanswered question. This is your only warning. Please believe me when I say that I will not hesitate to do so. If you cooperate, I will leave without harming any of you, out of a professional courtesy from one career criminal to another.

I assume you won't want to contact the authorities to discuss your recent illicit activities."

Mrs. Frazier shook her head in confusion, frowning, as James turned his gaze to her.

"Oh my. Isn't this interesting? It seems Mrs. Frazier isn't up to speed on your extracurricular money-making ventures. Well, time to come clean then, James. It will do your conscience good. Okay, here we go."

James Frazier cried out in pain as the hitman ripped the tape from his face.

"Careful James, I could misconstrue that as a cry for help."

"No, I wasn't, I was—"

"Sshhh. You speak after I ask you a question. You're having trouble following instructions, James, and we haven't even begun yet. Do I need to shoot someone to get your attention?"

Mrs. Frazier began to whimper and shake her head as the children huddled closer to her. James gave his head a violent shake.

"Good. All right then. First question. Are you acquainted with Samuel Murphy, formerly of the Drug Enforcement Agency?"

"Y-yes," answered James.

"Good. You're doing good, James. Next question. Did you recently procure identities for a woman and her teenage son at the request of agent Murphy?"

"I…he, yes," said James, sighing and dropping his head to his chest.

"Excellent. We are moving right through this in no time. Now for the most important question, James. What are the names of the new identities of the woman and the boy?"

When James didn't reply immediately, the hitman turned and leveled his gun at the terrified mother and her children on the couch.

"Kathleen and Jared Sorensen. No wait. It's Katherine. Katherine Sorensen," James blurted out at the sight of the gun trained on his family.

"Katherine and Jared Sorensen. S-O-R-E-N-S-E-N?"

"Yes."

"Great. Well, it seems that you and the missus probably have some things to discuss, James, so I'll leave you to it."

Walking out the front door, the hitman crossed the street to his van. He pulled off the mask, ran his fingers through his hair, and drove away from Frazier's house. The only reason the family was still alive was because the hitman knew if he killed them, it would eventually lead right back to Sam Murphy when the police checked James Frazier's phone records. He was also certain that James would keep his mouth shut out of fear for his family's safety.

In the passenger seat, the dog lifted its head and showed its teeth to the hitman. Once again, he regretted taking the dog from his victim on impulse. It was as if Sam Murphy was taunting him even after death.

THIRTY-FOUR

It was just after four in the morning when Kendra and Kyle touched down in Nashville. Even at that hour the humidity was higher than what they were used to. After Kendra collected her bag from the luggage carousel, she called for an Uber. She had researched hotels on the plane, and they settled on a midrange hotel in the downtown area. To check in early upon arrival and avoid waiting until 2:00 p.m., she paid for the previous day. She planned to start looking for a house rental right after they got a few hours of sleep. Saving every penny possible for housing was Kendra's goal, so she asked the Uber driver to take them through a fast-food restaurant rather than order room service at the hotel. She still had to furnish a new place and that required everything from silverware to beds. It was a daunting thought.

They checked in to the hotel and went to sleep right away. After a long night of flying, they were both exhausted. Showered and refreshed after waking up just after 1:00 p.m., they headed downstairs for a light lunch. Kendra was in a hotel in an unfamiliar city, which would ordinarily feel like a vacation. But worry still plagued her mind, despite being eighteen-hundred miles from home. She attempted to convince herself that they were momentarily safe from the Sinners' grasp, but her anxiety lingered.

Kyle was in awe of the flashy lights and music-inspired vibe of Nashville. Even in the afternoon, it felt like a miniature Las Vegas. They strolled down Broadway Street, the heart of Nashville, where they were swept up in the live music and art that seemed to emanate from every corner. While sitting on a bench under a large tree, they enjoyed a shaved ice as Kendra searched the Zillow website for rental houses. She scribbled down notes for three possibilities, organized appointments for later that afternoon, then called for an Uber. Kendra's second priority, right after housing, was to purchase an inexpensive car, as she had made up her mind to start job hunting without delay. With school starting in a couple of weeks, it was pointless for her to stay home alone. She ran through the things she had to accomplish in her head. Her to-do list included registering Kyle for school, securing housing, furnishings, transportation, and a job. She had just under two weeks to complete everything, with no clue how she was going to manage the mammoth task.

Luckily, they both loved the second house they viewed. The property was on a tree-lined street, and came with a spacious yard, a basketball hoop, and an aboveground pool. Priced within their budget, the house had two bedrooms and two baths, giving them both their own space. Kendra skipped the appointment to view the third house and paid cash for the rent and deposit to the landlord on the spot. The old man who owned the home was more than happy to take her money, saying that he always relied on his gut feeling when choosing renters and had never been wrong before. They signed a lease, and he passed her the keys. Kendra was amazed by how simple the entire process had been, and by the time they got back to the hotel that afternoon, she felt a huge weight lifted from her shoulders. The plan was to visit every thrift store they could find the next day, then go to Walmart to buy anything else they needed. Kendra had decided to surprise Kyle with a new Xbox and a cell phone of his own. She wanted to ensure that he had a way to contact her once he started school.

They were up and out of the hotel early the next day. Kendra had their Uber driver take them to a U Haul rental location where she rented a small truck to load furniture she planned to buy. They spent countless hours scouring thrift stores until they had nearly everything they needed. They got lucky and stumbled across a mattress store going out of business and bought beds. On their way to drop off furniture at the house, Kendra spotted a late-model Hyundai in a small car lot. On a whim, she pulled in to check it out. The Sonata was in great condition with low miles. The sticker read $15,200. But Kendra understood the power of a cash sale. Soon after they arrived, the salesperson approached them.

"Good evening, ma'am. You're interested in the Sonata, I see," he said, smiling at Kendra.

"I am. I'll give you $10,000 cash right now."

He blinked at her. "I'm not sure we can go quite that low."

"Well then, let's talk to whoever can make that decision. I have about an hour at most to make this thing happen, otherwise I'll have to keep looking elsewhere tomorrow," Kendra said.

The salesperson, seeing his commission slipping away, led them to the sales trailer located at the far end of the dealership. Directing them to a desk in the corner, he stepped into the manager's office. The sales manager's name, Allen Harrison, was on a plaque outside the door.

The manager followed the salesperson to where Kendra and Kyle were sitting and extended his hand to Kendra.

"Allen Harrison, I'm the sales manager here."

"Ken—Katherine Sorensen," Kendra said, flustered. She reminded herself to be more cautious. She came close to introducing herself as Kendra. "This is my son, Jared,"

"Pleased to meet you both. Why don't you follow me into my office and let's see if we can get you into that Sonata today," said Allen.

A little over an hour later, Kendra became the owner of the silver 2013 Hyundai Sonata. Prior to leaving the dealership, Kendra purchased insurance online and listed herself and Kyle as drivers. She received an excellent rate, as both their new names had clean driving records. She handed over the keys to Kyle to follow her to their new house to unload furniture, and then to the U Haul location to return the truck.

Their first night in their new house was a mixture of good and bad. Kendra was relieved to have finally found a place to settle down instead of always being on the run or in an unfamiliar motel. Although she tried, she couldn't relax completely. Letting go of the anxiety was tough after so many days on high alert. Her habit of being constantly vigilant for danger was still in full force, and she wasn't able to let it go yet.

A light rain in the morning made it an ideal day to stay inside and organize the house. In the afternoon, Kendra took Kyle to the Walmart supercenter where they purchased an Xbox, household items, and groceries. She looked forward to eating something that wasn't fast food. She spent the evening scouring every online employment website she could find. Putting together a believable resume would be a challenge for her. She had spent twelve years as a nurse but couldn't mention that experience without revealing her identity, and she lacked any other marketable skills. As a teenager, she worked in fast-food, and later as a part-time receptionist while she went to school. Those positions were not considered high-level by any means. She was on the verge of giving up for the day when she came across a job opening for a private party in-home health care aide.

Full-time position available immediately. Experienced health-care aide for eighty-nine-year-old woman needed in downtown Nashville private residence. Monday through Friday, 8:00 a.m.–5:00 p.m. No weekends required. Duties include cleaning, feeding, dispensing medication, and accompanying patient to and from medical appointments as needed (transportation provided). Must be proficient with a BP cuff. Experience with a Hoyer lift is desirable, but not required. Requires maturity and thick skin. $27.00 per hour, plus an annual bonus for the right fit. Call Emmett at (615) 622-0894.

The ad had Kendra so excited she practically jumped off the couch. Despite the lower pay compared to that of a nurse in California, living costs in Nashville were lower and she had savings, thanks to Sam. She dialed the number, hoping the job was still available.

"Emmett Kent," said a deep male voice with a southern drawl.

"Yes, hello Mr. Kent. My name is Katherine Sorensen. I'm calling about the open position for a health aide. Is that still available?"

"Yes, ma'am, it most certainly is. If my mother didn't find fault with every single applicant, it would have been filled weeks ago. I don't mean to scare you off . . . Katherine, was it? But my mother is very particular. And to be very frank with you, my wife and I are tired. I have a job I can't concentrate on, and my wife is dang near to the point of divorcing me if we don't get someone in here to help with Mom. We have interviews set up tomorrow. Can you come by at about three o'clock tomorrow afternoon?"

The job's requirement for thick skin was becoming apparent to Kendra. But dealing with a difficult elderly woman would be a cakewalk in comparison to her past two weeks.

"Yes, I can make that, absolutely."

"Great. Text me your full name and I'll send you the address and put you down at three o'clock tomorrow."

"Thank you so much, Mr. Kent. I look forward to meeting you and your mother tomorrow."

Kendra wondered just how bad Emmett Kent's mother was after hearing him chuckle before he hung up.

THIRTY-FIVE

The hitman dialed Senator McLeod's number, anxious for him to pick up.

"I hope you have some good news for me," said Steven McLeod.

"I have their new names. It will be much faster if you have your contact at LAPD run this down. Have him check flights out of San Francisco and San Jose for the last week. If he doesn't get anything there, then try Sacramento. She probably has a credit card under her new name, so have him look for any activity on that as well."

"Well, that *is* good news. I'm ready for the information whenever you are."

"They're going by Katherine and Jared Sorensen."

He spelled the last name for McLeod and ended the call after the senator agreed to get back to him once he had a lead from Gutierrez.

Senator McLeod immediately called Gutierrez to give him Kendra and Kyle Thompson's new identities. The senator was thrilled that they were getting close to wrapping things up.

Gutierrez put aside everything else he was working on and started on finding Kendra Thompson and her son. Gutierrez's partner was getting suspicious because he was carrying the majority load of their cases on his own, but Gutierrez told him he was investigating the

McLeod murder full time because of the pressure from the DA's office. That was a half-truth. He had motives other than making an arrest while working on Devon McLeod's murder case. His constant worry was that evidence would lead back to him or the senator. He had no doubt the senator would be quick to point a finger at him if he was found out. The sooner he located Kendra Thompson, her son, and the video, the better he'd sleep at night.

It didn't take him long to find Kendra's hotel records at the Coventry Motor Inn in San Francisco. Based on that information, he speculated they had taken a flight out of SFO. The question was, where did they go? To access airline records, a warrant would be necessary. Obtaining hotel records wouldn't require him to have a warrant because they could trace credit card activity on Kendra's new name. But the system needed some time to search the database using just a name. Kendra and her son could be literally anywhere. He submitted a request to Amelia in records with a plea to expedite it. Gutierrez was aware of Amelia's romantic feelings toward him, so he went to the records department for an in-person appeal after submitting the request. Amelia promised to prioritize it once he turned on the charm. For now, there was nothing else to do but wait.

Two days after submitting his request, he received an email from Amelia telling him she had found something. He went straight to records the moment he saw her email.

"Hey, Ramón," said Amelia, smiling.

"Hi, Amelia. Thanks for getting on this so quickly."

"It was my pleasure, Ramón."

Amelia handed him the printout. "She stayed at the Hampton Inn and Suites in Nashville, registered for two nights. That was several days ago, but at least you have a starting point now."

Gutierrez nodded and smiled at her. "I can't thank you enough for this, really."

"Sure you can. You can take me to dinner."

"I'd love to. I'll be in touch about that as soon as I can."

Amelia really wasn't his type, but it wouldn't kill him to take her to dinner. She had proved to be a valuable source for quick information. Saying goodbye, he made his way back to his desk. To get an idea of its location, he pulled up the website for the Hampton Inn and Suites in Nashville. There were two possible explanations for Kendra checking out after just two days. Nashville was either a temporary stop or she had found something more permanent there. Amelia didn't find any other hotel reservations, so Gutierrez believed the Thompson's hadn't left Nashville. His gut told him they were still in the area.

He relayed the latest information to McLeod and told him to send the hitman to do the legwork. If McLeod's guy was any good at all, he would find them.

McLeod wasted no time getting the information to the hitman, and in turn, the hitman was on the road to Nashville within the hour. Two reasons kept him from flying whenever he could avoid it. First, he detested the notion of being confined in a metal enclosure hurtling through the atmosphere at five-hundred-fifty miles per hour. Second, the smaller his job footprint, the better. His alternate identities were used sparingly, and only when it couldn't be avoided. Once he used an alias, he considered it burned and never used that name again. He was exceedingly careful and had never been linked to any of his jobs because of that.

He felt a heightened sense of excitement as he loaded the dog into the van and started the drive out of his neighborhood. He would soon have his targets in his sights. He reached over to ruffle the dog's ears, and the animal snarled in response. Despite admiring the animal's tenacity, he was growing weary of the dog's hesitance to warm up to his new master. He'd always heard that animals had the ability to judge one's character. Maybe the dog sensed something in him that most people didn't. The hitman's profession and his pleasure in doing it would lead most people to label him as a psychopath.

He ignored the dog and calculated his trip time in his mind. If he drove twelve hours a day, he would reach Nashville in three days at the most. That allowed him breaks for food and sleep, and made allowances for any unexpected traffic delays or detours. By that time, Kendra Thompson would have begun to feel safe. She would think that they got away when no one came for them.

He took pleasure in knowing that she would be wrong.

THIRTY-SIX

Kendra busied herself with household chores to pass the time until her 3:00 p.m. interview, while Kyle was glued to his Xbox for most of the day. While she wasn't fond of his all-day video game session, she recognized his need for a break. Despite that, she was adamant that he go with her to the interview and wait in the car. She didn't feel comfortable leaving him alone just yet. She couldn't be sure they were safe, since they had only been in Nashville for a few days. Kyle initially complained, but eventually he exchanged his Xbox for his new phone to keep himself entertained during the drive to Emmett Kent's house downtown.

A large plantation style house came into view as Kendra pulled up to the address her GPS directed her to. More of a mansion than a house. Kyle shifted his attention to Kendra after putting his phone down, eyebrows raised.

"What does this dude do for a living?"

"I have no idea. Wait here and honk if you have an emergency."

"Oh my God, Mom. *So* lame," he said, rolling his eyes for emphasis.

Kendra made a face at him and headed toward the double front door. With the hope of portraying herself as a healthcare professional, she wore navy blue scrubs with a stethoscope hung around her neck. A middle-aged woman answered the door and led her to a hall around the corner. Two other women sat on chairs in the hallway, resumes in hand. Dressed in tailored slacks and silk blouses, they were the epitome of business professionalism. She instantly regretted her impromptu wardrobe decision as she glanced down at her scrubs and sneakers. There was nothing she could do about it, so she held her head high and tried to appear confident.

A tall man in an expensive suit emerged from the room at the end of the hallway ten minutes later, followed by a young woman.

"I'm very sorry, Ms. Berry. Please excuse my mother's rude comments."

While shaking her head, Ms. Berry headed toward the front door, looking very unhappy.

Kendra kept her eyes on the man as he turned toward them and took a deep breath.

"Who's next?" he asked.

An older woman stood. After shaking her hand, Emmett Kent introduced himself and led her into the room he had just left. Kendra noticed the woman sitting across from her glance in her direction before looking back at the closed door.

"Everyone comes out of that room looking ticked-off. Nope, not happening. I'm out. Good luck," she said, as she stood up and walked toward the front door, leaving Kendra alone in the hall.

The interview with the older woman was brief. Within ten minutes, she was walking down the hallway on her way out, clearly not happy. Kendra's first impulse was to turn and bolt. Whatever was happening in the interview room, it was evident that the last two women were displeased. Although Kendra had reservations, she decided to see it through, since she was already there and in dire need of work.

"You must be Katherine," said Emmett, walking toward Kendra with his hand outstretched.

"Yes. Pleased to meet you, Mr. Kent."

"Please, call me Emmett. Mr. Kent makes me feel so old."

"All right, Emmett."

"Right this way, Katherine. Her majesty awaits," he said.

Kendra entered the room to find a petite elderly woman in a wheelchair scowling at her.

"You're in scrubs, young lady," she said with a sneer.

"I am. Most health professionals wear them when working," Kendra said.

"Now, Mother. Don't start already. Katherine, this is my mother, Margaret Kent. Mother, this is Katherine Sorensen."

"In my day, a young lady dressed up to meet a potential employer. It's absolutely disrespectful to show up like this," said Margaret, waving her hand at Kendra.

Kendra came very close to laughing out loud. This was the woman who sent the other three applicants running? Kendra had dealt with much worse than this woman on an hourly basis at the hospital. She decided to approach Margaret Kent the same way she approached all patients, and not consider her time with her as an interview. Which meant she had to take immediate control of the situation.

"Well, Mrs. Kent, I prefer to wear scrubs when working in this capacity. You never know when a patient might have an unexpected bowel movement or experience uncontrollable vomiting. That is particularly commonplace in elderly patients such as yourself. Medication adjustments, urinary tract infections, even just something to eat that was too spicy can trigger those symptoms."

Margaret's jaw moved as if she was going to speak, but shock left her silent. Emmett Kent chuckled softly. Walking to the couch, Kendra picked up a pillow and headed toward Margaret.

"Now, let's get this behind you to support your back or by bedtime tonight, your sacroiliac will be giving you a lot of pain."

Kendra used a gentle touch on Margaret's back to move her forward in the chair, then positioned the pillow behind her. "That's right, dear, just like that."

Kendra was under close scrutiny from Margaret, who had yet to say anything since her initial attempt at insulting her. Following that, Kendra picked up the blood pressure cuff that was draped over the wheelchair and wrapped it around the woman's frail arm.

"This cuff is too big for her," she said, looking at Emmett. "You won't get an accurate reading with this. It will show her blood pressure is low when it probably isn't."

"Her pressure has been very good. The doctor just adjusted her meds over the phone based on her readings," Emmett said.

"He didn't require she come in for an office check first?" Kendra asked, glancing at Emmet.

He shook his head.

"Have you had any headaches or dizziness since he lowered your dosage, Margaret?"

"Well, er, I . . . well, yes, I have been a bit lightheaded."

"Okay. That's probably because your BP is a bit high after lowering your medication. We need to get the right size cuff as a first order of business."

Kendra removed the stethoscope from around her neck and placed it on Margaret's chest, then her back, listening to her heart and lungs. "Take a deep breath for me. Now exhale. Good. Again please." She picked up Margaret's hand and pressed her fingers to her wrist to time her heart rate. "Your heart rate is fine, and your lungs are clear. But you really do need a smaller cuff so we can get an accurate BP. You should take your readings several times a day. Are you having any pain or uncomfortableness anywhere?"

"No, just my lower back most nights."

"Well, once we get you the proper support, that will improve greatly. This pillow will help for tonight."

Kendra turned to Emmett. "Do either of you have any questions for me?" Looking back to Margaret, she raised her eyebrows at her in question.

"Just two. Where the hell have you been hiding yourself and when can you start?" said Emmett, smiling.

THIRTY-SEVEN

It was late morning on his third day of travel when the hitman crossed the border into Tennessee, and three hours to make it to the hotel after that. He had reservations at the Hampton Inn and Suites, the same hotel where Kendra and Kyle had stayed. He dressed his dog in a service vest he got online, parked his van in the guest area, and with his suitcase and dog in tow, he approached the front desk to check in. Using one of his alias identities, Walter Smith, he took the key card from the desk clerk and rode the elevator to the fourth floor. Once he had given the dog food and water, he took a shower to rinse off the road dust after three long days in the van. He spent his afternoon lounging on the bed and scrolling through the TV until late afternoon, then he made his way to the front desk. The same desk clerk who checked him in was still on duty. Leaning on the counter, he smiled and propped himself up on his elbows.

"Hello again. I'm hoping you can help me. I was supposed to meet my sister here a few days ago, but I was delayed. I told her I would call her when I got into town, but she has a new phone number, and dolt that I am, I seem to have misplaced it. I know I should have put it into my phone right away, but I didn't, and now I don't know how to reach her."

"Oh, that's a shame. I'm sorry, sir, we aren't allowed to disclose any information about guests."

"Of course not. How silly of me. Would you mind just looking at her picture? She and my nephew will be so disappointed if I don't make it to his birthday party. I didn't tell them, but I've started a college fund for my nephew," said the hitman, grinning at the desk clerk. "It's a surprise, because he wants to attend Nashville State. Maybe she mentioned where they were going or if they had found a place yet? She's so busy, I'm not sure she'll call me. I don't know what I'll do to find them if I don't hear from her soon. Martin, that's my husband, he's always telling me how forgetful I am. I really don't want to have to tell him what I've done."

The hitman pulled up a picture of Kendra and Kyle on his phone, one he copied from Kendra's Facebook page. They were posed in front of the Staples Center, smiling for the camera.

"This is my sister, Katherine, and my nephew, Jared," he said, turning his phone toward the clerk.

"I remember them. She was really nice," said the desk clerk, glancing around to make sure no one was listening. "All I can share with you is that she had the same Uber driver for the couple of days they were here. Maybe he can help you. I know him. He does a lot of rides out of the hotel. His name is Manuel Torres. You can request him, but probably don't have to. He usually gets all the ride business here."

"Oh, that's wonderful. Thank you so much for your help," said the hitman, slipping a hundred-dollar bill across the counter to him.

The clerk lit up like a Christmas tree. "It was my pleasure, Mr. Smith. You let me know if I can be of any further help."

"Actually, if you wouldn't mind setting up a ride with Manuel for tomorrow morning at nine o'clock and charging it to my credit card on file, that would be most appreciated."

"Absolutely, sir. I'm happy to do it."

The hitman thanked the clerk again and walked out of the hotel to downtown to find a restaurant for dinner. He returned to the hotel after his meal and spread out a map of Nashville on the desk. He studied the area, looking for a remote area outside the city. The Beaman Park Nature Center, a nature preserve thirty minutes outside of the city, caught his eye and he marked it with a pen. That would do nicely. Confident with his plan, he brushed his teeth, changed into pajamas, and settled into a real bed for the first time in three days. Sleeping in the van had taken a toll on him, and he was feeling the effects.

He had trouble falling asleep, thinking about how much he wanted this job to be over. The longer it dragged on, the more his profit decreased. Despite his high fee, he had to factor in overhead and travel expenses. His plan was to retire to a sunny beach in the near future, but he had specific financial goals to reach first. He drifted off sometime after 11:00 p.m. and slept peacefully until his phone alarm woke him at 7:00 a.m.

He fed the dog and got dressed, then he ordered breakfast through room service to save time while he took the dog outside for his morning business. After breakfast he arrived downstairs fifteen minutes before his scheduled ride and waited for Manuel on a bench in the passenger pickup area, reading a newspaper. When the Uber driver pulled up, he lowered the passenger window.

"Mr. Smith?" he asked.

"Yes indeed. You must be the famous Manuel, who shuttled my sister and nephew around the city last week."

"Maybe? I drive many people. I am sorry to say I don't remember them all."

The hitman pulled up the photo of Kendra and her son on his cell and showed it to Manuel as he got into the backseat.

"Oh yes! I remember this lady. She was a very good tipper. Where am I taking you today, amigo?"

"I would like to go to the Beaman Park Nature Center in Ashland."

"Okay. I know the place. It will take us thirty to forty-five minutes, depending on traffic."

"Fine. I want to take some pictures for my high school class. I'm a science teacher."

"Very nice. I enjoyed science in school."

Manuel pulled out of the hotel lot, and they began their drive to the preserve. They made good time, arriving in thirty-five minutes. The hitman directed Manuel to avoid the reception center and keep moving deeper into the wooded region. He was satisfied they were alone after driving a couple of miles into the preserve, and told Manuel to stop the car so he could take some photos. As soon as the Uber driver pulled over, the hitman pulled his gun from his backpack. He spoke clearly and calmly, with the barrel pressed against Manuel's neck.

"Manuel, do you have a family?"

"Yes," he said, shakily.

"If you'd like to see them again, then you will answer my questions truthfully. Do you understand?"

"Yes," he said, nodding quickly.

"Good. I want to know every single place you took Katherine Sorensen and her son. I mean every stop you made. Am I clear?"

"Yes, but I don't remember so good. I drive many people."

"You have records of where you take your clients, do you not?"

"Yes, but only until I am paid for the ride from Uber. I don't have those records anymore."

"Well, that's going to be a problem for you, Manuel. Without that information, I have no further use for you."

"No, wait! I will remember."

Manuel recounted Kendra's travel to the hitman, including the two houses he took them to. The hitman's mood improved upon hearing that. The day after Manuel took Kendra to the houses, she checked out of the hotel. He hoped Kendra had rented one of them and wasn't staying with friends. If she was a guest in someone's house, that would complicate things. But he was on the verge of finding them either way. He instructed Manuel to take him to the two houses while reminding him of the gun pointed at him from the backseat. The first house appeared to be empty, with a sign that read "for rent" in the front yard. However, the second house had a car in the driveway and the sprinklers on in the front yard. There was no doubt that someone lived there. Having seen enough, he directed Manuel to drive him back to the hotel.

They pulled up to the passenger drop off where Manuel held the hitman's gaze in the rearview mirror.

"I don't want to come after you and your family, Manuel. But I will, if I have to, make no mistake about that. Let me see your driver's license, please."

"What?"

"Your license. Let me see it."

Manuel took his license from his wallet and passed it back to the hitman. The hitman snapped a picture of it and handed it back. "Don't make me use that information, Manuel. And I assume it goes without saying that you are not to go to the police or anyone else to report me or this ride today. That includes your family. If you warn Katherine Sorensen that I was looking for her, your children will die a very unfortunate and painful death while you and your wife watch, helpless to save them. Am I understood?"

Manuel shook his head vigorously. "Say yes, Manuel, so I know you understand. I'm a bit of a stickler for details."

"Yes, I understand. I will say nothing to anyone, ever. I never saw you before in my life. Please, just don't hurt my kids."

"You'll never see or hear from me again, Manuel, as long as you keep your mouth shut."

"I will not say anything. I promise."

The hitman patted Manuel's shoulder and gave him a smile. "Good man, Manuel. Have a pleasant day, my friend," he said, exiting the car.

THIRTY-EIGHT

Kendra was not oblivious to the irony of Emmett Kent asking where she had been hiding. She cleared her throat to stall for time.

"I've just relocated to Nashville with my teenage son, Jared. We've only been here for a little over a week. He'll start school next week, so I can start then."

"We were hoping to have someone start immediately. Would that be possible?" Emmett asked.

Kendra bit her bottom lip anxiously. "I'm not comfortable leaving him alone in a new city. I understand if you need to keep looking or offer the position to another applicant," Kendra said.

"Emmett, give Katherine and me a moment alone, please," Margaret said.

"What? Now, Mother, we need to get someone hired. Let me handle this."

"Emmett, leave us. Now," Margaret repeated, shooing him away like he was a pest.

Emmett sighed and left the room, glancing back at them nervously before closing the door behind him.

"Sit, please," Margaret said.

Kendra sat on the couch across from Margaret, hands folded in her lap. Margaret didn't make her nervous, but she was curious as to why Margaret wanted to talk to her alone.

"I like you, Ms. Sorensen. You have what we used to call gumption, in my day. But if I am going to employ you, particularly for my personal care, I must insist that you be completely truthful with me. I may be old, but I am not stupid. And I can see as plainly as day that you have extensive medical experience, and for some reason, you've chosen not to share that with us. Which tells me you're hiding something. Emmett is a loving son, but that man can be as dense as a loaf of rye bread. He trusts everyone. I, on the other hand, do not share that same outlook. If you're on the lam from the law, then this job isn't for you."

Margaret's gaze was unflinching. Kendra looked down, considering her choices. Lies had taken over her life, and they continued to pile up. She was so weary of constantly lying. Although she knew her lies were manifested through necessity and fear, it didn't make her any less dishonest. The truth was becoming a vague memory for her. She wasn't even sure she wanted to remember the truth.

"I am not a fugitive from the law." That was not entirely true, but Kendra was sure hiding from a crooked cop was not what Margaret had meant.

"Well, that's good to know. Care to elaborate further?" Margaret asked.

"I am trying to keep myself and my son safe, Margaret. That's all. I do have nursing experience, you're right about that. But working in my previous field is no longer possible. At least for the time being."

"And why is that? Was there a legal issue? Perhaps a malpractice suit?"

"No! Nothing like that. I was a good nurse. I *am* a good nurse. My skill and professionalism have never been questioned. Not once in all the years at my hospital."

"Again, good to hear. Then what or whom are you running from, Katherine?"

Kendra couldn't explain the reason for her intense emotions as she glanced up at Margaret. It was possible that the strain of their circumstances had ultimately caught up with her, and the tears came on without any warning.

"Whatever is said in this room will stay with me, Katherine. I won't even speak to Emmett about it. You have my word."

Kendra let her guard down in a rare moment of fragility, and the words rushed out before she could stop them. "The truth is, my son witnessed something terrible. Something unthinkable that could get us killed by the people involved. The most ruthless people imaginable. They know he saw them, and now they want us dead. I can't go to the police because someone there is involved, and I don't know if he is the only one. So we got lucky and ended up with new identities thanks to a very nice retired federal agent. But they killed him, and now we're here. On our own."

Kendra reached for a tissue from her purse and blotted her eyes. At that moment, Emmett opened the door to peek in. Turning away hastily, Kendra concealed her tear-stained face from him.

"Emmett, when I want you back in here, I will let you know," Margaret said.

"Is everything all right?" he asked.

"What did I just say, Son? Now go away."

Emmett backed out the door, closing it behind him.

"Where is your son now, Katherine?"

Kendra blew her nose before looking up at Margaret. "He's in the car. I understand you won't want me working here after hearing my story. And I don't blame you, Margaret. I'll make my excuses to Emmett and go," said Kendra, standing.

"Sit down. And stop putting words into my mouth. I'd like to meet your son."

"What?"

"Your son. I'd like to meet him. You said he was here, right?"

"Yes. Waiting in the car."

"You know, Katherine, I was a single mother myself. I raised Emmett on my own after his father passed away. Lord knows, it wasn't easy. Boys are a handful, and without a father to guide them, they're even more difficult."

Kendra nodded in agreement. "I think my son resents me for moving him away from everything he knew. He's only sixteen, and this has been so traumatic for him."

"For both of you, I would imagine. But this doesn't sound like it was your fault. Or his, for that matter. Maybe it was just one of life's many potholes."

"More like a crater, honestly."

They both laughed, and it was a welcome moment of levity.

"Emmett!" called Margaret.

Emmett was in the room in seconds, looking nervous.

"Katherine's son is in her car outside. Can you bring him in, please?"

Emmett looked at Margaret, confused. "Emmett, please go get Katherine's son from her car. I'm not sure why you force me to repeat myself so often."

Emmett left and reappeared with Kyle a few minutes later. Emmett and Kyle both wore the same confused expression. Kyle walked toward Kendra and sat next to her on the couch while Emmett stood where he was.

"Jared, you've met Emmett Kent. This is his mother, Margaret Kent," Kendra said.

Kyle looked at Emmett and then Margaret. "It's nice to meet you," he said.

"Lovely to meet you as well, young man. Your mother is going to be working here, so I thought we should meet each other. I have some gardening and other minor jobs around the house I need taken care of. Would you be interested in that position after school? We could have our driver pick you up from school and bring you here each day until your mother is off work at five o'clock. The position pays $15.00 per hour."

"Yes! I can do that! Thank you so much," Kyle said.

"Well, it's all settled then. Your mother can drop you at school on her way here each morning. Albert will pick you up, and then you can drive home with your mother. This should all work out fine."

"Mother, I wasn't aware we were hiring a second gardener or," Emmett hesitated, glancing at Kyle, "a *handyman,*" he said.

"Well, now you know, Emmett. That will be all, dear. You can show Jared to the living room to wait for his mother. Have Hilda get him a snack and something to drink. Katherine and I will be finished up here shortly."

Kendra nodded at Kyle, and he followed Emmett out of the room.

"I hope I didn't overstep by offering your boy that position. I thought perhaps it would be safer to have him here after school, knowing he is being picked up and not on his own."

"You have no idea how grateful I am, Margaret."

Margaret chuckled. "Oh, don't worry, you will both earn your pay. But I have a good feeling about you. I'm aware that most people think of me as nothing more than an ill-tempered old woman. I'm sure Emmett warned you that I can be cantankerous. He isn't wrong about that, by the way. But the incompetent simpletons he's hired in the past to take care of me would challenge anyone's patience."

"I make my own judgments about people, Margaret."

"Good. We are going to get along just fine, dear. But can I offer you one bit of advice? The longer you walk in someone else's shadow, the longer it takes to cast your own."

"I understand what you're saying, Margaret. And I wish it were that simple. But it's not. I can't come forward and have my son testify against these people. Ever. It's just not an option."

"Well then, I suppose that is your decision. I won't press you any further on the matter. You know what's best for you and your son.

Now, as your first official duty, please take me to say goodbye to Jared. I'd like to sit in the living room for a bit. You can start work next Monday after you drop Jared off at school."

Kendra and Kyle waved goodbye to Emmett and Margaret from the car as they pulled out of the long driveway. As they drove back to their new home, Kendra was filled with the first rays of hope for their future.

THIRTY-NINE

The hitman sat in his vehicle across the street and two houses down from the house Manuel had pointed out to him yesterday. A removable sign advertising Martin's Plumbing was attached to the side panel of his van. Despite his gut feeling that it was Kendra Thompson's house, he hadn't seen any activity after hours of waiting. The Hyundai in the driveway meant someone was probably home. He decided to take action when there had still been no activity by 1:00 p.m. He relocated the van around the corner to a spot where it couldn't be seen from the house. He worried that the van had been parked there for too long, and he didn't want to draw attention to himself.

Once the van was out of sight, he climbed into the back to go through the bag of disguises he always carried with him. He dressed himself in a checkered flat cap with tufts of gray hair sewn into the lining, a fake gray mustache, and cardigan sweater. A cane and metal rim glasses were the finishing touches to the look. In a matter of minutes, he had aged himself by thirty years. Stepping out of the van, he leaned heavily on his cane as he began walking toward what he believed to be Kendra's house. Maintaining his character caused him to make slow progress. He leaned on the cane as he walked up the pathway leading to the house and rang the doorbell.

Inside, Kendra was humming to herself while she washed the lunch dishes. The sound of the doorbell startled her, causing her heart to escalate. She wondered who could be at their house. Emmett and Margaret Kent were the only people they knew in Nashville. The sound of an unexpected visitor brought Kyle out of his room, worry etching a line across his forehead. Kendra shook her hands dry and gestured for Kyle to move aside before grabbing a dishtowel. She looked through the peephole and saw an elderly man standing on the porch. With a frown, she took a step back. Next came a knock, followed by a frail voice.

"Brian? It's grandpa."

Kendra sighed and turned the deadbolt. She swung the door open, but kept the security screen closed.

"Hi, can I help you?"

"Oh. I'm sorry. Are you Brian's new babysitter? I'm Arthur, Brian's grandpop. Didn't Melissa tell you I was coming to see him today?"

Kendra held her hand up. "I'm sorry, but there's no Brian here. You must have the wrong house."

"Oh dear. I apologize for bothering you. My daughter just moved, and I must have the address wrong. I guess this isn't 1226 South Second Street?"

"You're close. This is 1226 South Third Street."

"Oh, my. My sense of direction just isn't what it used to be, I'm afraid. So sorry to bother you. You wouldn't happen to know which direction Second Street is, would you?"

"No, I'm sorry. We just moved here, so I'm not very familiar with the area."

"Well, welcome to the neighborhood, and again, my apologies. Have a nice day," he said, touching the brim of his hat in a farewell salute as he turned to walk back to his van.

Once he rounded the corner from the house, he lifted the cane and jogged back to the van. There was no question that he had located Kendra and her son. All that was left to do was to come back tonight and finish things. The risk was too high to force his way inside and take care of them now. He had spotted a neighbor watering their lawn two houses down, and a couple of teenagers skateboarding in the driveway across the street. There was no need to complicate things unnecessarily.

He drove back to the hotel to wait until that night. When he was ready to go, he removed the plumbing sign from the van, loaded the dog inside, and headed toward Kendra's house.

The Thompson household was dark as he checked the time. It was after two in the morning. He parked the van across the street and slipped on leather gloves. Checking his pants' cargo pocket for his tools, he patted the gun in his jacket pocket. He didn't need to wear a ski mask for this visit. The occupants of the house were not going to make it out alive. Satisfied that he had everything he needed, he exited the van and closed the door softly. He crossed the street without making a sound, then jumped over the gate into the backyard. He stayed hidden in the shadows while searching for the breaker box along the house. He found it around the corner near the kitchen window. He opened the panel and clipped the necessary wires as the electricity powered down with a series of short beeps. Following that, he approached the back door and quickly picked the lock with his tools. Although the deadbolt was difficult, he managed to remove it within minutes. He took the gun from his pocket and tucked it into his waistband, then opening the back door, he slipped inside and waited for his eyes to adjust.

In the bedroom at the end of the hall, Kendra sat up as her fan stopped blowing cool air in her bed's direction. She glanced at the bedside clock, but it was dark. Checking her phone, she saw that it was 2:13 a.m. She suspected that one of the breakers had tripped. The landlord had warned her that it would happen occasionally with the old house, but she didn't plan on going outside tonight to mess with the breaker box. It would have to wait until the morning. She swung her legs over the side of the bed, then sliding her feet into her slippers she padded down the hall and into the kitchen for a drink of water.

The hitman stood perfectly still, concealed in the shadows between the large refrigerator and the counter. As Kendra filled a glass with water, she balanced on her elbows over the sink and stared out the kitchen window. Movement in the reflection of the glass caught her eye, and she froze. She peered into the darkness, searching the backyard for any sign of an intruder.

The hitman took Kendra by surprise when he grabbed her from behind and covered her mouth with his large, gloved hand before she could scream to warn Kyle. Her attempt to fight him was useless—he was too powerful. He held her head stationary with one hand and pinned her arms to her side with the other. With Kendra struggling, he twisted her around and shoved her against the pantry cupboard, dazing her as he slammed her head into the cabinet. Her water crashed to the floor, shards of glass flying through the air. Powerful hands wrapped around her neck, and he tightened his grip, choking the life from her.

Pinpricks of light danced in front of Kendra's eyes as she began to lose consciousness. She struggled to remove the man's hands from her throat while her lungs screamed for air, but he simply dug in deeper, squeezing her neck with all his strength. She kicked and clawed at him but he remained unscathed. This couldn't be how it all ended. Not after everything she and Kyle had been through. The thought of Kyle caused a rush of adrenaline to shoot through her. That's when she spotted the butt of his gun tucked into the back of his waistband. She hadn't seen it at first, but now it was all she saw. She realized he was going to strangle her and then shoot Kyle. Kendra grabbed for the gun, but it was just out of her reach, her fingers barely grazing the grip. An image of Sam's face and their training flashed through her mind, and she heard him with such clarity, it was as if he was standing right in front of her. The fragmented memories flooded her thoughts as she fought for her last desperate breaths.

Break a finger. Head-butt. Go limp. Crush their foot. Groin kick. Uppercut to the nose.

Kendra locked onto the man's small finger with a firm grip and pulled with all her strength. His finger loosened a fraction of an inch, and that was all the motivation she needed. Using her last bit of energy, she yanked his finger back and heard it snap like a twig. He cried out and his grip loosened for a second, just like Sam had told her it would. Kendra dragged in a lungful of air and delivered an uppercut to the man's nose with the hard heel of her palm. The hit landed with a sickening thud. He staggered backward as blood gushed from his nose. She lifted her leg, ready to knee him in the groin.

It was do or die. This ended for one of them tonight. Right here, right now.

The man cursed but recovered swiftly and came at her again, reaching into his waistband for the gun, his finger bent at an unnatural angle. But he was too late. Before he or Kendra could make a move, the hitman crumpled to the ground in a heap. Kyle stood over him, brandishing a cast-iron skillet in one hand.

Rushing toward Kyle, Kendra wrapped her arms around him. She allowed herself a moment with her son before her survival instincts took control. She tried to speak, but her throat was too sore after being strangled. She coughed, then sipped cold water to try to ease the pain. When she spoke, she didn't recognize her own voice it was so raspy.

"Grab a long cord, something we can tie him up with. Cut it from the vacuum cleaner and a lamp if you have to," Kendra said to Kyle.

"Why? Let's just go, Mom! While he's still knocked out."

"No. I want some answers. Now go. Hurry, before he wakes up."

Kyle hit the switch for the kitchen lights, but nothing happened.

"The lights aren't working, Mom."

"I forgot about that. Here, take this," she said, grabbing a flashlight for each of them from the junk drawer in the kitchen.

Kyle rummaged through the drawer for the kitchen scissors and hurried to the coat closet to cut the vacuum cord. Kendra shut the blinds over the sink and dragged a dining room chair into the kitchen. She pointed the flashlight at the man on the floor, then kicked him once to make sure he was still unconscious. Next, she grabbed the gun from his waistband and searched his pockets. She discovered his phone, but it was password protected, rendering it useless. His wallet proved to be no more help. According to the driver's license inside, he was forty-five years old. The face in the picture was oddly familiar. She held the flashlight over the license, focusing on the driver's picture before her gaze darted to the man on the floor.

Then it hit her.

The picture looked like a younger version of the elderly man who came to their door earlier that day. The person looking for his grandson. But now he had a shaved head, no mustache, and appeared several years younger that the picture. Minus the gray hair and mustache, they were one and the same.

She dropped into the chair. Hired assassins were supposed to be menacing. Ruthless. Savage. Just like the man on her kitchen floor. We should be able to spot them immediately because they wear their callousness and disregard for human life like a badge that warns us to keep away. They weren't supposed to be harmless old men with canes who smile at us and get lost looking for their grandson's house. Kendra was angry at herself for falling into his trap. She had allowed her guard down and look where that got her. It was a mistake she wouldn't make again.

Kyle rushed into the kitchen holding two long cords.

"Help me get him into the chair," Kendra said.

Kendra's father had been a boy scout leader for many years. It was one of the clearest memories she had of him. He used to take her camping and fishing, and he taught her how to start a fire and set a trap. He also taught her how to tie a proper knot. She concentrated on remembering the steps as she wove the cord around the man's hand and feet. Once Kendra hogtied the hitman to the chair, she was satisfied he wasn't going anywhere anytime soon.

Kyle brought two more chairs to the kitchen for them, then they sat and waited. Rubbing her neck gently, Kendra winced. The inside of her throat felt swollen. Although the hitman hadn't squeezed her for very long, as a nurse, Kendra knew that the injury was caused by the strength of the squeeze, not the duration. She would have pronounced bruising where his thumbs dug into her.

It wasn't long before the hitman began to stir. He came awake suddenly, trying to break free from his restraints. There was no mistaking the hatred in his eyes as he looked at Kendra.

Kendra leaned forward in her chair, grinning at him.

"Good morning, sunshine. I sure hope you're feeling better than you look, because we are going to have a little question-and-answer session," Kendra said.

FORTY

With dried blood obstructing his nostrils and a very swollen nose, the hitman was forced to breathe loudly through his mouth.

"Fuck you, Kendra," he said, spitting out blood.

"I don't go by that name anymore. But it seems you already know that. You obviously aren't a member of the Sinners gang, so who are you, then? Who sent you after us?"

The hitman smirked at Kendra, as if he were sizing her up. When he spoke, his words dripped with venom.

"I am truly going to enjoy killing your son and making you watch it. And it won't be quick."

Kendra saw Kyle squirm in his chair out of the corner of her eye.

"Really? Because you seem to be doing such a bang-up job of things so far. That was me being facetious, by the way, in case you didn't catch the sarcasm."

"I might even enjoy gutting your boy as much as I did that DEA agent friend of yours. Don't worry about his dog, though. I took him."

He leveled his gaze directly at Kyle when he said the last sentence.

Kendra balled her hands into fists, and she was on her feet before she could stop herself. She landed a hit to the man's nose, causing fresh blood to spurt out. Kyle grabbed onto her arm tightly and led her back into the chair. She nodded at him to signify that she had regained control of her emotions, but she couldn't control her trembling hands as she looked at the man.

"I will never stop coming for you. I found you this time, and I'll find you again. You can kid yourself all you want to, Kendra. But I *will* get you. And you're going to watch your son die. I give you my word on that. Don't underestimate what I'm capable of."

"I think I'll take my chances. And I would caution you to be careful. You, whoever sent you, and that gang have done *nothing* but underestimate me. You have no idea how far I am willing to go to protect my son."

"Do you know what I think?" he said.

"I have no interest in your thoughts, and trust me, you don't want to hear what I'm thinking right now. You all assume I'm just a nobody. A nurse running scared. Well, guess again. I'll tell you what I really am. I'm a desperate mother. And that makes me very unpredictable and even more dangerous because I have nothing else to lose at this point. My one goal is to keep my son alive. So come and get me, asshole. But you'd better be ready when you do."

Kendra surprised herself as she channeled all her fear and anger into her words. As he watched her with wide eyes, Kyle couldn't believe this was his mother talking.

"Kyle, go get me the blue pill bottle in my medicine cabinet. The sleeping aid pills. And bring me the bottle of Motrin too."

Kyle sprung up and jogged to the back of the house.

"You're going to take a little nap, and when you wake up, the police will be here. A very detailed letter explaining who I am, and why you broke into my house, will point them in the right direction. I expect they are going to have some rather difficult questions for you."

The hitman glared at Kendra. His nose continued to swell, and she knew the injury needed ice and someone to attempt to reset the fractured bone. However, she had no intention of doing so. He came to her home with the intent to murder her and Kyle, so as far as she was concerned, he could sit there and suffer until the end of time for all she cared. She hoped his nose swelled shut.

"Of course, if you're willing to tell me who sent you and give me the details about your arrangement with that person, then I might be persuaded to send the letter later. That would likely leave you out of the fray. At least temporarily," Kendra said.

"Go fuck yourself, lady. The next time we meet, it will be with my gun to your head so you can watch your kid die."

"All right. Suit yourself, then."

Kendra wasn't surprised at his response. She never honestly expected him to break ranks and side with her. His employer would expect him to be completely loyal and confidential. She had to give it a shot, though, even if it seemed impossible. And now that she had, he had clearly made his choice.

Kyle came back into the kitchen holding the bottle of over-the-counter sleeping pills in one hand, and the Motrin in the other. Kendra grabbed them and crossed the room to the sink. After reading the label, she crushed three sleeping pills into a cup of water. It was more than the recommended dosage, but she needed to be sure he remained unconscious. The haziness and unsteady feeling would stay with him for a while after waking, but it wouldn't kill him. Convinced that he would not take the sleeping aid on his own, she pinched his swollen nose until he had to open his mouth to breathe. Then she forced the water into his mouth. He tried to resist, but she tipped his head back and the water slid down his throat. She shook two Motrin from the bottle and swallowed them. Her larynx wasn't crushed. That was the good news. The bad news was that there was nothing she could do but leave her neck alone and let it heal.

Next, she went to the desk in the living room for a pen and a notebook pad. With Kyle by her side, she sat opposite the hitman and composed a letter to the Nashville police. She started by telling them her real name. She provided a detailed account of everything, starting with Kyle's video of Devon McLeod's murder, Sam's assistance in escaping through the tunnel, and ending with the hitman's break-in at their home that evening. She provided the Bank of America safe deposit box information so they could find Kyle's phone, and she intended to include the key with the letter. She shared with them Sam's suspicions about Senator McLeod and her interaction with Officer Gutierrez. The hitman was snoring loudly, sucking in air through his open mouth by the time she finished. By then, his face was a complete disaster. He was unrecognizable because of the swelling. Kendra tried again to muster even an ounce of empathy for him, but couldn't.

Next Kendra wrote a quick note to Margaret Kent, apologizing that she wouldn't be able to accept the job caring for her, and thanking her for the opportunity. She explained that their pursuers had tracked down her and Kyle and she asked Margaret to give the letter to the Nashville police on her behalf. Kendra couldn't help but chuckle when she thought about Emmett discovering that she was running from killers and Margaret had already known about it. She'd love to be a fly on the wall when that conversation took place.

Kendra placed both letters in a manilla envelope and sealed it, addressing it personal and confidential to Margaret Kent.

"Go pack your things, Kyle. We're leaving. Take clothes, and toiletries, your Xbox and whatever else you need. We are not coming back here, so make sure you get everything you want."

"But this guy found us. He obviously knows our new names. Where are we gonna go now? This is stupid, Mom! We keep running, and they keep finding us."

"The police in Nashville will have all the information they need to make arrests. I'm giving them the video. But you are not going to testify. It's not safe. I don't care what they say. We're going to disappear, and they can sort it all out. When and if it's safe again, we'll go home. But for now, this is our safest bet."

She gestured for Kyle to follow her to the back of the house, where she pulled the duffle bag of cash from under her bed.

"I didn't tell you about this before, because I didn't think we would need it. But I found this," Kendra said, hoisting the bag on the bed.

She dumped the bundled money on the bed and reached into the bag, pulling out a file folder hidden under the lining. She handed the folder to Kyle. He unfolded a handwritten note from Sam.

Kendra,

If your Sorensen surname is ever compromised, these new identities are untraceable. I hope you never have to use them because if you do, that means someone found you and your identities are burned. The Sorensen IDs should be adequate, but if someone locates you, then it also likely means I am dead, and they have gotten to the forger to trace you. The chances of that happening are slim, but this is an alternative—just in case. There is no technological trail to the forger who did these IDs. These were generated by someone on the dark web, someone who cannot be traced to me. That is not a resource I would ordinarily tap into or recommend, but I am a firm believer in having a back-up plan. If you ever decide that being on the run isn't working, contact Special Agent Matthew Clarke at the San Francisco DEA field office at 415-430-7600. You can trust him. Good luck and stay safe.

Sam

Kyle opened the passports. Sarah Williams was the name under the picture of his mother staring back at him.

He opened his new passport next and read his new name out loud. "Bryant Williams." Sitting on the bed, he looked up at his mom. "So, what now?"

"How do you feel about an extended vacation in Australia?" Kendra asked, grinning at him.

"What about the guy in San Francisco? Matthew Clarke? If Sam trusts him, then why can't we just call him?"

"Because I really don't trust any law enforcement right now, Kyle. I'm only giving the video to Nashville PD because they are so far removed from the situation, they can't possibly be involved. But I need to see what happens once they turn the video over to the LAPD. Hopefully that will be enough to spark an investigation. If not, then they will want your testimony, and I don't want you anywhere near a murder trial that involves the Sinners. It's too dangerous."

"Yeah, that's too dangerous, but you're not worried about running from the dude tied up in our kitchen? I'm sick of it, Mom. We can't keep running away. I want my life back. This sucks, and I'm over it."

Kyle made a good point. Kendra was over it too. But with nowhere else to turn, she had to rely on her gut reaction. And in that moment, her instinct was screaming at her to run. Once they got out of the country, where she felt safer, she could explore other options. Maybe she would even call Matthew Clarke. Because Kyle was right on point about one thing—they couldn't spend the rest of their lives running.

FORTY-ONE

Earlier that week, Kendra had purchased a new suitcase from Walmart, and now she was throwing clothes onto her bed beside it. She was fortunate to have had the foresight to buy new luggage. Maybe she sensed something like this was coming. She told herself at the time that she was sick of seeing their old duffle bags. They had seen better days after being dragged across California and Tennessee. But maybe it was her subconscious preparing her to run again.

She touched her neck gingerly. Although the Motrin dulled the throbbing pain a bit, she may need something more potent in the upcoming days. She definitely needed something to help hide the bruising that would last for the next three to seven days. Packing a scarf wasn't a priority when she fled from Los Angeles in fear for her life, and with summer in full swing now, wearing a scarf wasn't weather appropriate, anyway. Her best bet now was to cover the bruises with make-up and wear a short, chunky necklace. Although the thought of something, anything, around her neck again wasn't appealing, she knew the inevitable bruises would spark questions.

After folding clothes into the large suitcase, she went to the bathroom and swept everything off the counter into the smaller of the two cases. She cleared out the medicine cabinet and checked the drawers for anything else she might need. She was completely packed and ready to leave within fifteen minutes. She perched on the edge of the bed and pulled out her phone. Using her new name, she reserved a flight for two to Brisbane International Airport on the Kayak website. They would depart at 2:00 p.m. that afternoon. In order to avoid using her Katherine Sorensen alias to finalize buying the tickets, she would need to obtain a prepaid credit card. Their current names were unusable after being burned.

The sun would be up soon, and she needed to get them securely settled at the airport before it got too late. Kendra pushed the heavy suitcase off the bed, swung her purse over her shoulder, and went to Kyle's room. He was busy throwing clothes into his suitcase, but stopped and glanced up at her when she entered the room.

"We need to go soon. How much longer until you're done?"

"Just a couple of minutes, Mom."

"Okay, I'll meet you in the living room. We're going to be fine, son," Kendra said, forcing a smile that anyone else might buy.

Kyle nodded and resumed tossing clothes into his suitcase. Kendra knew there was nothing else she could say at that moment to make things better, so she left him to finish packing. She rolled her bags next to the front door and snatched the hitman's gun from the hall table. Removing the bullets, she looked around the room before deciding to hide them in the couch cushions and put the empty gun on the hall table. She peeked into the kitchen to check on the man, who was still snoring loudly, with his head hung to one side. She scrawled a short note to the police stating that the gun and keys were his. She left his wallet and phone next to the pile, then tossed the Motrin bottle into her purse. She left an envelope addressed to her landlord on the dining room table that contained her house keys, a note to sell anything left in the house, and next month's rent money. It was the least she could do for bailing without any notice.

Kyle joined her in the living room, placing his luggage next to hers.

"Okay, let's get out of here," Kendra said.

Kendra pressed her key fob to open the trunk while they placed their luggage on the small porch. The otherwise quiet night was interrupted by the sound of the suitcase wheels on the sidewalk. While loading the trunk, Kyle suddenly stopped and looked around.

"What's that noise?"

"Huh? What noise?"

"Shhh. Listen."

Kendra heard it then too. The muffled sound of a dog barking. She glanced in both directions down the street, just as Kyle caught sight of what they were looking for. He pointed and smiled. From inside of a work van parked two houses down, a large yellow Labrador was pawing at the front windshield.

"Mom, I think that's Buddy! That guy said he took Sam's dog, remember? Where are his keys?"

Kendra squinted at the van. It *did* look like Buddy. She hurriedly returned to the house and grabbed the man's keys. They rushed toward the van, clicked the key fob, and unlocked the door. Buddy wasted no time launching himself out of the van and heading straight for Kyle as soon as he pulled the door open. With his tail wagging, he whined, barked, and spun around in circles, excited to see them.

Kyle bent down to hug the dog and was met with a tongue face wash.

"Mom, we can't leave him. We have to take him with us!"

Kendra opened her mouth to protest, but then thought better of it. "Okay. All right. Let's see if we can find his leash."

They searched the van, where Kendra found a receipt for the Hampton Inn and Suites. She left it on the dashboard for the police to find. The idea of searching his hotel room crossed her mind for a brief moment, but she dismissed it as not worth the effort. Even if she found something to identify him, what would be the point? Knowing his name wasn't helpful, so she decided to let the police handle it. Kyle found the service dog vest and held it up to show Kendra.

"We can try it," Kendra said, shrugging.

They loaded Buddy into the car and Kendra drove away from their newly rented house with a deep sense of sorrow. She liked Nashville and had looked forward to starting work with Margaret Kent. Now that wasn't possible, and they were headed out of the country. As Kendra traveled to the Kent residence, she reflected on the direction her life had taken. There was no doubt that she felt resentful. She didn't fault Kyle for recording Devon McLeod's murder. Although he was wrong to record someone being jumped, he didn't know what was going to happen. But she would have changed his actions if given the choice. Her anger was directed at Senator McLeod, Gutierrez, the South Side Sinners, the Satans 13 gang, and whoever the man tied up at her house was. Since she couldn't change her situation in the long term, she focused on what she could do right now. Though she racked her brain for another solution, running seemed like the safest thing to do.

She reached for Kyle's hand, doing everything in her power to keep her expression steady.

"We're going to be fine, Kyle," she said, as much for her own benefit as his.

"Yeah. You already said that, Mom."

"I know. I just want you to know that I mean it."

Kendra smiled when he squeezed her hand in response. This was progress. Maybe he truly believed in her ability to protect them, rather than just relying on their luck so far. And Kendra realized that they had been exceptionally lucky thus far. She really needed that luck to last a little longer.

FORTY-TWO

Kendra and Kyle arrived at the Kent mansion and parked in the driveway. The house was still dark as the sun began to peek over the horizon, while sprinklers tended to the rose bushes and front lawn that bordered the driveway.

"Wait here and try to keep Buddy quiet. I just want to slip this in the mail slot and go."

"Okay. C'mere, Buddy," Kyle said, patting his lap.

The front seat received a sudden visitor in the form of a seventy-pound Labrador, whose tail grazed Kendra's face. Brushing her hand over her face, she spat out dog hair.

"Nice, Buddy. Thanks a lot," she said, stepping out of the car.

She followed the driveway to the side of the house, then tiptoed over the wet grass to reach the porch. As she made her way up the steps, tears formed before she could stop them. After hurriedly wiping them away, she stepped forward and prepared to push the envelope through the mail slot.

"You're up early this morning, Katherine," came a voice from the corner of the porch.

Kendra spun around to see Margaret sitting at a patio table, shrouded in the shadows.

"Oh my God, Margaret! You almost scared me to death," said Kendra, her hand flying to rest over her heart.

"I imagine I did. Why are you sneaking up to my front door at this time of morning? You're not due to start work until Monday."

"I wasn't sneaking, I was just, well, I wanted to leave this for you," she said, holding out the manila envelope to Margaret.

Margaret took the envelope and laid it in her lap. "You're not coming to work for me, are you?"

After a quick glance back at Kyle in the car, Kendra took a seat opposite Margaret.

"I'm sorry, Margaret. I can't. They found us. Well, he, a single someone found us. I'm not even sure who he is or how he figures into all of this, to be honest. But he was here to kill us, and that's all that matters. I can't stay. I'm sorry. We have to leave today. We're leaving the country."

While Kendra spoke, Margaret stayed quiet, then leaned in. "That's going to be a nasty bruise around your neck," she said.

Kendra touched her neck. "Yes, it will be. I'm going to have to do a major make-up job and stop and get a necklace of some sort to try to hide it. I was just waiting until right before we got to the airport to allow as much of the bruising to form as possible. That way, I can cover all of it. But Margaret, I need to ask something of you. First of all, can I use your phone to call a taxi for us? And would you mind donating my car to a charity or church if I leave it with you? Second, I need you to get that envelope to Nashville police for me right away. Will you do that?"

"Where is the man who did that to your neck?" asked Margaret.

"He's tied up at my house."

"That is somewhat risky, don't you think?"

"I gave him sleeping pills. And my father was a scout leader and taught me to tie a handcuff knot. Then I hogtied him. I think he's secure for a bit."

"I see. To answer your questions, of course I can donate your car. But let's have Albert drive you to the airport. Best for you not to leave a trail, I would imagine. And I'll give you a necklace to cover the bruises.

You shouldn't waste any more time by stopping for that. And whatever is in this envelope will get to the chief of the Nashville Police Department immediately. I donate rather handsomely to the Police Officer's Association each year. Chief Whitmore can finally do something for me in return."

"Margaret, I can't thank you enough."

"Oh, hogwash. What's important is that you and your son are safe. This is the most exciting thing that's happened around here in years. I'll be the envy of all the ladies at my bridge game on Tuesday," she said, winking at Kendra.

"I do still need to have Albert stop by a drugstore, though. I can't purchase airline tickets under Katherine Sorensen. It's too risky. And I need a crate for Buddy," said Kendra, nodding her head toward the car.

"I assume it would be safer to purchase the tickets with my credit card rather than under whatever name you will be using. You can give me cash for them."

"Really? Would that be all right?"

"I don't see why not. Of course, Emmett will probably pass out later, but I am a grown woman with my own money. So I don't see where it's any of his business, really. Why don't you have Jared come out of the car and we'll have a quick bite to eat while we get everything together?"

Kendra signaled Kyle to join them on the porch. Before Kyle could close the door, Buddy bolted out of the car and headed straight toward Kendra. He kissed her hand and then moved on to Margaret, giving her a quick kiss before lying at her feet.

"What a beautiful creature! When did you get him?"

"Today. We have a history with Buddy, though."

Kendra wiped tears away as she told Margaret about Sam.

"Well then, you are going to need my vet, Dr. Hill, to issue a health certificate to travel, vaccination records, and authorization to sedate."

"I don't have time for that, Margaret. Our flight leaves at two o'clock this afternoon."

"Nonsense. Dr. Hill will come here."

The same middle-aged woman who let Kendra in for her interview a few days ago peeked onto the porch. "Is everything all right, Mrs. Kent?"

"Yes, I'm fine. But I do need my phone and purse, please. Also, I need you to bring me a few of my chunkier silver necklaces. Something that sits high on the neck, please."

While Hilda retreated into the house to search for the items Margaret wanted, Kendra updated Kyle on their plan.

"So, we really get to take Buddy with us?"

"Yes. Buddy's coming with us. I know Sam would want that."

"Yes!" said Kyle, reaching down to pet Buddy.

Hilda returned with Margaret's cell phone, purse, and a few necklaces. Margaret called the vet immediately.

"Dr. Hill, Margaret Kent here. No, Chloe is just fine. Yes, I realize it's early, but I have an emergency. I have a canine who will be traveling abroad, and I need shots, a groom, a health certificate, travel authorizations, sedatives, and a permission to sedate letter. Oh, and bring an extra-large crate please and dry dog food as well. No, tomorrow won't do. His flight leaves at two o'clock today. Yes, I'm sure you're dreadfully busy. Well, I don't know, but I expect you'll figure that out, Doctor. See you soon."

After disconnecting the call, Margaret's gaze shifted to Kendra. "You can't give that man any room to say no, or he will. But he's the best vet in Nashville. Now, let's get those flights paid for."

Kendra pulled up her reservations, and Margaret made the purchase with her card. Kendra then contacted the airline and arranged for Buddy to join them on the flight. In order to fly, he would need to be in his crate in the cargo hold. Given the last-minute booking and the absence of a service dog certificate, it was the best they could do. But at least he would be joining them.

The next thing Kendra did was take their phones, remove the sim cards, and crush them under her shoe. It pained her to do that. All the money she had spent in the past week to get them settled was a complete waste. She didn't dwell on it, though. She had more pressing concerns at that moment. Namely, leaving the country undetected by making it to the airport before anyone else found them. She had no idea who else might be on their trail.

Margaret spread the silver necklaces on the table in front of Kendra. "Which one do you prefer, dear?"

"Margaret, these are far too expensive. I can just pick up a cheap costume jewelry trinket at a drugstore on our way to the airport. You've already done too much."

"I won't hear of it! Where do you think I would wear any of these, anyway? I don't go to formal events anymore, and the bridge ladies don't dress up. Please, it would make me happy to know someone was enjoying one of them."

Picking up one of the necklaces, Kendra thanked Margaret by squeezing her hand. It was a choker style, and she couldn't help but notice the irony. Despite fastening it on the loosest setting, she still felt the tightness on her sore neck. She would have to deal with it.

Hilda served them scrambled eggs and toast while Buddy had ground beef crumbles. Dr. Hill arrived not long after. The vet assistant took Buddy to the mobile grooming van for a bath and nail trim, and the vet administered shots. He gave Kendra a health certificate, a letter confirming Buddy's travel fitness, a few sedatives, a letter permitting sedation, and his updated shot records. It was a long flight to Australia, and Kendra had no idea how Buddy would tolerate twenty hours in the air. She wasn't even sure how she would do on such a long flight. She was grateful that Buddy had sedatives. She wished she had her own.

With the vet gone, it was time for Kendra and Kyle to leave. Albert backed the town car into the driveway behind Kendra's Hyundai, then loaded their luggage inside. After paying Margaret for their airline tickets and Buddy's care, Kendra made sure to keep the duffel bag of cash with her. Now, more than ever, that cash was essential for their well-being. The money wasn't going to last forever, and she wouldn't be able to work in a foreign country. While it wasn't a permanent fix, it would give them about a year before they had to seriously consider an alternate source of income.

Kendra was finishing up her goodbyes to Margaret just as Emmett stepped onto the porch. Wearing a silk robe, he looked like he had just woken up.

"What on earth is going on out here, Mother?" he asked, looking from Margaret to Kendra, and then to Albert waiting by the town car.

"Nothing, Emmett. We'll talk in a minute," she said, winking at Kendra.

A smile crept onto Kendra's face. She leaned down to give Margaret a final hug and whispered in her ear. "You told me I had gumption. But you're the one with gumption, Margaret Kent."

Margaret chuckled and waved while Kendra and Kyle walked to the car.

FORTY-THREE

SIX MONTHS LATER
BRISBANE, AUSTRALIA

Kyle leaned his surfboard against the house and shook the water from his hair.

"Mom! Can you get me a towel?" he shouted through the back door window.

"Just a second," said Kendra. "No need to yell. I'm right here."

Kendra grabbed a beach towel from the linen closet and headed toward the back door of their small bungalow house. Buddy sprinted past her and into the house when she opened the door to give Kyle the towel, leaving a trail of wet paw prints everywhere.

"Buddy, no!" shouted Kendra.

But her scolding was too late. Buddy stopped to gaze at Kendra, then shook his coat, spraying seawater on everything within six feet of him.

"Oh, for heaven's sake, Buddy. Get outside. Kyle, call Buddy, please!"

"C'mon, boy," Kyle called.

Buddy ran to the sound of Kyle's voice, sliding across the wet hardwood and colliding with the back door before Kendra could open it.

"You are a hot mess, Buddy. Now you're gonna have to get a bath," said Kendra, letting the dog outside. "Don't let him back inside until you hose him down and dry him off."

"Can't you do it? I'm supposed to meet Aiden and Noah and some other people at the beach for a bonfire."

Kendra sighed. "Fine. But this is the last time. And I mean it. If you let Buddy swim in the ocean, then you bathe him. Got it?"

"You're the best, Mom," said Kyle, giving her a quick peck on the cheek as he passed her on his way into the house.

"Yeah, yeah. I'm the best. Come on, Buddy."

Buddy enjoyed every moment of his time in the water as Kendra used the hose to wash him. While she was drying him off, Kyle came out of the house wearing shorts and a t-shirt.

"I'll be back later, Mom."

"Don't be out late, please. You know your curfew."

"I know. We're just gonna be at the beach. You can literally see our bonfire from here."

"Okay. Have a good time. And no drinking. You're only seventeen."

"Only another year and I can drink whatever I want in Australia," he said, grinning.

"Yeah, well, we'll cross that bridge when you turn eighteen. Which, I will remind you again, you are not."

"Whatever. We're just gonna hang out tonight. Stop freaking out," he said, as he turned to leave.

Kendra looked at Buddy. "Was I freaking out? Wow. Kyle's knife, say hello to my heart," she mumbled, as Buddy whined, watching Kyle leave. "No, you can't go with him. You're stuck here with me, pal."

Once she was back in the house, Kendra switched on the kitchen fan. Their old house lacked air conditioning, and February was the most humid month in Brisbane. When they arrived in Australia last September, she was puzzled as to why the rent was so cheap for such a prime location. She soon discovered why. Since September had the lowest humidity, she had no idea what she was getting into with no air conditioning. Now that the humid season was underway, the weather was almost unbearable for two expats from southern California. She missed climate control desperately.

She fixed herself a salad for dinner and fed Buddy. Then she got comfortable on the couch for an evening of television. When Kyle got home at midnight, she woke up, still on the couch. They said goodnight, and each retired to their respective rooms.

Kendra had a good night's sleep and woke up shortly after sunrise. Kyle would undoubtedly sleep in since it was Sunday. After making coffee, she opened her laptop. Every morning, she looked through the online job postings, hoping to see a private health care position. She hoped there would be someone willing to pay her under the table until she could obtain a work permit to work legally in the country. Disappointed, she saw that there was still nothing suitable, so she decided to check out the Los Angeles Times website on a whim. A couple of times per week, she checked the online paper, looking for any updates on the Devon McLeod murder investigation. Until that morning, she hadn't seen anything, and assumed there had been no movement on the case despite her turning in Kyle's video. But now the screen's headline jumped out at her.

Authorities Make Arrests in Devon McLeod Murder Case

The investigation into the death of Devon McLeod, 26, nephew of Senator Steven McLeod, who was found murdered in Los Angeles last year, has taken a shocking turn as new evidence emerged yesterday.

A joint operation between the FBI and DEA led to the arrest of Senator McLeod, along with a decorated LAPD gang task unit officer, and several members of the South Side Sinners gang. McLeod will face multiple charges, including campaign fund improprieties and charges related to his involvement in the murder-for-hire scheme of his nephew, according to LAPD sources. The FBI reportedly has video evidence of the murder, identifying several members of the South Side Sinners, and incriminating evidence linking LAPD gang officer Ramon Gutierrez and Senator McLeod to the conspiracy.

Senator McLeod's wife Marilyn could not be reached for comment. The LAPD will hold a press conference today at 2:00 p.m. Follow us for more news as the story unfolds.

After reading the article twice, Kendra searched the news channels but found no additional information. She sat in silence, staring at the laptop screen in disbelief. Twenty-four hours ago, she was beginning to feel like their lives were becoming almost normal again. Then, in an instant, life became anything but normal. Kendra had been waiting for this news for the past six months, but now that it had come to fruition, she wasn't sure how she felt.

Kendra didn't move from the couch and kept the laptop open until Kyle woke up two hours later. She called him over and swiveled the laptop toward him. He sat down next to her and read the article. Neither of them spoke for several minutes.

"So, what does this mean? Can we go home now?" asked Kyle.

"I thought you loved it here?"

"Yeah, I do. But I miss home too. This feels like a vacation, not home. And you said after our visa extension expires that we might have to leave Australia anyway."

"I know. I'm honestly not sure what this means for us. But I think it's time for me to call Sam's friend at the DEA. He can answer our questions and then we can decide what's best for us."

"Okay, but I want to hear what he says. This is my future too. And in another year, I can decide for myself what I want to do."

Kendra's heart skipped a beat at the thought of Kyle out on his own. She doubted she would ever feel completely safe again, no matter what happened. But Kyle couldn't live with her forever, and it felt like the right time to do something to change their situation. They had been on the run for too long already, and it was wearing on both of them.

"Agreed."

Kendra took a deep breath and headed to her bedroom to get Sam's letter containing Special Agent Matthew Clarke's number.

Truth has the power to heal us. It frees us. So why did she feel so uncertain? She prayed she was making the right decision and not putting them in the line of fire.

FORTY-FOUR

Kendra unfolded Sam's letter and dialed agent Clarke's number. It took her a couple of tries to get it right. She was anxious and forgot to use the country code when dialing the United States-based number the first time. She and Kyle huddled over the cell phone as she put it on speakerphone.

"Agent Clarke." Kendra froze at the sound of his voice. She had secretly hoped it would go to voicemail, giving her more time to prepare what to say.

"Hello?" he said.

Kendra cleared her throat to speak.

"Agent Clarke? I got your number from Sam Murphy. Before he was killed. He said I could trust you."

Kendra rolled her eyes in self-annoyance. She was struggling to explain this properly.

"All right. And who am I speaking to?"

"My name is Sarah Will—no. Actually, my name is Kendra Thompson. I'm here with my son Kyle. Do you know who we are?"

Special Agent Clarke took a deep breath. "Yes, Ms. Thompson, I do. The FBI and DEA would both very much like to speak to you and your son."

"I'm sure they would. We're calling you because if Sam trusted you, then we trust you. I hope I'm not making a mistake."

"Ms. Thompson, Sam Murphy was a dear friend of mine for over thirty years. I know he helped you. And that's good enough for me. I assume you've heard about the latest developments in the Devon McLeod case against the Sinners, Officer Gutierrez, and Senator McLeod?"

"Yes. I'm not sure what that means for my son and me. And there was another man who came after us in Nashville. I don't know who he is or how he fits in to all of this. But he told us he was the one who murdered Sam. And the night he found us in Tennessee, he had Sam's dog, Buddy. We rescued Buddy from his van."

"His name is Richard Eastman. He's a professional assassin who was hired by Steven McLeod. You and Kyle were very lucky, Ms. Thompson. Richard Eastman murdered Sam and three members of the Satans 13 gang the night you escaped. And by the way, Sam's sister was worried about Buddy. Everyone thought the gunfire scared him off that night, but Lou knew Buddy was accustomed to hearing gunfire. He went shooting with Sam on a regular basis. She'll be glad to know he is being taken care of."

The mention of Lou's name caused Kendra's heart to lurch. She believed that Lou had every right to blame her for Sam's death. If not for Kendra, Sam would still be alive today.

"Is Lou okay? I know she must hate me. But there hasn't been one day that I haven't thought about her and her kindness to me and my son. If not for her and Sam, we would surely be dead by now. But I got her brother killed, and I wouldn't blame her for hating me."

"Lou is fine. And she doesn't hate you. Quite the opposite. In fact, she calls me once a week to check on the case and to see if you've made contact yet. She is worried about you and Kyle."

"Really?" Kendra's eyes filled as happiness flooded through her.

"Yes, really."

"So, what do these arrests mean, agent Clarke? Is it safe for us to come home now?" asked Kendra.

"Neither I nor any other agent can ever guarantee your safety, Ms. Thompson. Even though the Sinners captain who green-lighted the hit on you and Kyle will be going to prison, that probably won't make much difference. Gangs have just as much control from prison as they do from the streets. This particular person is a respected member of the Sinners, and he may remain in charge of the street warriors under his leadership. But even if he is replaced on the outside, his hit will remain active unless he calls it off. Which, if I'm being honest, he is unlikely to do."

"So then, the arrests change nothing for us? Do I understand that correctly? How is that possible? I tried to do the right thing. I made sure that the FBI and DEA got the video. And yet we still can't come home. Do you have any idea how frustrating that is for us?" said Kendra.

"I do, yes. And I agree that it's not fair. But it's where we are right now. I'm sure Sam spoke to you about the Witness Security Program. It used to be called Witness Protection."

"He did, yes," sighed Kendra.

"Mom, maybe it's time we did it. I feel like we are on borrowed time everywhere we go."

"Kendra, I'm sure you have reservations about the witness program. I don't blame you, given your experience with Officer Gutierrez. But here's what I can promise you. Both you and Kyle would be protected twenty-four-seven during the high-threat period before the trial and until the trial concludes. Once that's done, your new locations and identities are assigned. You would receive financial assistance for housing and basic living expenses, and job retraining under an innocent victim witness status. If you come back, I will personally escort you to the Assistant US Attorney's office for processing. Their office will vet you, and so will the US Marshals Service. The Department of Justice's Office of Enforcement Operations makes the final determination for eligibility into the program, but I cannot imagine a scenario where you would not be approved into the program immediately. I'll finish by saying that no witness following proper guidelines has ever been harmed or killed while under protection in the history of the program. You stand a far better chance of remaining safe under federal protection than you do on your own, Kendra. That's an indisputable fact."

"What happens to the people we know back home? Do they just think we fell off the face of the earth or something? Like, they'll never know what happened to us?" asked Kyle.

"A back story would be created. Usually something like you perished in a car accident and the bodies were charred beyond recognition. A boating accident with no body recovery. Something along those lines. We don't leave any loose ends," replied agent Clarke.

Kendra looked at Kyle, who shrugged. "Agent Clarke, I'd like to talk to my son. I will call you back shortly with a decision."

"Please do, Ms. Thompson. I know you think you're safe, but trust me when I tell you, you aren't."

"Trust me, Agent Clarke, I am under no such delusion."

Kendra ended the call and turned to face Kyle. She was so conflicted. On the one hand, they seemed to be safe for now where they were. On the other hand, how long would that last?

"If we do this, there's no coming back. We don't have any other identities to pull out of a hat and run with. We would be in the program for life. Forever." She allowed her words to evaporate into the air. They hung between them for a moment as they both considered the finality of what agreeing to Agent Clarke's plan meant to them.

"Yeah. I know. I do worry about being on our own, Mom. The other guy found us. What if the Sinner guy is more pissed off because he's going to prison? He could send someone after us. Or the senator guy could just hire someone else. I mean, we would never see it coming. At least with the witness program, we'd have help if we needed it, right? It would kind of be a relief not to be on our own anymore."

"They'd want you to testify against the Sinners. That terrifies me, Kyle."

"Yeah, it scares me too. But I can handle it. I'm not a kid anymore. You heard what he said. We'd be under their protection and then in the program."

"Are you absolutely certain this is what you want to do?"

"What else is there to do, Mom? There's nothing left of our old lives, anyway. Not now. What do we do in six months when our visas expire? Start over somewhere else? No, thanks. That would suck. I want to live somewhere I can stay without having to disappear again. I'm seriously sick of running."

Kendra nodded and, with shaky hands, dialed agent Clarke's number again.

"Clarke."

"We'll book the first flight to Los Angeles. Will you meet us at the airport?"

"Count on it."

"I'll text you our flight information. Thank you, Agent Clarke. Please don't make me regret this."

"I won't. I give you my word."

Kendra placed the laptop on the coffee table and purchased a pair of tickets from Brisbane to Los Angeles for a midnight departure. Next, she called the airline to get Buddy on their flight, thankful that she had obtained a service dog vest and certificate from an online registry. Answering a couple of questions was all it took, and Buddy was registered as an emotional support dog. Kendra thought Buddy might actually have to live up to his new title very soon, given what she and Kyle were about to face.

Now all that was left to do was pack.

Again.

FORTY-FIVE

It was a sunny day with heat waves shimmering off the runway's asphalt as the plane approached Los Angeles International Airport. The pilot announced the temperature as a mild seventy-five degrees. Kendra attempted to calculate the day and time, but failed. Flying eastward, and due to the time difference, they gained a day somewhere about halfway over the Pacific Ocean after crossing the International Date Line. Her head pounded, thinking about it. All she knew for certain was that she was exhausted. Buddy slept at her feet and Kyle was out next to her. They both woke up as the plane touched down. Kyle stretched and peered out the window.

"Are we here? Are we in LA?"

"Yes," said Kendra. She felt a surge of anxiety at the thought of what they were about to do.

Buddy stretched and yawned, letting out a little howl, much to the delight of the toddler across the aisle from them.

Passengers all over the airplane stirred as they rolled to a stop. Flight attendants walked the aisles, making sure passengers knew how to unload and secure their carry-on baggage properly. Kendra kept a tight grip on her purse, which held the remaining cash from Sam rolled up inside an empty make-up bag.

They waited until most of the passengers had disembarked before standing to leave. With all their luggage checked before leaving Australia, they didn't have any carry-on bags. Kendra took the lead as they exited the plane and headed through the air bridge toward the terminal, with Kyle and an enthusiastic Buddy close behind. She scanned the crowds, searching for anyone who seemed out of place. Anyone who wasn't moving with the flow of people toward the customs area. She hoped she was just being paranoid in believing that a gangbanger could make it to the customs checkpoint, but that didn't stop her anxiety from spiraling. What if the gang, or the senator, had bribed a customs employee to gain access? With an LAPD insider under their belt, it wasn't a huge stretch to imagine they had a customs agent on the payroll too. Her paranoia ran wild with thoughts of a gangbanger suddenly emerging from the crowd and peppering them with gunfire. She stopped walking and took a few deep breaths to compose herself. Kyle stood beside her, his gaze darting over the crowd. She thought she had come to terms with their decision to come back to the US, but now that they had arrived, doubt started to creep in. People rushed around them, all in a hurry to get into the immigration line. Kendra wanted to turn and run back to the airplane, overwhelmed with second thoughts about returning home. They waited at the end of the tunnel for another five minutes until everyone had made their way through the tunnel and it was just the two of them and Buddy on the air bridge. They had no choice but to move forward. There was nowhere left for them to run.

She glanced at Kyle and nodded toward the crowd. It only took them a few minutes to reach customs and immigration. This was their first point of entry to the United States, and Kendra was nervous as they waited in line. They no longer had their government-issued IDs with their real names. Renting houses and flying to a foreign country with a fake ID had made her anxious, but the idea of reentering the US with one was a whole new level of nerve-wracking. Agent Clark had promised to meet them at customs, but upon looking around, she realized she had no idea what he looked like. Kyle's worried look confirmed that he shared her concerns. They gradually moved forward until there were just two people ahead of them. Kendra's anxiety intensified with each passing minute. Just when she was ready to grab Kyle and bolt for the bathrooms, a man in a dark suit waved to her from behind the booth. He stepped clear of the kiosk and moved his jacket aside so she could see the badge clipped to his belt. She nodded her head to let him know she understood. They approached the booth as Agent Clarke leaned over to speak to the customs agent, showing him his DEA badge and identification and handing him paperwork. Speaking into his handheld radio, the immigration officer waved Kendra and Kyle forward. They stepped up to the booth where he stamped the paperwork and passed it back to agent Clarke.

"Morning, ma'am. Your names please."

"Kendra and Kyle Thompson."

After so many months of using fake names, it felt good to introduce themselves using their real names. She knew it was short-lived, and they would soon adopt new identities again. Until then, she would savor the freedom of not having to remember who she was supposed to be.

"Do you have passports?"

Kendra looked at Agent Clarke, unsure how to answer.

"Here are copies of their passports. They are being remanded to the protective custody of the DEA pending the Assistant US Attorney's approval to transfer them to the US Marshal's Witness Security Program."

The immigration officer looked at the passports and back up at them. He reviewed the paperwork from Agent Clarke one final time, then ushered them through the gate and into the terminal.

"Kendra, Kyle, it's nice to meet you both," said Agent Clarke, shaking their hands.

"Likewise, Agent Clarke," said Kendra.

Buddy wagged his tail and tried to jump on the agent. "Hey, Buddy. Remember me?"

Buddy licked the agent's hand in response.

"Let's go get your luggage. I have another agent from the LA field office who will be accompanying us to the US Attorney's Office. Once we get you through that paperwork, we'll take you to the safehouse where you'll be living until the trial is over. The only trial you will testify at is the Sinners' murder case, Kyle. Immediately after that, you will go into protective status permanently."

"Where will we be going?" asked Kyle.

"If you're asking about the safehouse, I can't disclose that to you. As far as a permanent residency, you won't know that until you are on your way to your destination. The Marshal's deputy will review that with you. That information is confidential and highly secured. I won't even know where you are."

"Oh. Okay," said Kyle.

"I know this is a lot. But I'll be around until the trial ends and you enter the witness program. There's agent Medina," he said, pointing to a tall man in a suit at the luggage carousel.

They collected their bags and followed the agents to a black SUV with tinted windows. They merged onto the 105 Freeway toward downtown, and Agent Medina switched on the emergency lights as they sped into the heart of Los Angeles. It was good to be back in their hometown. Kendra took in the views and committed them to memory in case she was never able to come back again. Kyle stared out the window, and she knew he was doing the same thing. They got to the US Attorney's Office, Central District of California, a little after noon. The parking garage was nearly empty because it was the weekend. Clarke made a quick call to let someone know they had arrived and then led Kendra and Kyle to a door marked stairs.

Two minutes later, a man who Kendra guessed was in his mid-thirties opened the door and ushered them inside.

"Ms. Thompson, Kyle," he said, extending his hand. "I'm Assistant US Attorney Martin Page. Thank you for coming in. If you'll follow me upstairs, we can get your paperwork done and then Agents Clarke and Medina can escort you to the safehouse." He started up the stairs, then turned back to Kendra. "You should be proud, Ms. Thompson. You did a good job of keeping your son safe. But you can relax now. We'll take it from here."

Despite the Assistant US Attorney's reassurances, Kendra couldn't shake the feeling of a lamb being led to slaughter. She glanced over at Kyle, then took his hand in hers. His palm was damp, and her hand quivered. Buddy trailed closely behind as they climbed the stairs leading to Martin Page's office, where their new lives would officially start.

FORTY-SIX

FIVE YEARS LATER
JACKSONVILLE, FLORIDA

Terra Thompson fussed with the tie on her son's tuxedo, straightening it.

"Look at you. Your wedding day," she said, beaming at him. "You're happy, right?"

"Yes! Of course, I'm happy, Mom. I love Emma," said Sean.

"Good. Because I couldn't ask for a better daughter-in-law."

"Dan remembered to bring the rings, right?" he said, smoothing his hair down.

"Yep. He's out there just itching to get you hitched."

"Do you think I'm too young? To get married, I mean."

Terra stepped back, holding her son at arm's length. "No. You're the most mature twenty-three-year-old I've ever known. Plus, you and Emma are hopelessly in love with each other. Why wait?"

"Can I ask you something, Mom?"

"Of course. What is it?"

"Do you ever feel guilty?"

Terra ran her hand over the silver choker on her neck, conjuring up memories from what felt like a lifetime ago. She didn't need to ask Sean what he meant. Terra lived it every day, just as he did.

"Sometimes, yes. Do you? Is that what's bothering you?"

"Yeah. I do feel guilty. It's like I've lived this entire other life before I met Emma that she knows nothing about. I can't even share any of my childhood memories with her. I guess it feels like I'm lying to her, and it bothers me."

"I get it. I feel the same way sometimes. But you know we can't tell them."

"Did you seriously just say that to me, Mom? And just in case I might forget, the two US Marshals in the audience out there are a constant reminder, anyway," he said, nodding his head in the direction of the chapel's sanctuary.

Sean was right. It wasn't necessary for Terra to remind him not to talk about their pasts. The Marshals, Assistant US Attorney Page, the DEA, and the Department of Justice had all hammered it into their heads so many times she couldn't count them all.

"Hey, I thought you wanted Marshals Howe and Campbell to be at your wedding?"

"I did. I *do*. I'm glad they're here. They're not just our handlers, they're practically family. So it makes sense for them to show up as my uncles. I'm just saying you don't have to tell me I can't tell my soon-to-be-wife about my past. Just make sure you don't share anything with the good doctor, Dan, either."

"Ha! Dan probably wouldn't believe me, even if I did. He believes I am as pure as the driven snow. Hey, I'm sorry your dad can't be here."

Sean let his head drop for a minute before looking up at his mom.

"Don't be sorry, Mom. He gave his permission for me to enter the witness program as a minor. He knew that meant that he'd never be able to contact me again. Besides, you more than made up for me only having one parent."

Terra blinked back tears. "Don't make me cry and ruin my make-up. You know your dad only did that to keep you safe. Not because he didn't care."

"I know. I think that was the only time I ever saw my dad cry. The day we said goodbye at the Marshal's office."

They had both given up so much. Terra wiped a tear from the corner of her eye but recovered quickly. This wasn't the time or place to get melancholy over the past.

"I almost forgot. I have something for you," she said, handing Sean an envelope from her clutch bag.

Sean smiled and took the envelope, opening it carefully. "Airline tickets to a fabulous honeymoon?" he asked, grinning.

He reached inside and withdrew a check. He was stunned as he looked at his mother.

"What the heck, Mom! This is too much. I can't take this."

"Yes, you can. Dan and I want to help you with medical school. We have the money. I don't exactly make pennies as a nurse, and Dan's a successful surgeon. We do all right."

Before Sean could react further, Terra's husband, Dan, poked his head through the door.

"Terra, are you two almost ready? The natives are getting restless. Sean, if you're not out there in two minutes, I won't be able to stop my brother from cornering every guest he can get his hands on and trying to sell them insurance."

"We'll be right there," said Terra.

For a long time after their induction into the witness program, Terra sometimes slipped and called Sean by his given name of Kyle. Just like everything else in their lives, it took time to adjust. Surprisingly, she hadn't thought of herself as Kendra, or her son as Kyle, for a few years now. The US Marshals allowed them to retain their surname, as it was common enough to be untraceable, and that made the transition easier. Being Terra and Sean Thompson had been a part of her identity for so long now, it was who she was. And they were happy. The Marshals relocating them to Florida had turned out to be the best thing that had ever happened to both of them.

Even after a series of tragic murders and life on the run, they found themselves with a happy ever after. Terra hugged her son one last time, took his arm, and together they walked toward the church for his wedding.

THE END

ACKNOWLEDGEMENTS

No author pours their blood, sweat, and tears into a book without a little help, and I am no exception to that. I have a few people to thank for making *Run* a reality. All the people below made an impact on this book.

A special thanks to the professional contributors. Your input was absolutely invaluable, and I thank you from the bottom of my heart.

Ted Encinas, Retired Gang Intelligence Agent, Riverside, California Police Department. Look for an upcoming autobiography from Ted, which promises to be outstanding, based on the career stories he shared with me.

Jeffrey James Higgins, Retired DEA Supervisory Special Agent. Author of *Furious: Sailing into Terror,* and *Unseen: Evil Lurks Among Us*

Dr. Gary Gerlacher, MD Author of *The Last Patient of the Night: An AJ Docker Thriller*

Cynthia Bosch, RN. Not only an outstanding nurse, but a stellar human being I have had the pleasure of being friends with for fifty years.

A huge thank you to my circle of early readers, who selflessly gave their time to help mold this book into what it is. And to catch my early typos, of which there were many!

Tiffanie Steik - Future best-selling author.

Eileen Cotto - Your enthusiasm always encourages me, and you added so much to this book. I am eternally grateful to you.

Adrienne Williams Stucki - Reader extraordinaire.

To my fellow authors, who graciously agreed to read and critique this book. Your expert advice made all the difference. By the way, I highly recommend all the books listed below by these very talented authors.

Haris Orkin - Author of *The James Flynn Escapade Series*

Scott Michael Powers - Author of *The Murder Plague*

Regina Buttner - Author of *Down a Bad Road*

Stephen Bray - Author of *Night Shadows*

Ellen Ricciutti - Author of *One Time or Another*

Pamela Taylor – My fantastic editor and author of the *Second Son Chronicles*.

Thank you to my son, Mychael, for always having my back and being my biggest fan. I love you to the moon and back.

Last, but certainly not least, thank you to my dear friend, Tom McCaffrey, author of *The Claire Trilogy*. Thanks for continually encouraging me to write and for totally getting my sense of humor. You really are the male version of my personality. Anyone who hasn't read Tom's books, you are truly missing out.

ABOUT THE AUTHOR

Christy Cooper-Burnett is an award-winning author from southern California with a degree in Administration of Justice, where she lives with her rescue beagle, Gertie. She has one grown son who inspired her to write her award-winning debut novel, *No Way Home*.

Christy began her writing career later in life, but once she got started, she never stopped. Her work focuses on creating relatable stories and characters that transcend genres and encourage readers to imagine what they would do if thrown into the imaginative situations her trademark strong female protagonists end up in.

Her books have been awarded spots in the California Indie Author Project, the Pencraft Awards, International Book Awards, Literary Titan Book Awards, and the Indies Today top five-time travel novels.

"Immersive science-fiction and a moving character drama."
–Brian Carmody, author of Hellish Beasts
CHRISTY
COOPER-BURNETT
NO
WAY
HOME

NOTE FROM CHRISTY COOPER-BURNETT

Word-of-mouth is crucial for any author to succeed. If you enjoyed *Run*, please leave a review online—anywhere you are able. Even if it's just a sentence or two. It would make all the difference and would be very much appreciated.

Thanks!
Christy Cooper-Burnett

We hope you enjoyed reading this title from:

www.blackrosewriting.com

Subscribe to our mailing list – *The Rosevine* – and receive **FREE** books, daily deals, and stay current with news about upcoming releases and our hottest authors.
Scan the QR code below to sign up.

Already a subscriber? Please accept a sincere thank you for being a fan of Black Rose Writing authors.

View other Black Rose Writing titles at www.blackrosewriting.com/books and use promo code **PRINT** to receive a **20% discount** when purchasing.